A MARRIAGE OF CONVENIENCE

"I'm not some naïve young thing," Leah said. "I can't explain it any other way. The minute Matthew realized I couldn't have *kinner*, he . . . changed."

"And you think that's because a woman who can't give birth is somehow less appealing. Less attractive," he said.

"Jeb, we agreed that our relationship—" she began.

"And you think that's because I'm *not* attracted to you?" he burst out.

She blinked at him. "Yah."

Jeb laughed softly. It was ridiculous, but then, she'd been through a lot.

"That's not true at all. Look at you. You're gorgeous. I've thought so for years. You've got this way about you that draws a man in. I notice you—your eyes, the way your lips purse when you're deep in thought . . . this part of your neck—right here—" He ran his finger over the soft flesh just above her collarbone. "I can see your heartbeat there . . . I can't explain Matthew. He's an idiot. I can pretty much guarantee you he didn't love you as much he claimed if he could just change course like that, but that wasn't because you aren't a beautiful woman."

She opened her mouth to speak, then slowly closed it.

"I'm attracted, okay?" he said, and he lowered his voice. "*Very* attracted. I see you in my home, in my kitchen . . . and I feel a whole lot. So never think our arrangement is because you aren't beautiful enough . . ."

Books by Patricia Johns

THE BISHOP'S DAUGHTER

THURSDAY'S BRIDE

JEB'S WIFE

Published by Kensington Publishing Corp.

Jeb's Wife

PATRICIA JOHNS

ZEBRA BOOKS
KENSINGTON PUBLISHING CORP.

www.kensingtonbooks.com

ZEBRA BOOKS are published by

Kensington Publishing Corp.
119 West 40th Street
New York, NY 10018

All Kensington titles, imprints, and distributed lines are available at special quantity discounts for bulk purchases for sales promotion, premiums, fund-raising, educational, or institutional use.

Special book excerpts or customized printings can also be created to fit specific needs. For details, write or phone the office of the Kensington Sales Manager: Attn.: Sales Department. Kensington Publishing Corp., 119 West 40th Street, New York, NY 10018. Phone: 1-800-221-2647.

Zebra and the Z logo Reg. U.S. Pat. & TM Off.
BOUQUET Reg. U.S. Pat. & TM Off.

First Printing: September 2020
ISBN-13: 978-1-4201-4913-5
ISBN-10: 1-4201-4913-X

ISBN-13: 978-1-4201-4916-6 (eBook)
ISBN-10: 1-4201-4916-4 (eBook)

10 9 8 7 6 5 4 3 2 1

Printed in the United States of America

To my husband.
I couldn't do this without you.
I love you!

Chapter One

"Rebecca's far enough along in her pregnancy that she's showing," Rosmanda said, nudging the plate of shortbread cookies toward Leah. "I'm sorry to be the one to tell you, but you'd notice it on Service Sunday. She's not exactly being modest about it. It's as if she refuses to let her dresses out until the last minute. I'd tell her that it's not proper, but it isn't my place. She'd got a *mamm* of her own. All I can say is, I'm much further along than she is, and I'm perfectly capable of letting a dress out. And as for my girls, I'll make sure they act with more propriety than that."

Leah forced a weak smile, but she didn't touch the plate of cookies. It wasn't right to be talking behind someone's back—but sometimes an update was necessary so she could smother her natural reaction to seeing her ex-fiancé's new wife. Leah had been gone for eight months while she taught school in another community, and a lot had changed.

"You have a few years yet before you have to worry about your girls," Leah said with a short laugh. "They're only four."

"I'm thinking ahead," Rosmanda replied, but humor didn't glimmer in her eyes. She was serious.

"The thing is, Matthew wanted children," Leah said. "At least he's getting them."

It was the kindest thing Leah could think of to say. Matthew had broken her heart and tossed her aside, then immediately begun courting a girl just off her Rumspringa.

"That isn't your fault," Rosmanda said, lowering her voice. "Leah, I don't know why God allowed you to be born with a malformed uterus, but it isn't fair to cast aside a woman because she can't give birth."

"Maybe it is fair." Leah shrugged. "Matthew wanted children—what Amish man doesn't? And I can't give that! So, if he knew what he wanted, and we weren't married yet, he wasn't in the wrong. Technically."

"So he's married himself an eighteen-year-old wife," Rosmanda said, and she shook her head. "I don't mean to degrade her. She's family, after all. Rebecca is beautiful, sweet, and from what my husband says, she's a good cook. But she's *young,* and Matthew is—how old is he now?"

"Twenty-five," Leah replied woodenly.

Leah was thirty, and dating a boy five years younger than her had already been a stretch. She'd prayed for a husband since she was a young teenager. And now that she was advancing into her old maid status, she'd thought that Matthew was the answer to her prayer—her reward for patient waiting. God rewarded the good girls, didn't he? He worked miracles. He made a way. But her wedding had never happened. He'd dumped her, and she'd accepted a teaching position that would allow her to get out of town to try to heal from the breakup.

"Rebecca's only eighteen . . ." Rosmanda grimaced. "When you're eighteen you think you're ready to take on marriage and children, but you're not quite so grown-up as you think. She married a man who'd been dating another woman for *three years*. And no one warned her that there would be complicated feelings left between you and Matthew."

"I don't want to hold him back," Leah said. "She has nothing to worry from me."

"I might have wanted to hold *her* back!" Rosmanda retorted. "I've told you about Mary Beiler, haven't I? Many a girl plows ahead with a marriage and lives to regret it. I didn't want that for Rebecca. But she's related to my husband, and I'm just an in-law there."

"Matthew made his choice," Leah replied.

"Did you know that Matthew's been asking about you?" Rosmanda replied. "And spending a whole lot of time with your brother."

"They're good friends," she replied. "They have been for years. And if he still cares what becomes of me, maybe I should be glad that some of his feelings might have been genuine."

Rosmanda sighed. "And I also know you, Leah. I'm not saying Rebecca has anything to worry from you. . . . You're a good woman, and he's officially off-limits. But that doesn't mean this will be easy on Rebecca."

And maybe it wouldn't be, but Rebecca had won. She had Matthew as her husband, and she was pregnant with his child. Uncomfortable or not, Rebecca would survive just fine.

The side door opened, and four-year-old Hannah came into the kitchen, followed by her twin sister, Susanna. They weren't quite identical twins, but it was close. Hannah had always been just a little bit blonder than her sister, and right now, their dresses were covered in dirt from the garden and their bare feet were brown with soil. Rosmanda heaved a sigh.

"Little girls need to stay clean," Rosmanda said, rising to her feet, her own pregnant belly doming out in front of her as she rose. "We'll have to wash your dresses now, and that's even more work for your *mamm!*"

"Sorry, Mamm . . ." Hannah wiped her dirty hands down the sides of her dress, and Leah couldn't help but smile. The girls started toward their mother.

"No, no!" Rosmanda said. "Stay right there. I don't need dirty footprints all over the house."

Those girls were a handful, and in a matter of months, Rosmanda would have a new baby to add to the mix.

"I should get back home," Leah said, standing, too. "Thank you for the chat."

Rosmanda grabbed a cloth from the sink and shot Leah an apologetic smile. "So soon? You've hardly eaten a thing."

Leah didn't have much appetite anyway.

"I've got to start dinner for my brother, and I can't be holding you up either," Leah said. "I'll see you again soon, I'm sure."

Leah smoothed her hand over Hannah's hair as she passed the girl on her way to the door. *Kinner* . . . she'd never have any babies of her own, and there was a part of her heart that ached when she saw her friend's little girls. This was the goal for an Amish woman—to marry and have a family of her own. Leah hadn't managed to do either of those things, and at the age of thirty, her chance at any domestic joys were past. It was best to admit it and face the truth.

Outside in the warm June sunlight, Rosmanda's husband, Levi, helped Leah hitch up the buggy. Rosmanda and Levi Lapp lived on two acres of land near the town of Abundance and a short buggy ride from the Amish schoolhouse. That would be convenient for them when the girls were old enough to start school. They had family concerns . . . and they were fortunate. Other women were married, having babies, raising kids. And Rebecca was already round with her pregnancy. That mental image was an uncomfortable one, and Rosmanda's warning had been well-meant.

No one had written to tell Leah. That was how pity worked, though. People smiled sadly and kept their mouths shut. Was that the point she was at now—being pitied?

Maybe she was grateful not to have had that thought of Matthew's impending fatherhood the last few months. And maybe she wasn't, because it meant that she was beyond hope in the community's eyes.

When the buggy was hitched and Leah had hoisted herself up onto the seat, Levi gave Leah a friendly wave.

"Thank you, Levi," she said. "It's much appreciated."

"Take care now," he said, giving her a nod, and she flicked the reins and the horse set out for home.

The sun was high and bees droned around the wild-flowers that grew up out of the ditch beside the road. Coming back to Abundance for the summer was more work than teaching in Rimstone. She'd have canning to do to refill their pantry, herbs to dry, a thorough cleaning of their little house to accomplish, too. Her brother, Simon, had been working at an RV manufacturer in town, but he'd been laid off, so his money had dried up. Besides, he was a man, and he only did as much women's work as would keep him fed and clothed in her absence. Finding a wife might be prudent for her brother, except he'd made a bad name for himself already with his worldly ways and the daughters in Abundance stayed clear of him.

Leah felt more responsible for Simon than most. Their parents died in a buggy accident when Leah was sixteen, so she'd skipped her Rumspringa and raised her eight-year-old brother the best she knew how.

And this was the result. She'd done her best, but Leah obviously failed him. So, while she never would have *kinner* of her own, she'd already raised her brother, and she'd had her chance to make a good man of him. But Simon's grief over their parents' death had taken him in a different direction, and she hadn't been able to drag him back.

Her mind was moving ahead to dinner, though. Simon liked her fried chicken, and this being her second day back in the community, she wanted to make something special they could enjoy together. They'd stopped by the grocery store when her brother picked her up from the bus station, so the cupboards were stocked once more, and she was looking forward to cooking in her own kitchen again.

Leah enjoyed her teaching position in Rimstone, but she was a guest, and in Rimstone, it was Cherish Wittmer's kitchen. Cherish was warm, understanding, and the closest to a mother she'd had since her own mother's death . . . but a woman of thirty needed some counter space to call her own.

The horse knew the way home and plodded steadily down the road toward the little house she'd rented on an Amish farm. The rental agreement was under her name, and she and Simon kept the bill paid between them. The horse turned into the drive without any need for her guidance, plodding past the main farmhouse. She looked over at the house, silent and empty at this time of day. But then, the most they ever saw from that house was a kerosene light in the kitchen after dark. Two widowers used to run this farm together—Peter and Jebadiah King. Uncle and nephew. They acted as landlords for the cottage, too, but the older of them had passed away, and now it was just Jebadiah, a scarred and mysterious man, running the farm alone.

Leah had never seen much of him. Peter had been the friendlier of the two. Jeb kept to himself, but there were rumors enough that passed through the community in waves every time they were reminded of his existence. Jeb made her uneasy—he always had. He was tall, muscular, and badly scarred from a barn fire. His halting gait was recognizable from a distance, and it always gave her a shudder.

As Leah approached their rented, one-story cottage, she saw a buggy pulled up next to the house. And there was Jeb, reaching up and steadying her brother as he climbed down from the seat.

Simon moved slowly, and he wasn't wearing his hat. Simon looked toward her, and she saw smears of blood under his nose and mashed, bruised skin around one eye. Her heart skipped a beat and then hammered hard to catch up.

"Simon?" she called, and she pulled her buggy up short, tied off the reins, then jumped down. She lifted her skirt to keep it from tangling with her legs as she ran toward him.

"Hey, sis . . ." Simon grimaced as he took a step toward the house. "It's not as bad as it looks—"

"I find that hard to believe," she said, but her voice didn't sound as firm as she would have liked. "Simon, what happened to you?"

Simon leaned on the larger man, and she turned her attention to her brother's rescuer. Jeb was about forty, and he stood head and shoulders taller than Simon. The burn scars went down one side of his face, then disappeared under his beard. His neck and left arm were burned, too, and his limp suggested the burns hadn't stopped there. Jeb adjusted his grip on Simon's shoulder.

"Nothing, nothing . . ." Simon murmured. "Don't worry about it. Just a misunderstanding."

"Yah?" Leah looked toward Jeb. "What happened to him? I want the truth."

"I found him like this, walking by the side of the road

on my way home from town," Jeb replied, but when he looked down at Simon, his gaze lacked proper sympathy.

"Simon!" Her voice was rising, and she couldn't help it. "Who did this?"

"What are you going to do, drag them off by their ears?" her brother muttered. It was a jab at her job as a schoolmistress, but she wasn't amused. She was about to retort when Jeb cut in.

"Who do you owe money to?" Jeb interjected, pinning Simon with a hard stare.

"Some men . . . it's nothing—"

"It's enough to have yourself beaten like a tough steak," Jeb retorted. "So I'm thinking this isn't legal. That leaves gambling and booze, and you don't smell like alcohol."

Leah's gaze whipped between them. Jeb was only voicing what she was already thinking.

Simon grimaced. "It was a sure thing. I thought I'd beat him. I had the perfect hand, and I was so sure he was bluffing . . ."

Leah took her brother under the other arm and she and Jeb both helped him into the cottage. She could feel Jeb's wrist brushing against her waist. When they got him inside, he hobbled to a kitchen chair and Leah stepped back. Jeb seemed to fill up more of the small kitchen than both she and Simon combined. Simon winced as he lifted his shirt to inspect his bruised ribs, and Leah went straight for the sink.

"How much do you owe this time?" Leah asked, turning on the water and putting a fresh cloth under the flow.

"How much did you make for teaching?" Simon asked instead.

"Enough to pay my room and board in Rimstone, and keep our rent paid. Not a penny more than that," she retorted. "How much have you got saved?"

Simon didn't answer, and maybe she should have expected that much. Simon didn't save, he spent. Besides, they weren't alone.

"How much do you owe?" she repeated. This was a more important question, and she wrung out the cloth and came over to where her brother sat. She dabbed at the blood beneath his battered nose. Whoever had done this to him was a monster, and she had to hold back tears as she dabbed at his swollen flesh.

"Fifty thousand," her brother said.

The breath whooshed out of her lungs, and for a moment, the room felt like it was spinning. A strong hand caught her elbow and lowered her into a kitchen chair. She looked up to see Jeb standing over her, his expression granite. But there was something close to sympathy shining in his dark eyes. He pulled his hand away and she sucked in a wavering breath.

"Fifty thousand dollars?" Leah breathed. "Simon, where on earth are we going to get that kind of money?"

Jeb should leave—he knew that. He wanted to leave, in fact. Everything inside him wanted to bolt for the door and get some space again, but when Leah had blanched like that and just about fainted, he didn't have a whole lot of choice.

He went to the sink and opened two cupboards before he found the glasses. There were a few dishes inside, but not many. Jeb couldn't boast much more in his own cupboards. He and Katie had started out with some proper dishes, but after her death, he and his uncle had broken them one by one through their own clumsiness and he was down to an assorted few.

Jeb grabbed a water glass and filled it from the tap, then returned to the table. Leah was ashen, her lips almost as white as her cheeks, and when he handed her the glass, her gaze fell to his scarred hand with the puckered, stretched skin. She licked her lips uncomfortably. He still wasn't used to this reaction—the revulsion. He placed it on the table next to her and pulled his hand behind his back and out of sight.

He knew what he looked like now—his face was worse than his arm and hand were, and his left leg was probably the worst of all. *Kinner* stared if they saw him on the road, clinging to their *mamms'* aprons, and they burst into tears if they were faced with him in an aisle in the farm supply store and didn't have an easy escape.

"Thank you," Leah said, a beat too late.

Jeb didn't answer.

His hip ached, and the skin on his arm was so tight that he couldn't fully extend it. He'd worked on that alone in his room, pushing past the point of comfort, grunting with pain—but something had happened to the tendons in that fire and they'd shrunk. He wasn't going to be the man he was before ever again.

Simon sat at the table and wiped blood from his nose on the back of one hand. He might be beaten up, but he'd heal up all right. Jeb's damage was more permanent . . . and, he dared to say, it went deeper. He'd lost his wife and his naïve optimism all in one tragic accident. He'd gained both these scars and his freedom from a marriage to a woman who loathed him . . .

And he hated that he was relieved.

"We'll figure out the money," Simon said to his sister. "We always do."

"You mean *I* always do!" Leah's voice shook, and Jeb looked over at Leah. Her color hadn't come back yet, and she looked exhausted.

Jeb took the cloth from her fingers and he turned to Simon. The younger man's gaze jerked up in surprise, but

Jeb put a solid hand on his shoulder to keep him put and carefully wiped the blood and dust from his face.

When Jeb had seen Simon stumbling down the road, his hat missing and blood dribbling from his face, he'd felt about how Leah looked right now. This was bad—and if whoever he owed was willing to give this kind of message, it wouldn't stop either. But what could he do? He'd pulled his buggy to a stop and helped Simon up onto the seat. There would be blood splats Jeb would have to hose off his buggy floorboards before the day was out.

But there was no confusion as to what had happened . . . and fifty thousand dollars wouldn't be easy to come by.

Jeb finished wiping off Simon's face, then he crossed his arms, looking the young man up and down. "Your leg—what happened there?"

"It's my knee," Simon said. "It'll be okay—"

It very likely required a hospital visit, but that cost money, too. Jeb sighed, then crouched down in front of Simon and gently felt the joint in question. There was a fair amount of swelling, but nothing felt broken or dislocated.

"Who did this?" Jeb asked, his voice low.

Simon didn't answer, and Jeb's anger started to rise. This was no game, and the idiot might end up dead in a ditch next time if he kept trying to play with whatever Englisher crooks he was associating with.

"Just some people. I'll get them the money—" Simon said after a moment.

"How?" Jeb demanded. "You're going to make your sister come up with it?"

Leah cleared her throat. "It's okay, Jeb. My brother and I will discuss it."

He doubted she had the cash. A man leaning on a woman like that—it put a bad taste in his mouth.

"You should go talk to the bishop," Jeb said. "Maybe the community can step in—"

"They've already threatened to discipline me," Simon said, his words slurring past his swollen mouth. "We're not going to the bishop."

Leah looked away, and her expression was grim. She was a woman very much on her own—single and trying to fix problems too big for any solitary person. Jeb might like his privacy, but there were times when a community could be of help. He wasn't blind to that.

"You just inherited this farm, didn't you?" Simon asked after a beat of silence. "Your uncle Peter just passed, and you were named heir. I know that."

Leah looked over at Jeb in surprise, and he felt the heat hit his face. That was private business, and he preferred to keep it that way. But apparently word was out. He had his own problems at the moment—namely, finding a new home.

"Yah, I was named heir, but there are a few complications there," Jeb replied. "Peter stipulated that I had to be married within four weeks of his passing in order for me to inherit, so my cousin, Menno, will get this land."

It had been a cruel stipulation, because Peter knew exactly why Jeb wouldn't remarry after his wife's death, free or not.

"Do you have any savings?" Simon pressed.

"Simon, stop that!" Leah seemed to be getting her color back. "I'm sorry about your uncle, Jeb. And I'm sorry for how callous Simon is being. My brother isn't himself right now—"

"Yah, I know," Jeb said.

"I did hear about the funeral," Leah added. "And I was going to send a letter of condolence, but—"

No, she hadn't been. That was a lie he was willing to forgive.

"It's fine," he said, and he headed to the sink to rinse out the cloth. "The funeral was very nice. The community did well by him."

"God rest his soul," she murmured.

"God rest his soul," he echoed, then wrung out the cloth and tossed it toward Simon. "Put that under your nose." Then he turned to Leah. "If I were you, I'd bandage up his knee nice and tight. I got kicked hard by a horse once, and that's what helped most. Do you have any steak in the house?"

Leah shrugged weakly. "I've got an old sheet to use for bandages, but no steak at the moment."

"I have one in the icebox at home. It was going to be my supper, but you can have it for his face."

It was something. Someone had to help her. Simon had some of Jeb's sympathy for the pain he was in right now, but he'd brought that punishment on himself, the young fool. But Leah was caught in the middle, and she was doing her best to provide for herself without a husband.

"I'll bring you some dinner," Leah said. "And then you won't go hungry. If that's okay with you."

"Yah. A fair trade," he agreed. "Thank you."

A woman's cooking . . . it had been a very long time since he'd had some.

Simon adjusted himself in his chair, leaning forward as he nursed his nose. Leah looked uncomfortable, her gaze flickering toward Jeb uncertainly. Right. He wasn't exactly welcome here.

"I should go," Jeb said, and he turned toward the door. Leah stood up and followed him.

"Jeb—" she started, and he glanced back. She closed the distance between them, tipping her face up to look him in the eye. He saw her slight recoil as her gaze moved over those scars. "What do you know about what my brother has been up to?"

Jeb glanced back at the young man. He wasn't about to keep his secrets, and if Simon hated him for it, so be it.

"He's been gambling with some dangerous Englishers,"

Jeb said. "They do this kind of thing when a man hasn't paid up. I can only imagine how long that debt has been growing." Jeb rubbed his good hand over his beard. "I saw him with a black eye and a sprained wrist once, and another time with a bloody nose. So this isn't the first time he's been beaten up."

"And no one thought to tell me," she breathed.

"He's an adult."

"He's my brother!" she snapped, but her chin quivered. Was she angry at him for not writing to tell her? As if staying in communication with his late uncle's renters was his responsibility.

Jeb had bigger problems.

"Really?" was all he said.

She licked her lips. "If you could maybe keep me informed of what he's up to—" she started, but the words evaporated on her lips when she saw his face. Were his feelings about her brother that obvious? Or was it just the scarring that stopped her like that?

"I won't be here," he reminded her. "Menno will inherit this land, remember? I'm sure my cousin will be happy to keep you on as renters. It's income, right? So, if you want someone to keep an eye on him, you'd have to talk to Menno."

Leah nodded, and tears misted her eyes. Blast. It wasn't just a beautiful woman crying that softened him like this, it was this particular woman. Life hadn't been easy for her either.

"I'm sorry," he added feebly. "If there was something I could do, I would."

Jeb pulled open the door and stepped outside. He couldn't stay here. He had work to do, a farm to run on his own for the time being, and getting emotionally involved in other people's problems wasn't good for him. The community might be a great support for others, but it hadn't ever been for him.

"If I came by at six, would you be at the house?" Leah asked.

"Yah. I can do that."

"I'll bring some fried chicken, in exchange for that steak."

Jeb nodded his agreement, then headed toward his buggy, the horse waiting patiently. Chicken in exchange for steak . . . except an idea had started to form that just might be the solution to both of their problems. She needed money, and he needed a legal wife in order to collect on that inheritance.

He glanced back and saw her standing at the door, her dark eyes fixed on him with a worried expression.

Leah was beautiful, and he was scarred. She was ten years younger than him, and far less emotionally damaged than he was. But she'd been left over in the marriage market, and she needed money.

He could get that money, if he inherited the land under his boots.

Was this as crazy as it sounded?

Chapter Two

Leah went back into the house and shut the door behind her. Her hands felt cold despite the hot weather, and she stood there for a moment feeling entirely drained of all feeling. She'd come home, thinking it would be a pleasant summer of canning food and mending her brother's clothes, but instead she'd stepped back into some sort of bad dream, and she was halfway waiting to wake from it.

Simon struggled to his feet, and Leah pushed back the fog and hurried toward him.

"Sit down," she said. "I need to wrap your knee. Jeb was right—you need a tight bandage if it's going to heal."

Simon sank back into the chair.

"Hold on. I'll fetch an old sheet," she said, and she went down the hallway to the linen cupboard. She found the tattered sheet she'd been thinking of and shook it open. It would do. Using her teeth to start the tear, she slowly tore a long strip from one side.

"I thought you'd stopped with the drinking and gambling," Leah said when she came back into the room.

"I had," Simon said.

"Not for good," she countered.

"It was a big game," he said.

"Jeb said there were other times he found you battered."

"Just let me explain." Simon shot her an annoyed look, but he pulled up his pant leg to expose his puffy knee. "It was a big game—you didn't have to come with much, but some big players were going to be there, and I knew I had a chance to win. So I went. Except I didn't win. I got pretty high in the ranking, and then I lost. I had signed a few IOUs, and they roughed me up when I didn't pay up within a few days. Then there was another game, and I thought I could pay it back if I just won . . ."

"But you didn't." Leah began to wrap her brother's knee with careful precision.

"No . . . and the same thing happened. So this last game, I knew I had to win, because losing just wasn't an option!"

"Obviously, that didn't work out," she muttered.

"But there is another game coming up—"

"Would you just stop?" she snapped. "Simon, look at you! They'll kill you next!"

"I'm fine—"

"You're not!" She tied off the bandage, and Simon pulled down his pant leg once more. "If you needed extra money, you should have told me, not tried to gamble for it."

"And you would have told me to get a job," he retorted.

"You need a job!" She shut her eyes for a moment, trying to calm the rising anger. "How long has it been since the RV place laid you off?"

"I don't know. Three months?"

Leah had been doing her best since her parents died, for all the good she'd done. She'd kept him fed, clothed, and she'd made him memorize his scripture verses. She'd worked extra jobs and even accepted charity to keep food on the table, but her brother didn't seem to appreciate any of it. If he had, he wouldn't be doing this to her now!

"Peter King was giving you work," she said. "Wasn't he?"

"He's dead."

"Yah, but there's still a farm to run!" she said. "And Jeb is doing it all himself. Maybe he'll hire you—"

"If I can't win the money, I need to pay back what I owe within two weeks," Simon said. "Or—"

"Or?" she demanded.

"They'll do it again." Simon's voice trembled this time. "If you don't want me to win it back, you've got to help me! I didn't want to talk about this in front of Jeb. It's not his business. You'll have to tell him not to tell anyone, okay?"

"Jeb keeps to himself," she said woodenly.

"Last month, the elders came," Simon said.

Leah winced. "They didn't tell me—"

"I'm old enough to marry, Leah. They aren't going to tell you anything anymore," Simon retorted. "But they told me that they were close to sending me away. It wouldn't be shunning exactly, because I'm not baptized yet, but they thought it would be better for me to go to another community."

"They might be right," Leah said.

"Except the people who I owe won't stop!" Simon said. "Don't you get it? Leah, they know where I live. They'll come after *you*—"

Leah rubbed her hands over her face, her mind spinning ahead. "Then we both leave. I'll bring you to Rimstone with me, and you'll have to stay on the straight and narrow. Maybe we'll call you a different name so that if someone asks about you, they won't know who they're talking about—"

"These men will come to our neighbors. I know how stupid I've been to get involved with people like this, Leah, I do. But my only option is to pay them back. Once they have the money, they'll leave me alone. And then I promise I'll never gamble again. I've learned my lesson!"

"Pay them back with *what*?" Leah shook her head. "Even if I scraped up every penny I have under my name, it won't be a fraction of what you owe! This isn't a matter of talking me into it, Simon! I don't want you killed, and I'd pay them off if I had access to the money. People don't just have fifty grand in their cookie tins!"

"Maybe the bishop would part with some of the community fund—"

"That money is for medical emergencies, paying for doctors . . . not gambling debt!"

The bishop wouldn't part with a penny of that money, and Leah knew it. The elders would have to agree, and their community all contributed to that fund. If there was fifty thousand dollars there, the Amish community of Abundance wouldn't be willing to empty it out for the likes of Simon Riehl.

"We'll have to hide you," Leah said. "They won't come beat a woman."

"I wouldn't count on it," Simon whispered.

A chill ran up her spine. Would these Englisher monsters really track down a woman and do to her what they'd done to her brother?

"But Jeb could lend us the money," Simon said. "He doesn't spend anything—he's got to have some! And I see the way he looks at you."

"Exactly *how* does he look at me?" she snapped, anger rising up inside her.

"He likes you," Simon said.

"And you'd have me flirt with him for money?" A man who'd been severely injured in a fire . . . a man who, it was rumored, was so badly injured that a married relationship would no longer be possible?

"I don't know!" Simon said, his voice rising. "If I had an easy answer, we wouldn't be arguing about this, would we? I'm just saying, of anyone, I think Jeb is the most likely to help us. He doesn't think much of me, but he does like you a lot, and—" He stopped short, the words hanging in the air between them.

Simon wouldn't say it out loud. His silent suggestion was disgusting, and even Simon knew that. But she knew what he was getting at. If she could sweet-talk Jeb into giving them a loan, combined with the money she'd stashed away, it might be enough to cover the debt, or to at least put a large enough dent in it to keep those thugs at bay for a little while longer.

"I have to start dinner," Leah said, and she headed to the sink to wash her hands. Outside the kitchen window, the sun was shining with all the bright optimism of a summer day, and instead of feeling comforting and tranquil, it felt glaring and harsh.

"Leah, if you'd just think about it—" Simon started.

"Simon, stop talking," she said, turning to give him a baleful look.

She wouldn't even admit to thinking over his shameful idea. What would he have her do, give her body up to a lonely man in exchange for money? Jeb might have a fair number of rumors swirling around him to do with his dead wife, but he'd not once shown an inclination to be unchaste, even after her death. If she was desperate enough to offer her body, he wouldn't accept it—of that, she was utterly certain. Would Simon have her just pretend to feel something for a man in order to manipulate him? The very thought was revolting to her. She had lived her life so far by the Amish faith and her desire to please God. She wouldn't start lying now, or manipulating. If a woman lost her integrity, what did she have left? There had to be some answer that allowed her to stay on the narrow path, to keep her dignity and to protect her brother.

Lord, help us! she prayed silently. *I don't know what we'll do!*

And yet her brother might be right that Jeb King was

their hope of a loan. But Jeb was a peculiar man. He'd always been a bit of a loner, keeping to himself. But there were the rumors . . . He and his wife, Katie, hadn't been exactly happy, and the Amish didn't divorce. There were some people who suggested that her death was highly convenient to Jeb. And there were others who argued that if he'd let her die purposefully, why would he have rushed into the flames and been so badly hurt? But the fact remained, after his time in the hospital healing from the burns, Jeb became even more of a hermit than he'd been before, loyal to a dead wife. So, if Jeb King was their solution, she had no idea what would soften him.

Jeb was a man with a past, a man with scars, and she didn't entirely trust him. He was huge—muscular and intimidating. If he offered help, she'd accept it, but she wouldn't go courting trouble with someone like him.

Leah turned her attention to her more immediate concerns, and that was making dinner. She needed a meal that would make up for the inconvenience her brother had already caused Jeb. This meal was supposed to be a celebration of her coming home again for the summer, and now it was turning into payment for a steak to help her brother's face heal, and perhaps a payment for the man's silence about what he'd witnessed today.

"Simon, you will bring the food to Jeb at six o'clock," she said.

"I'm not the one he wants to see," Simon countered.

"I'm not going to use my feminine wiles to manipulate a man into giving us money! If you want a loan from Jeb King, you're going to have to gain his good opinion on your own. I'm not doing it for you."

"He doesn't like me," Simon said.

"He's picked you up and dusted you off three times that I know off so far!" she retorted. "He thought you were worth that much bother. He's our neighbor, and if, as you say, he's our only hope, then I suggest you convince him of it yourself."

Simon was silent. Leah pulled down a container of breadcrumbs and some spices in preparation for fried chicken. Her cooking might be good, but it wasn't worth fifty thousand dollars to anyone.

"Okay," Simon said after a moment of silence.

"And I suggest you spend some time in prayer before you go," she added. "Because what you're asking for isn't a favor, it's a miracle."

Right now, she was thankful that she wasn't beautiful enough or even desirable enough to lure a man, even one who had lost as much as Jeb had. It took away the temptation to use her looks for her own benefit. That kind of thing could change a woman if she weren't careful . . .

Jeb dumped the last load of manure into the pile beside the horse barn. He had more work to do tonight after dinner—the cow barn hadn't been mucked out yet, and there was a bottle-fed calf in there that would need another bottle before bed. He pulled off his gloves, then wiped the sweat from his forehead with the back of his hand.

The day had been a hot one, and working the farm alone was a huge amount of work. After the funeral, some men from the community had come to lend a hand, but he'd assured them that if he needed some extra help, he'd get Menno to pitch in. That had been enough to make the other men feel better about going back to their own work and ceasing to worry about him. Except Jeb and Menno had never really gotten along, and he knew full well that he was sending away honest help to work this land alone.

It might be backbreaking labor, but he preferred it this way. He could work alone without the scrutiny of the other men who'd compare notes later over their fences, no doubt.

He was an oddity, and people looked at him funny when he passed by in town. He'd spent this much time alone that it actually felt good to continue it. It felt safer.

He pulled a watch out of his pants and looked at the time. It was almost six—Leah would be coming by the house soon with that promised fried chicken. His stomach rumbled at the thought, but it wasn't just his own hunger that made him pick up his pace as he headed to the pump to wash off before he went back to the house.

Maybe he was lonelier than he thought if he was looking forward to having a woman look in to his miserable little kitchen.

He'd already written off his idea of a marriage of convenience as stupid. She was beautiful and sweet, a good cook . . . she'd marry. She could even go to another community. But he couldn't quite let go of her money worries.

Fifty thousand dollars—that number had made his chest tighten, too. It was a lot of money, and he had no idea how she and Simon would scrape it together. If they didn't, would Jeb be physically intimidating enough to make a difference if those Englishers came at Simon again?

He'd have to be with him for that to work, and right now, Jeb didn't have the money to pay an employee. Every time he thought he'd figured out a way to help, it fell flat. Simon had certainly made his own bed.

As he came toward the pump, which was just past the garden and before the chicken coop, he saw Simon sitting on the step, a basket beside him. Jeb sighed. So, she hadn't come, after all.

It shouldn't matter.

Jeb heaved the pump and a gush of warm water flowed out onto his outstretched hand. He rubbed his hands and splashed the water over his arms, then heaved the handle again. The next gush of water was considerably colder, and he rubbed the water over his cheeks and let it run through his beard. Still dripping but significantly cleaner, he headed toward the house. Simon stood up as he approached.

He'd rather leave Simon outside, but he couldn't exactly do that.

"Best come in," Jeb said. "I'll get you that steak."

"Thanks," Simon replied.

Jeb picked up the basket, the aroma of fried chicken and potatoes wafting up to meet him. It smelled amazing— better than he'd been cooking for himself these days. He pushed open the side door, going inside first and letting Simon come in after him, delaying the inevitable judgment for a few seconds.

The kitchen table was covered in various tools and dishes he used on a regular basis, one end clear for him to eat.

"Sit down," Jeb said. "You're sore still, I'm sure."

Simon's gaze moved around the dusty kitchen in a slow perusal.

"Yah." Simon's voice was slightly breathy as he bent down to undo his boots.

"Leave them," Jeb said. He took off his own boots, which had been in the manure, leaving them by the door, then he deposited the basket on the table. Simon sank into a kitchen chair. Simon's face was puffy and raw still.

Jeb opened the icebox and took out the paper-wrapped steak, then tossed it on the table in front of the younger man. Then he pushed a hammer, a plastic bucket of nails, and a chipped but clean pitcher aside to make more room, opened the basket, and pulled out the dishes of food.

"Your sister's a good cook," Jeb said. It was what men said. It was a compliment to be sent back. "It smells great."

"Yah . . ." There was something in Simon's voice that made Jeb look up at him. "She's a good cook."

"You shouldn't take advantage of her like this," Jeb said. "A man your age should be making a full-time living, not working odd jobs. She looks like she's under a lot of strain."

And he knew what an unhappy woman looked like. He'd been married to one.

"I would work if I could find the position," Simon replied.

"Right." Jeb didn't believe that. It was just another excuse from a lazy ne'er-do-well.

"I haven't been a good man," Simon said. "I know it, and it's going to change. I've gone too far. I've learned my lesson."

"I'm glad to hear it." But what he'd rather see was results.

"Still, it's hard for someone with my reputation to get a good job," Simon went on. "You know that full well."

Was that a jab at Jeb's own reputation, or a plea for understanding? Jeb looked at Simon for a few seconds until Simon squirmed and dropped his gaze.

"I'm not in a position to help," Jeb replied curtly.

"You might be."

Jeb laughed bitterly. This was rather forward. "My cousin will be taking over this farm in a matter of weeks."

Simon eyed him for a moment, his one puffy eye narrowing as he squinted. "But you want to keep this place?"

Jeb sighed. "Not that it's your business, but that isn't possible."

"You said you had to be married to inherit," Simon pressed. "Didn't you?"

"And I'm not," Jeb retorted. Nor would he ever marry again. He was done with that.

"What if you could find a wife soon enough?" Simon asked.

"I'm not interested," Jeb snapped. What did this young idiot know about marriage? Jeb had inflicted himself on a woman for long enough, and that was when he was whole and healthy. Now, he was hardly the kind of man a woman wanted, and he wouldn't attempt marriage again.

"Here's the thing," Simon said. "My sister is the kindest, sweetest woman in Abundance. She's honest, she's good, and she's taken care of me ever since our parents died. She's put me ahead of herself for far too long. I thought she'd finally get a chance at her own happiness with Matthew Schrock. He was going to marry her until he found out she couldn't have children."

Jeb froze. So that was what happened?

"Why can't she?" Jeb asked feebly. This definitely was not his business, but he hadn't stopped the words from coming out of his mouth soon enough.

"Leah has something that didn't form right inside, and that's the result. Matthew wasn't willing to face a life with no *kinner*, so he dumped her. I was furious. They could have adopted, maybe, or . . . I don't even know. But she loved him with her whole heart, and he crushed her."

Jeb didn't answer that. It was a lot of information, and it only made him feel worse for Leah.

"My sister won't marry, Jeb," Simon went on, pleading in his eyes. "Not with her condition, and she's already thirty."

"I think you're being a little loose with your sister's private business," Jeb muttered.

"I see the way you look at her. You think she's beautiful—and she is! But we need fifty thousand dollars, and you need a wife," Simon said. "I know this is crude, and trust me, my sister has no idea I'm even bringing this up. But I have an idea that might help us all. If you could get legally married in time, this land is yours. That solves your problem. You'd own this land free and clear and wouldn't have to uproot and find some other way to make do. And if you inherit this land, then I'm thinking there's a way for you get your hands on the money we need. . . ."

There was a certain amount in a bank account that came with the inheritance, as far as Jeb understood, so the kid had a point. He'd already considered this very option and discarded it. He eyed Simon distrustfully.

"And I know that you and Leah wouldn't be marrying for love, but I also know my sister. She'd learn to love you, and given any amount of time with her, I think you'd fall headlong in love with her, too."

"You don't know what I want, Simon," Jeb warned. "Marriage is tricky. It isn't just a matter of a good cook and a good farmer."

"She has no other marriage options. If she doesn't want to do this, she'll stay single. I think she deserves a chance at cooking for a husband instead of her brother. She needs more than me."

"And this is all about her happiness, and not about the money," Jeb said dryly.

"Look, the money factors in," Simon said. "I'd be lying if I wasn't thinking about it. I was trying to be brave in front of my sister, but I'm scared."

Jeb rubbed his hand over his mouth, then turned away. How much did he trust Simon's version of things? Simon had fifty thousand dollars to gain if they decided on this plan . . .

"You think I'll only rack up the debt again," Simon interjected.

"It occurred to me," Jeb replied.

"I'd promise you, between men, that I'll go straight. No more risk or bad behavior. I'll work the farm for you, if you want. But you won't have to worry about me again if you give me that money to pay off my debt. I'll swear to God Himself."

Jeb winced at the wording. "Don't toy with God, boy."

"I'm not toying."

Jeb licked his lips, crossing his arms over his chest.

"Do you think she's attractive?" Simon asked tentatively.

"Don't ask me about that," Jeb retorted.

"I'm just saying, she'll make a good wife, given the chance, and by the looks of things around here, you could use a woman—"

"Shut your mouth, boy!" Jeb snapped. "Don't think you can solve a man's bitterness by throwing an available woman at him."

Simon paled slightly but didn't open his mouth again. Jeb stood there, the smell of the chicken and potatoes curling temptingly toward him. Yah, he thought she was beautiful, but he'd seen the way she'd recoiled from him.

"I know you want to see her married, but does she want marriage?" Jeb asked at last. "Even without *kinner*?"

"I think it's worth discussing, the three of us," Simon replied, but a smile was already tugging at his lips. He sensed victory.

Maybe he wouldn't be so averse to the idea of a woman in this house again. With some safeguards, of course. His gaze moved toward the window, where he could see a corner of the barn and the broad expanse of garden with the leafy rows of vegetables.

This land that he'd worked for fifteen years, the barn they'd rebuilt together as a community, the acre after acre of memories and sweat . . .

Menno was the cousin who'd looked down on him for years, and who'd let him work his father's farm without ever once suggesting he pitch in and help. Having Menno taking this place over would be a blow, and if there was a way to keep it, maybe it was worth the conversation.

He peeled the foil off the first dish and put two chunky pieces of fried chicken on his plate. The third piece he passed to Simon.

"I've already eaten," Simon said.

"Eat more," Jeb retorted. "I don't like people staring at me while I eat."

A woman. A wife . . . Did he dare even entertain the thought of marriage again? He'd been disappointment enough for his first wife. But there was a tiny finger of hope that wormed up inside him. There were certain pleasures of having a woman in his home—the food at mealtime, that soft scent of whatever it was women used that made them smell so feminine. It used to linger in the upstairs hallway . . . He hadn't remembered it until now.

Was he just as foolish as Simon here to even be considering this?

Chapter Three

Leah dried the last fork and put it back into the drawer. The summer sun hung low and golden in the sky, but it would be past bedtime before it actually got dark. She stood with the damp dish towel in her hand, her mind spinning.

Maybe she should go to the bishop . . . but what if this was the last straw for her brother and they sent him away? What if this was the rejection that would push her brother right out of their community for good? She'd promised God that she'd do her best by her little brother, and she'd been afraid that he'd go English for some time now. Besides, as Simon pointed out, it wouldn't protect her if she stayed here and he left. And it wouldn't protect their community. When wicked men wanted their money, they'd stop at nothing to get it. There seemed no way to fix this. What she wouldn't do to go back to the days when her brother's antics were reparable, like when he'd stolen candy from a store and she marched him right back over and made him give it back and apologize. It wasn't so easy anymore, and the consequences could be deadly.

A pile of bloodstained cloths were still on the kitchen table, and she gathered them up and tossed them into the laundry hamper. Tears welled in her eyes at the memory of her brother's bleeding face.

"He's an idiot," she muttered, and she grabbed a cloth and a spray bottle of vinegar and water. "He'll get himself killed for a game of cards!"

Except it wasn't so simple as that. He'd been pulled in, and the more he struggled, the harder they pulled, like spiders in a web. She scoured the tabletop, scrubbing with all her strength. She hated feeling so helpless.

The side door opened, and she looked up to see both Simon and Jeb. They came into the kitchen and Jeb bent down to take off his boots. She eyed them uncertainly. What had happened out there? Did the men come to some sort of agreement?

"You're back, then," she said, and her voice sounded strangled in her own ears.

"Yah." Simon came inside and dropped the paper-wrapped steak onto the freshly washed table. He pulled out a pocketknife and cut the string.

"Sit," Leah said, and when her brother was seated, she carefully laid the piece of meat over his eye.

"Thank you for seeing him home," Leah said, nodding toward Jeb. "It's appreciated."

Jeb put the basket on the table. "It was good chicken. Thank you."

"I'm glad. You're welcome."

Jeb dropped his gaze and crossed his arms over his chest. He didn't seem in a hurry to leave, and that might be good news. Maybe her brother had succeeded in convincing their neighbor that he was worth an investment. She looked up at the large man hopefully, and Jeb met her gaze for a moment, the intensity in his eyes making a shiver run down her arms.

"Leah, we've been talking," Simon said, straightening

and holding the meat in place with one hand. "There's a solution here that might work for all of us."

"Oh?" She looked between them. Jeb was looking away again.

"Here's the way I see it," Simon went on. "We need fifty thousand dollars, and that's not easy to come by. If we don't get it, I'm in a lot of trouble. And Jeb here has been working this land for . . . how long?"

"Fifteen years," Jeb replied.

"And his cousin is about to inherit this farm right out from under him if he can't suss up a wife."

Leah felt the heat in her face. "Simon, you can't just arrange a marriage for money."

"Leah, you *should* get married," Simon said. "What do you have right now? You've got a loser of a younger brother who keeps messing things up and a job teaching school in another community. I know you were hoping to find some solid widower out there who might be interested in marriage again, and unless there is a man in Rimstone you haven't mentioned—"

"No," she said curtly. And that was true, she had been husband hunting in Rimstone. When Matthew dumped her and immediately picked up with Rebecca, she'd thought that perhaps the best way through a broken heart was to move on, too. She had the idea that maybe a widower with a houseful of young *kinner* might be happy enough to take on a wife who'd be happy raising the *kinner* he already had. But there wasn't quite the abundance of widowers as a discarded single woman might hope.

"Simon, you're very naïve in some ways. If this is your idea of fixing your own problem, then forget it. Marriage is for life. Jeb could marry again, and you can't just have some legal arrangement that will cut off any chance of a man finding love—"

"I won't." Jeb's deep voice reverberated through the

room. Did he mean he wouldn't find love again or wouldn't marry again? It shouldn't matter. The two went hand in hand.

"Well, then, you see?" Leah shot her brother an annoyed look. Simon was making them both look foolish.

"I don't have fifty thousand dollars," Jeb said. "I've saved a little, but my uncle didn't pay me much with the understanding that he'd leave me the farm. The money I did make, I sent to my *mamm*. However, the inheritance does include some money meant to be used to buy seed and livestock and the like. If I inherited this land, I'd get that money, too, and I could use it for your brother's debt."

Leah blinked at him. Jeb was seriously considering this?

"You said you wouldn't marry again," she said.

"I never meant to marry again," he replied. "That might be a more accurate statement."

"I'm not being a wife on paper," she said curtly. "I'd rather be single and keep my own name than do that."

"I'm not asking you to," Jeb said.

"Oh . . ." She felt the heat in her face, and she wished she could hide her embarrassment better than this. "If you're asking me to find you a wife—"

"I know what I am," Jeb said, his voice low and deep. "I know I'm . . . disagreeable and scarred. I'm not exactly the kind of man a woman dreams of marrying. But I've also got my integrity. I'm not going to try to cheat my cousin out of that land. My uncle made it clear before he died that he wanted me to have that farm, but his will clarified his wishes a little more—he also wanted me married. What would that make me if I went around his wishes and put a woman's name next to mine for money? I might have the farm, but I wouldn't have the respect of anyone in this community. I couldn't live with myself. It's not worth it that way. So I'm not interested in putting someone on paper just to get some land. That would be dishonest, and this community can think of me what they will, but I'm not a liar."

Leah looked back toward him. Jeb stood there, his arms still crossed over his chest, but that dark, direct gaze was locked on her. There was no escaping it.

His eyes were the most disconcerting, because they didn't seem to match the rest of him. He was tall and muscular, but the scars drew the eye with their puckered ugliness. His eyes, however, held her with the same demand of an attractive man who might think he had something to offer.

"Leah, walk with me outside," Jeb said. "This is a conversation that should be had in private."

Leah looked toward her brother, but he wouldn't meet her gaze, that steak held in place over the side of his face. She needed to clear this up—make sure Jeb didn't think she was throwing herself at him for some money. She had her integrity, too.

Jeb held the door open, a faint breeze feeling good as it pressed against his shirt. Leah followed him, passing in front of him to get outside. She was shorter than him, coming up just past his shoulder, but she felt like a more commanding presence than she looked. Maybe that was the schoolteacher in her.

The screen door banged shut behind them, and Jeb led the way, ambling away from the house and toward the small field where Leah and Simon's two horses grazed. The sunlight was golden and warm, and bees buzzed lazily over the patches of purple wildflowers that grew up by the fence posts.

"I'm sorry about my brother," Leah said as she got to his side. "I told him he needed to talk to you himself if he wanted to arrange a loan. I had no idea he'd—"

"I think it's a workable idea," Jeb said, cutting her off.

"You do?" She frowned at him.

"And you didn't suggest it?" he asked.

"No." She swallowed. "I'm not the kind of woman who makes a business deal out of a marriage."

And he wasn't that kind of man ordinarily either. He pulled off his hat and rubbed his fingers through his hair.

"I'm not going to find another woman and marry again," he said quietly. "That's just a fact. And I had made my peace with that. One marriage was enough for me. At least a marriage with all the expectations attached to it."

"What expectations . . . exactly?" she asked.

"Love. Passion. Connection." All the things *he'd* longed for in his first marriage to a woman who had loved someone else . . .

"Oh." She smiled wistfully, and he recognized that look in her eyes. That was a woman who still dreamed of love.

"You still want to marry one day," he said.

"I think my chances at marriage are past," she said. "For me, that is. I'm thirty, you know. I can't have children either. I know that's a lot of information, but it explains it, doesn't it? I'm both old and infertile. I'm not exactly in demand."

"You aren't old," he said with a low laugh.

"You know what I mean."

Yah, he did. There always seemed to be more women than men in Amish communities, and the marriage market could be competitive. There came a point when it was simply too late, and a woman had to make her peace with that, too.

"So maybe we could help each other," he said quietly.

"How?" she asked.

"By getting married."

She blinked at him, then a faint smile tugged at her lips

as if she were just getting a joke. "I don't think you're serious."

"I am, though," he said. "The thing is, my best days are behind me. What I want is to work this farm. My cousin Menno hates me. I know that's a hard thing to say about a family member for us Amish, but it's true. I don't even remember when it started now. Probably when we were *kinner*. My point is, my cousin and I aren't going to farm together. There is no cozy family reconciliation on the horizon for us. But I'm not inheriting this land without a wedding."

"Why did your uncle make that stipulation?" Leah asked.

"That was old Peter for you," Jeb replied. "Even after all my injuries, he figured I still had something a woman might want in a man. I disagreed with him on that point. Anyway, I think it was his attempt to make me more appealing to the available women if I came with a farm."

"He meant well," she said.

He shrugged. "Something like that. Thing is, I can't just go find some unsuspecting woman and ask her to marry me. I'm . . . well, you see me. I'm a bit of a romantic disappointment, I think. I know myself, and I'm better off single. But if there were a woman who could benefit from an arrangement with me . . . someone who wouldn't expect too much and might see the arrangement as mutually beneficial . . ."

Jeb paused, watching the emotions flit across her face. She didn't answer, and he didn't go on. She pursed her lips and looked down at her feet.

If there were a woman who didn't mind these ugly scars, who could see beyond them to the man in him. If there were a woman who might even learn to love him over time . . .

"Let's look at this logically, then," she said quietly. "Marriage could be beneficial to me in the community. I wouldn't be an old maid anymore. I'd be married. It would make things easier with the other women. I won't have *kinner*, but at least I could have a husband."

"Yah . . . I could be that," he said.

"If we were very clear on expectations, we might be able to make an agreeable arrangement," she said.

"Such as?" he asked, squinting.

"Well . . . I can't have *kinner*. You know that up front. And if *kinner* aren't part of our deal, then I'd want a bedroom of my own. That part of marriage would be off the table."

No intimacy. The words hung heavy in the air. His first wife hadn't wanted that kind of intimacy with him either. She'd been in love with an Englisher man, and her family had insisted upon their proper Amish marriage to try to make her forget about him. Jeb had no desire to push himself onto a woman in that way. If she didn't want him, she didn't want him. But they could still benefit, couldn't they?

"You don't want . . . to share a bed," he said softly.

"No." She shook her head. "I think it's better to just face this for what it is, don't you? If we both stand to gain from this marriage, we don't need to play games. Not between us, at least."

Marital intimacy was supposed to be a part of marriage, but he'd already been through a miserable marriage. He wasn't interested in talking a woman into intimacy, or taking what crumbs were tossed in his direction, especially not now with his scarred body. Maybe this was the better way—less rejection all around.

"What happens in a marriage bed, or doesn't happen for that matter, is private," Jeb said. "I can agree to that. I can give you your own bedroom so you can be most comfortable, too. But we'd have to live together. It would have to be a real partnership."

"A partnership?" she asked.

"A friendship, perhaps. We'd have to mean those vows—that we won't go looking for intimacy with others and embarrass each other that way, we'll have each other's best interests at heart, we'll take care of each other when we get old or sick."

"Yah." She nodded. "I agree with that. The important part of marriage."

So, they were going to pretend that the physical wasn't important . . . and maybe it wasn't. If they did this, it would be a unique arrangement anyway, and their private deal wouldn't be anyone else's business.

"Is there anything else we'd need to agree on?" Jeb asked.

"Perhaps what we wanted from the marriage," she said. "We can talk about what we don't want, but what do we hope to gain from it? It's a lifetime agreement, after all."

"Yah, a rather long-lasting one," he agreed. "What do *you* want?"

"I want social acceptance," she said. "I want our community to see me as a wife. I want to be a legitimately grown woman at the sewing circle. So there would be a few social gatherings we'd go to together, and we'd never let anyone know about our private arrangement, or the women wouldn't respect me at all. It would have to be seen as a real marriage, a love match."

"I could . . . keep up appearances," he said.

Whatever that might look like. He wasn't keen on going to barn raisings and hymn sings, but he could do one or two to help her solidify her position as a wife in the community. And maybe it would feel nice to have the same respect of "married person" afforded to him.

"And what do you want from this arrangement?" she asked. "Besides the farm, I mean."

"Peace in my home," he said quietly.

She raised her eyebrows questioningly.

"No fighting," he clarified. "No anger simmering beneath the surface. No name-calling. No jokes at the other's expense. I'd want quiet and respect."

"Quiet and respect," she murmured.

"Going both ways, of course," he clarified. "I'm not asking you to wait on me exactly, but the women's work would fall to you, obviously. I'd be working the farm on my own, so I'd be out there dawn to dusk . . . and maybe even later. So I'm not saying I'd be a hard husband or anything. It's just that in my first marriage—" No, he didn't want to get into that. The past was the past, and it wasn't even her business. "I'm just asking you not to . . . be cruel. That's all. And I'll do my very best by you."

"I wouldn't be mean to you," she said, shaking her head, and the look in her eyes looked genuinely confused. "I can promise you that much, yah. No name-calling—obviously. No teasing or barbed words. I don't know what you lived with before, Jeb, but that sounds awful to me, too."

"I suppose that's a good thing," he said with a nod. He already felt like he'd said too much there, but if he was thinking about marrying her, he'd better be clear about it. "I'm a private man, and I'd want my business to stay that way."

"Agreed," she said.

Jeb looked down at her, the wind having worked a tendril of her auburn hair free and her brown eyes meeting his earnestly.

"So that's the fine print, I suppose," he said, and he smiled faintly. "Do you need to pray on this? Sleep on it? Take some time? We have three weeks until my deadline to wed is up."

"I don't have three weeks," she said simply. "The

Englishers gave Simon two weeks to come up with the money."

"So, time is of the essence," he murmured.

"Yah." She sucked in a breath, looking at him hesitantly. She was waiting for him to do this—make it official.

Was he crazy here? He'd spent the last fifteen years convinced that being on his own was the best thing, and now within a space of a few hours, he was going to ask a woman to marry him for convenience, without any of the marital sweetness after the lamp was blown out?

Lord, am I making a mistake?

But the heavens were silent, save for the twitter of birds overhead, and he looked down at the woman in front him—her soft eyes, the lines just forming around them, her face looking pale with the pressure of the moment.

If he didn't want to lose this farm, he knew what he had to do . . . and it wasn't like he was going to marry again. He was scarred, ugly, undesirable to the women of Abundance. He'd be alone for the rest of his life otherwise.

"Well, then," he said, clearing his throat. "Leah, taking into account all the things we've just talked over, will you marry me?"

His breath caught in his throat as he looked down at her. Those pale cheeks pinked then, and she smiled.

"Yah. I think I will."

Jeb laughed softly. "Okay, then. Am I supposed to kiss you? Or do we skip that?"

"Maybe skip it," she said, and she dropped her gaze.

"Right." He cleared his throat. "I'll talk to the bishop, then, and see if he can read our banns this week at service, and then I'll go to the lawyer and make sure the papers are ready for the day after our wedding. Then I'll give you the money, and you can take care of that."

His mind was already skipping ahead. There would be things to do to get ready for a wife coming home to his house . . . but it would indeed be *his* house. The land, the house, the cattle, the very fence posts would be properly his, and no one could take them away.

"Thank you, Jeb," she said, and he felt her hand press against his scarred forearm, then she pulled her hand back and winced. "Sorry."

"It doesn't hurt," he said.

"No?"

"No."

She reached out purposefully, as if willing herself to do it, and touched his arm again. This time she didn't pull back, and she didn't wince. A lump rose in his throat. This was the first time anyone besides a medical practitioner had touched his scars, and it was oddly sweeter than a kiss would have been. Maybe she was right. There were more important parts to a marriage.

Jeb pressed his hand over hers, then nodded toward the house. "Best tell Simon."

Leah pulled her hand back. "I will."

Then she headed toward the house, leaving him by the fence in the warm sunlight and the low drone of the bees.

He was officially engaged. For the second time in his life.

Chapter Four

Leah couldn't attend service that week after all. Tradition held that when the banns were announced, the betrothed would be spending a day together at the bride-to-be's family home. She'd cook for her fiancé and they'd have a few hours together while everyone else was at service.

They didn't follow that tradition, however. She didn't cook for Jeb, and he didn't come to spend the day with her. He had too much work to do on his farm, and this wasn't exactly a chance for two lovers to play house. No one would know the difference anyway—and if Simon suspected they'd skipped their private meal together, he had his own reasons to keep that information to himself; this wedding was for saving his skin.

Rosmanda and Levi offered to host the wedding at their farm, a truly generous offer on her friend's part. And the community would pitch in with food and physical labor. By Thursday, with her community behind her, Leah would be properly wed. Jeb would be her husband, for better or for worse. With the Amish, there was no going back once those vows were said. Jeb King would be both their immediate salvation and her lifetime of penance.

* * *

Thursday morning, Leah stood in Rosmanda's daughters' bedroom on the second floor of the Lapp farmhouse. Rosmanda's in-laws were bustling downstairs, giving orders to arriving guests and helpers alike, and Leah could hear their voices through the floor.

The small bedroom had two slender beds on opposite sides of the room with a white-painted dresser between them. There were wooden boxes of books and toys that had been pushed out of the way to make room for her, although she had nothing left to do to get ready for the wedding but wait. She'd finished her blue wedding dress last night, and Rosmanda had provided a fresh, white apron and *kapp* for her, made by Rosmanda's mother-in-law. So, Leah stood by the window watching the process of guests arriving and buggies being parked in the nearest field like they did on a Service Sunday.

This was her wedding day, and her stomach was knotted in nervousness.

Behind the house on a stretch of lawn, the church benches had been set up for the service. Leah couldn't see them from her vantage point, but Rosmanda had told her the plan. It was a rushed wedding—not everyone would be staying for the meal afterward, and the games. Jeb's family—his cousins and aunts and uncles—would stay, as would Leah's brother and her particular friends with their husbands and *kinner*. All in all, only about forty people would be eating after the wedding, but even that small a crowd would be a lot of work.

Leah plucked at a loose thread at her side—she'd missed one, it seemed. She wrapped it around her fingertip and looked around for some scissors. She didn't see any, and she released the thread.

Another few buggies arrived one after another. The first one stopped in front of the house, and Rebecca Schrock carefully climbed down. Her movements were cautious and slow, making up for a swelling belly that Leah could clearly see from above. Rosmanda had been right about her snug-fitting clothing, and the sight of the younger woman's rounded figure was like a vice around her ribcage. Rebecca waved, and her voice could be heard floating through the air, calling a hello to Rosmanda.

Leah forced herself to inhale and she tried to calm the beating of her heart.

There she was—Matthew's preference, and the mother of his first child.

Tears misted her eyes, and Leah blinked them back. When she'd imagined her wedding day, it hadn't been like this . . . and in her fondest dreams, the man she was joined to was Matthew Schrock, not some older man disfigured by scars.

The buggy moved on, circling toward the field where Matthew would unhitch the horses and let them graze, and Leah's gaze followed that gray buggy, her heart tugging toward it.

Oh, Matthew . . .

Leah pressed her lips together, then stepped back away from the window. Why had he come? Why not stay away and let her have her wedding day without her ex-fiancé there to ruin it? But then, maybe this was for the best— let him see her properly married. She'd been teaching in Rimstone when he married Rebecca, and she'd stayed away. He should be doing the same . . . or maybe not. They were all part of the same community, and they had to find a way to work together. She couldn't avoid Matthew and Rebecca forever. Besides, everyone ended up related to one another somehow through the community's complicated web of marriages. That was how a community stayed united—not taking things too far in dating, and if it didn't work out, then forgetting and moving on.

Was it wrong, then, that she hoped that somewhere deep

in Matthew's heart, watching her take vows with another man would draw a little blood for him?

The bedroom door opened, and Leah quickly wiped her eyes and turned to see Rosmanda come inside. Rosmanda stood with her hand on her belly, her dress properly let out so as not to draw undue attention to her figure. Her face was rounder with her pregnancy, though, and she had little beads of sweat along her hairline. She blew out a long breath, then looked Leah up and down, stopping as she saw Leah's face.

"Are you all right?" Rosmanda asked, frowning.

"Yah. Fine." Leah forced a smile.

"Oh . . . you saw him," Rosmanda said.

"I couldn't see him from up here," Leah said. "I saw *her*."

They didn't need to use names. They both knew who they were talking about.

Rosmanda shrugged tiredly. "You're getting married, Leah. You're moving on, too. Don't let him ruin this day for you."

Because Rosmanda believed that this was a real marriage. She might not be fooled into thinking Leah had fallen in love with the older man, but she did believe they'd share everything and grow to love each other.

"I wish he would have stayed away," Leah said.

"Well, he came." Rosmanda dabbed at her forehead with a handkerchief. "For what it's worth, he wishes you well. He and Rebecca are giving you some canning jars— the good kind. Four whole cases."

"Yah, very kind," Leah said. "I'm sure he means well."

"Let Jeb see you happy and with eyes only for him," Rosmanda said. "That's my advice. This is your wedding day, and you don't want to mar it with hard feelings. You'll look back on today, and you'll want to remember it well."

"I'm fine," Leah said. Her gaze drifted toward the window once more, and she saw Matthew striding back toward the yard. His shirtsleeves were rolled up his forearms, revealing his deep tan. He waved and smiled, teeth flashing, as someone greeted him. He didn't look up toward the window. Leah turned back to her friend, lifted her arm. "I have a stray thread here—"

Rosmanda went to the closet and came back with a pair of scissors. She trimmed the thread, then stood back to look her over once more.

"You look lovely, Leah," she said. "I'm so happy you're doing this."

Leah looked into her friend's face, and for a moment, she was tempted to unburden herself of the truth. In a way it would feel good to say it out loud—that this marriage wasn't what anyone thought! She was doing this for her brother. But a confession, while good for the soul, wouldn't give her the respect in the community that she wanted so badly.

"Is Jeb down there?" she asked instead.

Had *he* changed his mind about this? She wasn't sure if she'd be relieved or mortified if he did . . . to be cast aside twice—it would be almost too much to bear, even if this marriage wasn't one of love and romance.

"Yah, Jeb is outside with the bishop and his brother-in-law. He's been pacing around all nervously," Rosmanda replied with a low laugh. "I've been watching him the last few minutes from the kitchen window."

"Rosmanda, is this a mistake?" Leah asked.

"A mistake?" Her friend shook her head. "You said you cared for him, and he wants to marry you, and—"

"You said you wanted to warn Rebecca, but it wasn't your place. Well, it is your place now, and I want you to speak plainly," Leah said. "If you were me, if you were in my shoes, would you marry Jeb King?"

"What does it matter what other people say?" Rosmanda asked. "When you care for a man, you care for him. You'll grow into loving him. I know it. Rebecca was young, marrying a man who clearly loved another and then callously tossed her aside. There would be emotional baggage there that she couldn't even begin to fathom. For you . . . you're no young thing. You know what you're doing. You know what this means."

Except Leah wasn't sure that she actually did know what she was doing, and that was the problem. But she didn't feel like she had any other choice either.

"Am I missing out on some harbinger of heartbreak?" Leah pressed. "Something I haven't anticipated yet?"

"Look at my husband—several well-meaning family members warned me off him, you know."

"Are you warning me, then?" Leah pressed. Because she knew the reasons why she didn't want to marry the man—and they were plentiful. But were there worse things than an older hermit she felt nothing for? At least he wouldn't be pressuring her for intimacies she didn't want to give.

Rosmanda was silent for a moment, then she shook her head. "I'm happy for you. Love is terrifying. I know that better than most. But it's worth it."

Love might be all those things, but Leah wasn't a woman in love. Still, unless she wanted to unveil all her secrets, she wasn't going to get any useful advice.

There was a tap on the door, and Leah clamped her mouth shut, wondering if they'd been overheard.

"Come in," Rosmanda called with forced cheeriness.

The door opened and Simon appeared in the doorway. He wore his Sunday best—a pair of black pants and a fresh, white, short-sleeved shirt. His hat sat straight across his forehead, but the bruises on his face were a mottled green color. He smiled at Leah hesitantly.

"You still up for this?" Simon asked.

Rosmanda and Simon both looked at Leah, as if both

wanted an answer to that. Was she ready to do this? No! Every part of her wanted to run away from this marriage, but if she did, her brother would be the one to pay, and she couldn't let that happen.

"I'm ready to get married," she said, and she met her brother's gaze solemnly. He nodded, and she saw the gratefulness in Simon's eyes.

He'd not only gotten himself into a heap of trouble, but rescuing him would leave consequences lasting a lifetime. And there was no one else on this planet who would be willing to take such a leap for him.

"Let's go, then," Rosmanda said, and Leah sucked in a shaky breath.

Jeb King might not be her first choice in a husband, but this wedding would help them both.

It was time to let her romantic hopes go and embrace the practical. It was all she had left.

The day was hotter than usual—or maybe it was just Jeb's new clothes that seemed to seal in the heat. His hip ached, as did his leg. When he stood for long periods of time without stretching, this was how it got. The new black shirt felt itchy around the neck, and the black hat, also new, was just a smidge too loose and he felt like the wind would take it away.

He never had been comfortable in crowds, or in formal clothing. He hadn't been around this many people since his first wedding, and it made him feel like he wanted to sink into the ground. He wasn't used to society anymore. He didn't trust them.

Jeb knew that his neighbors weren't here to celebrate *with* him exactly. They were here to see the wedding they'd all be talking about for the next year, and not because of the size of the event either. This was a small affair. They'd be talking about the strange hermit who married the old maid and inherited a farm as a result.

Menno hadn't come. Jeb had been looking for him since he'd arrived, wondering if his cousin would bother attending. Was Menno that angry about the farm? Probably, and a wriggle of guilt wormed up inside him. Peter could leave the farm to anyone he chose, but an only son tended to have a few expectations along those lines, and with this wedding, Jeb was taking the land.

"You look good," Isaiah said, and Jeb startled as his brother-in-law seemed to materialize beside him. Isaiah was Jeb's older sister Lynita's husband.

"Yah?" Jeb heaved a sigh. "Thank you."

"You don't have to look so grim," Isaiah said with a low laugh. "You're getting married. Look the part."

"I'm happy. Just nervous," Jeb assured his brother-in-law.

"Marriage is a blessing," Isaiah said, lowering his voice. "You didn't get to experience that before, but it is. Look at Lynita and me. You'll have the happiness now. I'm sure of it."

Jeb glanced at Isaiah. "And I'll start out with a farm."

Isaiah's lips twitched up into a rueful smile. "You're allowed more than one blessing, Jeb."

Jeb couldn't help smiling at Isaiah's humor. "I know. It's just . . . it will be easier this time. We'll be comfortable. That's all I meant."

"Yah." Isaiah patted his shoulder. "Definitely."

But there was a certain look in Isaiah's eye that Jeb didn't like. It was a little too close to pity. How much did his brother-in-law suspect? Because when he'd told his sister about his plans to wed, he hadn't told her the whole truth. He'd just said that it might be quick, but he and Leah were certain of their decision. He'd hoped that was close enough to the truth without outright lying to her. Maybe they'd seen through him.

The benches were all set up on the stretch of grass behind the Lapp farmhouse. Tall, rustling trees threw welcome shade. The women milled next to their side of the benches. Jeb's instinct was to move toward a back bench, but today was about him, and he wouldn't have any easy escape from public view.

With only a few days to prepare, this wedding didn't have the usual trappings—he didn't have any friends standing with him in matching black shirts, for example. But he did have Lynita, who was helping in the kitchen, Isaiah standing guard, and their *kinner*, the youngest of whom was thirteen already, milling about. Even if he didn't make enough effort to see them, they'd made the effort for him today, and he was deeply grateful for that.

Jeb's first wedding was tense and hopeful. This wedding was tense, but realistic. And just like last time, he was about to be united to a beautiful woman who had no real desire to marry him.

Jeb looked past the milling guests toward the house just in time to see Leah and Rosmanda come outside with Simon behind. Leah was pale, and her gaze flickered over the crowd of neighbors before landing on him. Jeb smiled hesitantly. She didn't smile back, but she did meet his gaze and hold it. They were in this together, if nothing else.

The guests moved toward the benches to take their seats, and Jeb allowed Isaiah to nudge him toward the center of the benches between the women's side and the men's, where an opening had been left for the main event—the ceremony. Rosmanda led Leah to the same spot. Two high-backed chairs sat side by side, and Jeb waited until Leah smoothed her dress behind her and sat. Then he took the chair next to her. Sitting was a relief to his aching hip, and he straightened out his scarred leg to get more comfortable.

There would be an hour and a half of sermons before they took their vows together, then at least another hour of preaching, if not more, afterward. Jeb looked over at Leah, his gaze moving over the details of her new blue dress, a starched apron with one stray thread, and her pale hands clasped in a white-knuckled grip on her lap.

"Hello," he whispered, hoping to break some of that tension.

Leah looked over at him, and she smiled hesitantly. "This is it."

"Yah. You look very nice."

She seemed to notice the stray thread just then because she reached down and tried to tug it free, then folded it carefully out of sight.

"It'll be all right," he added.

"You sure?" she whispered.

"I promise." He caught her gaze and held it. "I'll be good to you, Leah."

Some color touched her cheeks then, and he was relieved to see it. He was serious, too. He wouldn't argue with her. He wouldn't make demands. He'd give her her own bedroom and a respectful distance.

"And the money for Simon?" she breathed, her words so quiet, he almost didn't catch them.

"Tomorrow morning I'll bring our wedding license to the lawyer. I won't waste any time."

"Thank you . . ."

In the moment, it was easy to forget that this was all about money, but it was, and the fact sobered him.

"Leah—" His mouth felt dry now, and when she raised his gaze to meet his again, he deeply hoped this wasn't another mistake. He didn't know what he was looking for—reassurance, maybe? Because he was scared, too.

He didn't have a chance to say anything more, because Bishop Yoder joined them at the front. And maybe it was for the best, because Jeb had nothing left to say, just some fleeting desire to connect with her on a human level—to see something in her deep brown eyes besides wariness and determination to see this through. The bishop opened a hymn book and began to sing the first few lines of a familiar hymn. The congregation joined in, and as the voices rose up in harmony around him, Jeb adjusted his position slightly, looking for some comfort for his aching hip.

Jeb didn't sing, and when he stole a look at Leah, he found her mouthing the words, but no sound came out of her.

This was their wedding.

Lord, he prayed. *Are You able to bless this?*

Because everyone knew that God didn't bless lies.

The sermons commenced, and they were lengthy and filled with biblical confirmation that a marriage was a holy union, not to be entered upon lightly or without due prayer and solemnity. Two different preachers stood up to speak, and between them there was more singing. After the last preacher spoke, the bishop rose and everyone fell silent.

This was the moment.

"Please stand, Jebadiah and Leah," Bishop Yoder said.

Jeb rose to his feet, but it wasn't a graceful movement. He winced as he got his leg underneath him again, and his damaged tendons screamed against the sudden change in position. Leah stood, too, and a warm breeze swept around them, carrying the scent of wildflowers and hay. Overhead birds twittered, and from the house he could smell the aroma of food cooking. For just a moment, if he shut his eyes, he could imagine that they were alone with the bishop, alone with the birds and the flowers and the softly scented breeze.

"Jebadiah," Bishop Yoder intoned. "Do you take Leah Riehl as your wife? Do you promise to stand by her and protect her, to provide for her and the children you will have together . . ."

Jeb glanced at Leah at those words—there would be no children, and he saw her tense. No one had told the bishop, it seemed. Or the bishop had simply forgotten.

". . . do you promise to love Leah until death parts you?"

"I promise," Jeb murmured.

"And do you, Leah, take Jebadiah King to be your husband? Do you promise to support him and love him, to respect him and be faithful to him in all things? Do you promise to seek God with him and only be a blessing to him for all your days until death parts you?"

There was a beat of silence. "I promise."

Jeb let out a pent-up breath. She hadn't run . . . He only realized in this moment that he'd half-expected her to.

"Then I pronounce upon you the blessing of Abraham and Sarah," the bishop said, raising his voice, "the blessing of Isaac and Rebecca, the blessing of Jacob and Rachel. May your marriage be long and fruitful." The bishop smiled, then paused meaningfully. "You are wed."

There was clapping from both sides of the congregation, and then Jeb and Leah sat back down again.

There would be another sermon yet . . . but Jeb's heart pattered hard in his chest. It was done. He was married to this woman, and their life together would begin. He looked over at Leah. Her gaze was locked on her lap, her lips parted. Her chest rose and fell with her breathing, and just at the base of her neck, he could see the flutter of her pulse. Jeb could only guess at what she was thinking, but as of right now, Leah was his wife, and he felt a sudden surge of protectiveness rise up inside him at that realization. *His wife.*

Whatever their reasons, whatever they both stood to gain from this marriage, they were now joined, and she was his to provide for and care for. He would do well by her. He'd do his best.

Here was hoping that this time, it was enough.

Chapter Five

The sun had started to set, dusky shadows growing long, and guests were leaving at long last. Leah had slipped off by herself, away from the chatting groups of well-wishers, and around the side of the house where no eyes were on her. She felt tired, and happy, celebrated. She was a wife at long last, and she would be accepted. Somehow, she'd half-expected something to stop this event, but it hadn't, and now she was a fully married woman.

She looked around the corner at the few people who remained. Jeb stood with some men. He was listening to something one of the men was saying, nodding slowly. Marital advice? They'd both be given some. Leah knew how this worked.

For years she'd dreamed of getting married, and year after year, she'd sat on the women's side and watched as girls younger than her became wives. Then Sunday services, she'd watch those young wives as their families grew. Their lives had truly begun—a husband, a home, *kinner* . . . and Leah had stayed lonely.

Sometimes she felt like her name had been a curse. Leah, of the Bible, was one of Jacob's two wives, and she hadn't been loved by her husband. Rachel, the other wife, had been deeply loved, and Leah had been forced to watch her husband adore his other wife while paying Leah the respect that was due her and nothing more. Back then, the "respect" resulted in children of her own, but it never included his heart.

That was a pain that Leah had understood. She'd watched so many Amish girls move on to have the family life she craved. She'd watched Matthew court someone else, and she realized something when that happened—watching another's happiness from the outside could suck a soul dry given enough time.

But Leah was an Amish woman, and she didn't live in biblical times. She'd never have to share a husband. That was some comfort. Instead, the man she'd loved simply married another woman, leaving Leah free to marry a man who didn't love her, and whom she didn't love either.

Leah, the unloved. Would being married be enough? It hadn't been for her biblical counterpart.

Rosmanda came around the corner and laughed softly. "There you are," she whispered. "We have to talk . . ."

"Is something wrong?" Leah turned toward her friend.

"No, nothing's wrong," Rosmanda said, and then she laughed again. "I've been voted the one to tell you about . . . tonight."

Heat washed over Leah's face as she understood what Rosmanda was getting at. The wedding night and the expectations. A *mamm* normally gave this talk, but Leah didn't have a *mamm* to do it.

"I know that this is how things normally work, Rosie, but I'm sure I'll figure out what I need to know," Leah said.

"Every woman has this talk," Rosmanda said, not to be dissuaded. "It's important. Before you're married, no one tells you anything. But now that you're wed, there are some things you'd better know up front. Just trust me on that."

Leah looked toward Jeb again, and this time, his gaze

met Leah's for a moment as Rosmanda tugged her toward the house, and Leah's heart sped up with anxiety. Very soon, they'd be able to leave, but tonight they'd have to share a bedroom.

Rosmanda led Leah into the side door that led into the kitchen. Women were doing dishes and cleaning up, and when they saw Leah, they smiled in good humor.

"You're lucky this isn't your parents' house." One laughed. "You and Jeb would be washing up in the morning!"

"We can come back, and—" Leah started.

"She's teasing you," Rosmanda said.

"Are you coming to the games night on Saturday?" the woman asked.

"For at least two weeks, we should expect absolutely nothing from the newlyweds." Another woman chuckled. "Or that they'll arrive very, very late."

"For a month," an older woman said, and the other laughed. "A full month!"

"Come. Let's go upstairs," Rosmanda said. "We need some quiet."

A couple of older women gave Leah a knowing look as she went up, and then the clatter and laughter was behind them as Rosmanda tugged her into her daughters' bedroom, where she'd been preparing for her wedding just hours before.

"There," Rosmanda said, shutting the door firmly behind them. "Now, sit down, because we don't have much time. Jeb is going to be hitching up the buggy soon."

Leah did as Rosmanda told her, and she sank onto the side of one of the twin beds. There was a neatly stitched quilt on top done in blues and white. Leah ran her fingers over the pattern, then looked up at her friend. Rosmanda didn't sit. She stood in the center of the room, and then she rubbed her hands over her face.

"This is harder than you'd think," Rosmanda murmured.

"I've been married twice and I'm pregnant with my third child, and this is still hard to talk about."

"Then leave it," Leah said. "I don't need this, Rosie—"

Rosmanda had no idea how very little Leah needed this talk.

"Oh, stop that," Rosmanda said, and she dropped her hands. "Hard things are the most important. Now, the first thing to remember is that your wedding night is going to be awkward. It just is. Whatever romantic dreams you have for tonight—let them go. It's going to be awkward, but wonderful. Luckily for you, Jeb has been married before, so at least he knows the basics. But the best advice I can give to you is to take your time tonight. Don't rush things. And don't let him rush things either! Talk together, let him hold you, just relax. Because if you rush it, you'll hate it, and that's a terrible way to start a marriage—"

Leah shut her eyes for a moment. This lecture was entirely unnecessary. She and Jeb weren't going to be taking part in regular honeymoon activities, and the last thing Leah wanted was to hear the practical advice on how to make it all happen.

"Can we please skip this part?" Leah asked. "Like you said, Jeb's been married before. And I think I know enough. If I need advice after tonight, I'll come and ask, all right?"

Rosmanda nodded slowly. "You are still due *some* marriage advice, though."

"Like what? A good recipe?" Leah joked.

"No, as in how to be married," Rosmanda replied, refusing to even smile at Leah's humor. This time she came to the bed and sank down onto the mattress next to her. "The conjugal part isn't the only part of marriage. But I do have a bit of advice that might serve you well."

Leah looked over at her friend. Rosmanda's gaze turned inward. "This, I could use."

"My best advice is to never stop flirting with him,"

Rosmanda began. "Remember what it was like when you were courting, and don't lose that. You see, once a man is married, the chase is over, and for some men it feels like the excitement is over, too. He's already won. But if you keep flirting with him, teasing him a little bit, tempting him, sharing special smiles with him . . . If you don't stop those things, it keeps the fun alive in your marriage. Give him everything you're afraid another woman might offer him. Does that make sense? If you're ever insecure, then love him so well that you know he could never find another woman to love him as deeply and passionately as you do."

Leah dropped her gaze. All too much of her friend's advice was not going to apply to her, because it all seemed tied up in that conjugal bed they had already agreed not to share. And she knew that Rosmanda and Levi had a very happy marriage. They were in love, and she'd often seen Levi catching Rosmanda around the waist or giving her a kiss when no one else was supposed to be looking. Their marriage was a passionate one, and Leah didn't need reminders of what she'd never have.

"And when we fight?" Leah asked, hoping to change the tone of this talk.

"Make up with equal passion," Rosmanda replied. "Let the dishes stay in the sink and let the floor stay dirty that night if it has to, but you go upstairs and keep those priorities straight."

Leah nodded. Did any of this advice happen in the kitchen? Rosmanda was the wrong woman to give this talk. Leah needed a stalwart older lady rife with scripture and warnings, with advice about praying together and turning their focus to God instead of each other. That would make this easier.

"I know you don't know him well," Rosmanda said, her tone dropping. "I know this is awkward right now. But being his wife . . . Leah, it's the closest you can ever be to a man if you love him well. If you open your heart to him, and you cradle his with as much care as you can, the intimacy you will share will never be matched. Some people say it's like having a best friend, but I disagree. It's like being partners in a battle—having a warrior defending your back. And it's having a lover . . . for life. A man who cherishes and understands you—"

It would be none of those things, and Leah felt tears prick her eyes.

"And if he doesn't cherish me?" Leah interrupted.

Rosmanda looked at her, silent.

"If he doesn't?" Leah pressed. "Perhaps having a good friend in marriage is a good thing. I don't think I need him to cherish me. I could be happy with something less."

"Perhaps . . ." Rosmanda said quietly, but she was looking at Leah with a funny look on her face. Leah was saying too much, and she knew it. It was the emotional stress of the day, and her natural inhibitions seemed to be reduced.

"I'm just tired, I think," Leah said, forcing a smile.

"Marriage is going to be wonderful, Leah," Rosmanda said, taking her hand. "It will be. I'm not saying it won't be hard work, too, but it will be worth it."

Leah nodded, then rose to her feet. "Thank you. But I wish you would just give me a good recipe and be done with it."

Rosmanda laughed. "Put more milk in your piecrust."

"What?"

"That's your problem. You always complain it's not flaky enough, and it needs more liquid, not less."

"Oh, ouch . . ." Leah smiled hesitantly. "But you see? That was helpful."

"I'm glad." But there was still a certain amount of sadness in Rosmanda's gaze.

Leah went to the door and pulled it open. The sound of the women chatting downstairs as they washed dishes filtered back up to her.

"Leah?" Rosmanda said, and Leah turned back. "Don't feel pressured into anything. You can say no. That is part of a relationship, too. That's the last I'll say on the matter."

Leah gave her friend a reassuring smile.

"Thank you for the beautiful wedding, Rosie. From the bottom of my heart. Thank you."

Rosmanda gave her a misty nod. Then Leah headed out of the bedroom and down the stairs. Jeb was going to drive her back to the house she shared with her brother, and they'd spend their first night under her family's roof as a married couple. It was tradition, after all.

Tonight was her wedding night, and Leah's heartbeat sped up in her chest.

He'd abide by their agreement, wouldn't he? Rosmanda's advice *was* wasted . . . wasn't it?

Over on Jeb's own farm, some of the men had pitched in to complete his chores so that he'd have tonight with his wife. It was a kind gesture, something the community did for every newly married farmer for his first night of marriage. So, after he had unhitched the horses and finished settling the animals for the night with Simon's help, they headed through the twilight into the house.

Jeb's stomach was in knots. This was it—their wedding night. And while they'd both been pretty clear on expectations, they'd be spending the night in the same house.

Leah was at the sink. She wrung out a cloth and hung it over the tap. The kitchen was spotless—gleaming counters, a swept floor . . . a whole lot cleaner than the kitchen waiting for her in his own house, and he felt a wave of shame at that. He'd done his best to clean up in the days coming up to the wedding, but he still had the sense that it was in bad shape. It didn't look like this, that was for sure.

Simon headed for a pie on the counter—already half-consumed. He got a plate, then dished himself up a healthy slice. It looked like cherry. Jeb couldn't eat if he tried right now, and he looked over at Leah. The color rose in her cheeks, as if she were thinking the same thing. How were they going to do this? Were they going to sit up late into the night, avoiding the obvious and stuffing themselves with food they didn't want to eat?

"We should turn in," Leah said, and her tone was resolute—determined.

That answered that.

"Yah. Okay." Jeb looked uncomfortably toward Simon. "I'll be up early to help out with the chores here before I go to my own farm. If you wanted to start working with me, Simon, we can keep track of your days of work, and I'll pay you what I owe."

"Sure. Yah. Thanks. That sounds good."

It might be a good way to keep Simon away from those Englisher thugs, to boot.

Jeb cleared his throat. "Okay. Well. Good night, then."

Leah didn't say anything else, and she didn't meet his eye again. Instead, she led the way down the darkened hallway, leaving the lamp in the kitchen with Simon, and Jeb followed. She opened the door to the bathroom.

"In case you need it," she said.

"Thanks." He looked into the bathroom—also spotless.

"The towels are in here—" She touched the closed door of a linen closet, and her steps slowed as she approached the door beyond it. He saw her visibly stiffen as she stopped at the closed door. "And this is my—our—room tonight."

"You'd asked for your own room," he murmured, keeping his voice low.

Leah opened the door and led the way inside. Jeb paused at the doorway, unsure of what she was expecting from him. They'd had an agreement—had it just changed? His heart sped up at that thought. He'd gone through this entire day believing that tonight they'd be in separate rooms. He wasn't ready for this. It was supposed to be easier for the man, but he wasn't young and smooth-skinned anymore. He was damaged, older, and the scars that he'd grown used to would be a shock to her.

"Come in," she said, her voice low but urgent. He stepped inside and Leah shut the door behind him, then licked her lips. "I don't want people to know about . . . our sleeping arrangement. And that includes my brother. Some things aren't his business. He might know what made us decide on this marriage, but he doesn't need to know anything else beyond that."

Her desire to keep their business between them was a relief, and it softened him toward her just a little more. A woman with discretion was a gift—especially under these circumstances.

Jeb nodded. "Agreed. I prefer privacy with our business, too. Have you told anyone—"

"About our plans for intimacy?" She shook her head. "Jeb, this marriage is supposed to give us status in the community, and I hardly see how it's anyone else's business. I'd be embarrassed if anyone knew. Humiliated."

Jeb swallowed. Yah, there were a few things about their marriage that wouldn't be easy to explain to someone on the outside.

"So, I was hoping you would be okay with us sleeping in the same room tonight," she said, her cheeks flooding with color. "It's expected."

Jeb's gaze swept around the room. There was a double

bed in the center, covered with a hand-stitched quilt. A rag
rug lay beside it, and there was a full-length mirror in
one corner, an overstuffed chair in the other corner next
to the window.

"Sure," he agreed. "I'm fine with that. I'll just make
myself comfortable in that chair."

"I'm not sure you'll fit in it," she said quietly. "I could
take the chair, I suppose—"

Not that he'd agree to. He wasn't putting his new wife
in a chair while he slept in a bed.

"Or we could use the bed," Jeb said quietly. "We'll put
pillows between us—like bundling. I won't touch you. I
can promise you that."

Leah was silent for a moment, but he saw her gaze
move around the room. She was calculating space, too, he
could tell. She went to the dresser and picked up a box of
matches. She struck one and lit the lamp on the dresser
top, flooding the room with warm, golden light.

"Maybe I shouldn't have suggested that," he said. "I can
sit up tonight in the chair. It's fine."

He could squeeze himself into it. He spotted a wooden
chest he could move to make a footrest. It wouldn't be easy
on his leg, but he could find a way.

"No," Leah said at last. "We can share the bed."

"Are you sure?" he asked.

She nodded. "With the pillows between us."

"Right." Jeb put his overnight bag down on the bed.
"Should one of us change in the bathroom, then?"

Leah's gaze flickered toward the door, then she shook
her head. "No. Let's just turn our backs. We can change,
and not turn around until we're both in our nightclothes. I
know my brother's enjoyment of a funny story, and I'd
rather not give him anything to work with tonight."

Leah had been thinking this through, he realized. She
had a plan already, and maybe he was grateful for that.

She was obviously as nervous as he was, and he caught the cautious look she cast in his direction. He wasn't exactly easy to look at . . . and maybe he'd forgotten that today.

"Okay," he said. He pulled his pajamas from his bag. "I'll face this way, and you face the other wall. We'll both say when we're finished, but there is no turning until we're both done."

Leah went to her closet and pulled out a nightgown, then she crossed to her side of the room. Jeb glanced over his shoulder at her, and she looked back.

"No peeking," she said solemnly.

Jeb chuckled and turned forward again. "No peeking."

He pulled off his shirt, and he felt the exposure of his scars on display, even if she wasn't looking. He fumbled with the pajama shirt, relieved to pull it on. He was about to do the same with his pants when he glanced up and, from the full-length mirror, he realized in a rush that the angle of the mirror gave him a view he shouldn't have—

He couldn't see all of her—just her bare back, shining white in the low light of the bedroom. She had a few beauty marks scattered over her skin, and he couldn't tear his eyes away. She reached for something and disappeared from the mirror, then came back into view as the nightgown slipped over her shoulder and tumbled down around her. He felt his cheeks heat.

He shouldn't have seen that.

"I'm finished," she said softly.

"I'm not." He cleared his throat and hurriedly pulled his pants off, then got his pajama bottoms on. He shook out his pants so he could hang them. "I am now."

"Then we turn?" she asked.

"Yah."

She was no longer the properly dressed Amish woman. Her *kapp* was gone, her auburn hair hanging loose around her shoulders. Her nightgown was white, and it covered her from collarbone down to her ankles—not an inch exposed. But the glimpse he'd had of her bare back was seared into his mind.

Leah reached for a comb and hurriedly began to try to arrange her hair again.

"You don't have to rush," he said.

"My hair—" she started.

"Is for your husband," he said. "And that's me. It's okay. You can comb your hair properly and take care of it."

Leah's movements slowed, and he watched her as she pulled the comb through her long hair that reflected glossy and luxurious in the low light, then separated it out into sections and deftly braided it. Jeb pulled the covers back on the bed to expose fresh, white sheets, and he grabbed a couple of pillows, dropping them down the middle in a makeshift wall.

So much like bundling. Some communities used this for setting a couple up—putting them together for a night with blankets and pillows between them . . . Not their community, though.

Leah approached the other side of the bed, looking down at it with an unreadable expression.

"I can go to the chair if you want," he repeated.

She shook her head. "No. It's okay. Can you get the lamp?"

Jeb blew out the lamp, and as he did so, he heard the squeak of the springs as she crawled under the quilt. He came back to the bed and found her lying on her side, her back to him. He eased into the bed and let out a careful breath. He was half afraid of moving, and when he looked over at her, her braided hair was so close, he could smell the soft scent of her shampoo.

She lay there, completely still, and he let his gaze move over the soft mound of blankets next to him.

His wife. This beautiful woman who smelled so good belonged to him. The thought was both terrifying and amazing, all at the same time.

"Jeb?" she said softly.

"Yah?"

"Why wasn't your mother at our wedding?" she asked. "You said you sent money to her . . . Has she passed away?"

"No, she's still alive," he said quietly.

"Why didn't she come?"

"I didn't invite her." It was complicated—an explanation for another time, perhaps, when he knew his own wife a little bit better. His mother hadn't attended his first wedding either.

"Good night," he whispered.

She didn't move, but her voice came to him softly. "Good night, Jeb."

And he lay in the ever-darkening room, listening to the sound of their careful breathing.

Chapter Six

Leah slept lightly, and twice she awoke to the sound of the springs squeaking next to her as Jeb rolled over. It felt strange, and even a little wrong, to have a man in her bed next to her, but there was nothing wrong with a husband and wife sharing a bed, and while this still felt strange, Jeb was very much her husband. Each time Leah managed to drift to sleep once more, but the third time she woke, she didn't know what had disturbed her. All was quiet and still, but she was wide awake nonetheless.

She lay on her back, very close to the edge of the bed, and Jeb was on top of the pillows that separated them, his arm pressed against hers. Leah rolled onto her side and looked at him in the moonlight that shone through the crack in the curtain.

They said that God worked in mysterious ways, and it seemed that He did. Because she'd prayed for years for a husband to call her own, and here he was. It was easier to look at him while he slept. She didn't have to worry about meeting that drilling gaze of his. Jeb was a large man, broad through the chest and muscular. His hair had some gray, and from where she lay, she could see the scars moving from his hairline down the side of his bearded face and down his neck, disappearing into his pajama shirt.

She hadn't had an up-close look at these scars yet, and she stared at them, mesmerized. They were ugly, to be sure, but ever since she'd touched his arm the day he'd asked her to marry him, her curiosity about that extent of his injury had been piqued.

Jeb had said the scars didn't hurt, but she could see him shifting painfully during the wedding ceremony. The way his scarred skin pulled taut when he stretched out his arm or turned his head—it couldn't be comfortable. But he didn't speak of it. He didn't complain.

And yet, the very size of him made her nervous. He was taller than other men in their community, and while those broad shoulders tapered down to a neat waist, she was struck by the size of his hand that lay limp on top of the quilt. He was nothing like Matthew. Matthew had been an inch taller than her. He was slim, not well-muscled like Jeb was, and Matthew had soulful eyes. She'd never felt at his mercy. Instead, she'd felt like she could drown in the emotions that he stirred up inside her.

Jeb was different. He was older, hardened, more experienced. There was nothing soulful about him that she could see—only scars and caution. She tried to imagine using Rosmanda's advice about her wedding night with this man, and the thought made her shiver. There might be wifely duties expected of a woman, but she couldn't do it.

Jeb shifted slightly, his arm pushing against hers. Jeb, even simply lying on his back, was using up most of the space. His finger moved along her arm, and as his touch moved in a gentle arc over her wrist, her heart hammered hard in her chest. He was asleep—this wasn't conscious—but his touch was insistent, and it held a request. She held her breath.

Jeb's snoring suddenly stopped, and then for a beat neither of them moved. Slowly, he pulled his hand away from her, and he rolled over onto his side, his back to her.

"Sorry," he said gruffly.

Leah didn't answer, but she turned onto her side, too, her back to him. She lay there as quietly as possible, listening to the sound of Jeb's uneven breathing. He wasn't sleeping—she could hear it. But somehow, listening to the silence between them, she fell back asleep until morning.

At four thirty, when Leah normally got up to start cooking, she blinked her eyes open feeling much more rested than she thought she would. She looked over her shoulder to see if Jeb was still there, but she found the other side of the bed empty, the quilt pulled neatly back into place.

She got up and went to the dresser, where she lit the lamp. Outside, she heard the tramp of boots, and she pulled back the curtain to look outside. She heard the chicken coop door shut and the kerfuffle of awakened chickens.

Leah rubbed her hands over her face and looked at herself in the mirror. She was barefoot, her sleeping braid hanging over one shoulder and her nightgown creased and wrinkled from sleep. She looked no different from any other morning, and yet she was different now. She was legally married—everything would be different.

Leah made the rest of the bed and got dressed. She brushed her hair, then rolled it up into a neat bun at the back of her head, then pulled a freshly laundered *kapp* from her top drawer and secured it over her hair with two hairpins. This morning she would make breakfast in the same kitchen she'd made breakfast for herself and her brother for years, except this morning she'd be feeding not only her brother, but her husband.

It felt strange—like a word game that hadn't really touched her life just yet.

Leah headed out into the cool kitchen and grabbed

some wood from the pile next to the stove. She bent down in front of the big metal unit and arranged the wood inside, then added some paper and twigs as kindling. She struck a match and the first lick of flame moved through the paper and zipped toward the wood.

She closed the stove once the fire had taken, and for the next hour she focused her energy on making a hearty breakfast of oatmeal, sausages, and scrambled eggs. It was Simon's favorite breakfast, and somehow this meal felt like a goodbye to her brother in a very tangible way. She'd be moving out of this house, and if she did cook for him still, it would be from the house she shared with Jeb. An era was ending, and it left a lump in her throat.

This was all for Simon. She could only hope he'd properly appreciate what she was doing.

Outside the kitchen window, the sky was softly pink, some streaks of orange clinging to wispy clouds. From the window she could see a light glowing from inside the stable, and the door opened, Jeb's big frame backlit in the doorway. She couldn't tell if he could see her or not, but then he grabbed the lantern and came outside, the golden light combined with the first blush of dawn washing over his features making him look more rugged.

Jeb's limp was more noticeable this morning. He didn't say anything as he came inside the house. He kicked off his boots and turned off the lantern.

"Morning," he said with a bashful smile.

"How did you sleep?" she asked briskly, turning away from him and reaching for a pot. She wasn't sure why she felt so exposed right now. But she did.

"Not great," he said. "I'm not used to sharing a bed anymore. I'm sorry if I sprawled."

"I don't remember. I was sleeping."

She glanced toward him, and she caught that direct gaze locked on her again, his dark gaze pinning her to the spot.

"No, you weren't," he said.

She felt the heat hit her face. She'd felt the way he'd touched her. Even if he hadn't been fully awake yet, that was the touch of a man who was thinking of more. Did they have to talk about it? "I just mean that it's okay. You don't need to worry about it."

"Then say that. Don't try to protect my feelings," he said. "I don't like that."

Leah turned away again to get the sausages from the iron skillet and onto a plate. She'd already upset him and they'd barely said a word to each other.

"It won't be a problem in the future," she said. "We'll both have enough space."

"But I mean it in other things, too," Jeb said. "I'm not a poetic man. I say what I think, and I like to have the same thing in return. Don't try to soften things for me. It won't help either of us."

Leah licked her lips. "Fine. You sprawled. Are you happy?"

A glimmer of humor came to his eyes and he chuckled softly. "Yah. I am."

The side door opened again and Simon came inside, a metal bowl of eggs in one hand. Leah went to take them while he took off his boots, and she put them on the counter.

"After breakfast, we'll go do Jeb's chores," Simon said. "And then we'll head into town to see that lawyer."

"All right," Leah said.

"As promised," Jeb said, his voice low.

"Thank you, Jeb," she said. "And when you're done for the day, I'll have dinner ready."

"Here?" he asked.

"At your house," she replied. *Their* house, although she was afraid to use that language just yet. Maybe she wanted to hear him say it first.

"You won't need more time to . . . set up over there?" Jeb asked hesitantly.

"I'll sort it out, if you'll give me a key," she replied.

Jeb reached into his pocket and pulled out a small ring. "I had that made for you."

She accepted the key with a nod and looked down at it. It felt so official suddenly. She'd be moving her things over to Jeb's house this very day, and cooking their first dinner together. Alone. She felt the breath squeeze from her chest.

"Will you be eating with us, Simon?" Leah asked suddenly.

"No," Simon said. "You're newlyweds. I'll fend for myself, thank you very much. I've been doing just fine while you were off teaching."

Leah smiled weakly. Of course. People were going to give them space. She licked her lips, then nodded to the meal.

"We should eat," she said, "before it gets cold."

Then she sat down at the table. She'd always said the blessing over the meals she shared with her younger brother in the past, but today she looked over at Jeb. It was his role now.

"Lord, we thank you for this food," Jeb said, his voice a low rumble. "And for the hands that have prepared it."

She closed her fingers into fists in her lap.

"Amen," she murmured.

Jeb finished chores earlier than he'd anticipated. Having the extra help in Simon was more welcome than he'd anticipated, too. The last time he'd had someone to work with, it was Peter, and having an extra set of hands to get the work done made everything go faster. All the same, it felt strange to have Simon out there with him. Uncomfortable. Restricting.

When the work was done, he and Simon went into town with the marriage certificate. The lawyer was available when they arrived, and he accepted the proof of marriage and then began the process of transferring funds in Jeb's bank account.

"It won't be done today?" Simon asked.

"These things take some time," the lawyer replied. "But the wheels are in motion."

"How long will it take?" Jeb said.

"You don't have a phone, do you?" the lawyer asked.

"No."

"Come back next week and check on the process," the lawyer replied. "We should be closer to releasing the funds and transferring them at that point. Why—is there a rush?"

"Yah. A bit," Jeb admitted. "We owe a debt, and it would be nice to pay it back in time."

"I'll put it on the top of my pile," the lawyer said. "It's the best I can do. And congratulations on your marriage."

"Yah. Thank you," Jeb said, and they shook hands. "I'll come back in a week."

"Oh!" the lawyer said. "Wait. There is one more thing for you." He unlocked a drawer and pulled out a white envelope. "Upon the event of your marriage, your uncle left you this."

Jeb accepted the envelope and looked down at it. His name was written on the front. "What is it?"

"I don't know. It's sealed. But it was to be given to you if you did manage to get married in the specified time."

His uncle's thoughts on the matter . . . Congratulations on having moved his life forward, or a lecture about how the love of money was the root of all evil?

"And if I hadn't married?" Jeb asked.

"There was a different letter," the lawyer said with a nod. "But you won't be receiving that one now. I have instructions to destroy it."

"Thank you," Jeb said woodenly.

As they headed out of the lawyer's office and walked toward the buggy parking, Jeb felt the crinkling presence of that envelope in his pocket. He wouldn't open it here. And certainly not in front of Simon. He glanced over at the younger man. Simon's expression was grim, and he glanced around himself nervously as they walked.

"Stick with me, then," Jeb said.

"What?"

"If you're scared, while we wait on the money, stick close to me. If you're working my farm, I'll be around, right?"

His farm. That felt good to say.

"Yah. I might do that." Simon nodded, but the fear didn't dissipate.

"Do they know where you live?" Jeb asked.

Simon shook his head. "I only ever saw them at a game. I wasn't stupid enough to say where I lived."

"But they could ask around," Jeb said.

"They won't need to if I pay them back," Simon replied. "Will they?"

Jeb didn't know, but the burden of that debt was going to haunt the boy until it was paid, of that he had no doubt.

Jeb led the way to the buggy, and while he tried to keep his own unease hidden, he did glance around to see if anyone was paying them any undue attention. But they got plenty of that on a daily basis—the Englishers loved nothing more than coming to the town of Abundance to buy Amish wares and stare at them in the streets. A whole family stood at the edge of the buggy parking lot taking pictures with their phones, and when they saw Jeb and Simon approaching, they turned their phones toward them.

Jeb hated this—being treated like a zoo animal for the Englishers' entertainment. He wasn't a curiosity, he was a man deserving of a bit of privacy, and he hated knowing that he was being recorded while he went about his own business.

"Excuse me!" the man of the group—the *daet*?—called out.

Jeb ignored him and went to take the feed bag off his horse's head. He patted the horse, then headed around to put the feed bag away. He glanced toward the family. The *kinner* were staring at him, and the two adults who appeared to be the parents were talking together, glancing in his direction. He looked studiously away.

"Let's get going," Jeb said, and Simon hoisted himself up into the buggy.

"Excuse me!" the Englisher called again.

Jeb muttered an oath, then looked over at the man who was coming in his direction. He wore a baseball cap and had a big camera around his neck.

"We're from out of town," the Englisher called as he approached. "And—" He stopped when Jeb turned toward him. "My God. What happened?" The man touched his own face. "A fire?"

Jeb didn't answer, and the man visibly rallied himself and pushed on. "Like I said, we're from out of town, and we just think your way of life is something great. The kids here would love to see how you hitch a wagon. Would you let them take a closer look? Maybe I could take a few pictures?"

"I'd rather not," Jeb said, trying to soften his tone. For all the irritation they caused him, the Englisher tourists fueled this town, and a lot of Amish wouldn't make a dime without the tourists.

The man balked in surprise, but the smile came back. "Without the pictures, then. They've been just dying to get an up-close look at one of your buggies. We figured we'd ask. It would mean the world to the kids."

"I said no." Jeb let the last of the politeness slide from

his tone. He was tired, stressed. He didn't have the strength for this.

"They're kids, man. This is their vacation—"

"And this is my *life*," Jeb said, shooting the man a look of annoyance. "Keep your *kinner* back. Buggies are no place to play."

"*Kinner*. Is that what you call kids out here? Is that German?"

Jeb shut his eyes for a moment, summoning up his self-control. "Keep your *children* away from my horses," he said in perfect English. "There will be no photo opportunities here."

The man blinked, then nodded. He headed back to the woman and the *kinner* who waited a few yards off. They all stared at him, wide-eyed, and he saw the woman cover her mouth.

"No," Jeb could hear him say. "Not this one."

"What happened to that man?" a small voice carried across the parking lot. "What happened to his face, Dad?"

Jeb clenched his teeth. Yah, he was used to that—the curiosity of everyone who saw him. What happened? They wanted a story, an explanation. All he had was a pile of heartbreak and scars that went deeper than they imagined.

"I think you scared them," Simon said as Jeb settled himself in the driver's seat and picked up the reins.

Jeb looked over his shoulder and saw the entire family staring at him. But it wasn't fear in the man's eyes—it was anger. He hadn't expected to be rebuffed, and as Jeb flicked the reins and the buggy started forward, the man's disgusted gaze met Jeb's.

"He'll live," Jeb muttered, and he turned his attention to the road.

Jeb had gotten used to people's stares—and not just the Englishers' either. The Amish treated Jeb with caution, too, so his hide was thick enough to take the sidelong looks of the English and the Amish alike. The Englishers would be satisfied with a story of a fire in a barn—the barn being the quaint part of the tale they'd cherish. The Amish, on the other hand, asked deeper questions.

The envelope weighed on him as they drove back, and when they finally unhitched the buggy and Jeb sent Simon off to clean the chicken coop, he pulled it out of his pocket.

Was I wrong, Lord? he prayed. *Am I about to get reprimanded from beyond the grave because I wanted this land?*

He did carry a small, nagging piece of guilt over his move to get the farm, and if it weren't for Simon's rescue at the same time, he might not have gone through with it. One man's victory wasn't enough. Even as one who preferred to keep to himself, he recognized the moral failure of prioritizing his own success over everyone else.

But he couldn't explain himself to Peter now, could he? This was no longer about him alone—it was about Leah, who deserved a home, and her brother, who, while perhaps less deserving, was still in desperate need of help.

He tore off the end of the envelope and squeezed it open. There was a piece of paper inside, and he shook it out into his work-roughened palm, recognizing his uncle's bold handwriting.

Jeb,

If you're reading this, you're married. Congratulations. I'm happy at the thought of you with a wife. A good woman is a blessing from God, and I know you'll have chosen carefully.

I couldn't let you go on alone, especially if I'm

gone. You're too much of a hermit. It's not good for a man to be alone. You need someone to care for you.

I'm glad you managed a wedding, because you deserved this farm, and it makes me happy to think of you running it. But you deserve a chance at a family, too. You're a better man than you think.

Menno will be angry. I know that, and I know he won't make this easy on you. But you've never much cared about Menno's opinions, and I hope that carries on. Menno is provided for already, and he has a wife and kinner *of his own. My daughters married well, and their husbands all have land already. You're the one I worry about.*

My last piece of advice to you is this: The past is the past, Jeb. Leave it there. And have lots of bobbilies.

Peter

Jeb looked down at the page, his heart filling with fresh grief. He could hear his uncle's gruff voice in those words, his plain way of speaking. It seemed almost ridiculous that his uncle should have made such a dramatic demand in his will for a reason as simple as this one. Peter had never been the meddling sort, but apparently, he'd decided to change his lifelong habit in death.

The *bobbilies*, or babies, weren't going to be an option for him and Leah. She couldn't have children, so he could let go of those hopes. If he'd stayed single, he wouldn't have *kinner* either. But he'd secured himself a wife, and that fulfilled his uncle's demands. Peter had been trying to help him move forward, and for better or for worse, Jeb had certainly taken a step. He looked toward the house. Yah, he'd most certainly taken a step. . . .

The rest of the day was spent in farmwork—watering cattle, mucking stalls, brushing down horses and checking on Simon, who wasn't quite the hard worker he claimed to be. Jeb had to send him back twice to finish cleaning out the chicken coop. He was already half-resenting his offer of employment, but if it wasn't Simon, he'd have to find someone else, and the loafer he knew was better than the curious son of some other family in this community.

He passed within sight of the house a few times during the day, and every time he did, his gaze would linger on that familiar structure. Was Leah in there yet?

He could have gone to check, but he didn't want to bother her, and he also knew it would be difficult to see her rummaging around in his space. The last time he looked toward the house, he saw the side door open and she came outside with a rug, and flipped it over the railing, then went back inside.

She'd come.

When the day's work was complete Jeb's stomach rumbled. He'd let Simon go an hour earlier, just for the solitude, so he walked alone toward the house, his leg aching but feeling good about the day all the same.

Jeb could smell the food already as he approached the house, and he kicked off his boots on the outside step, then carried them in.

"Hello," Leah said, poking her head around the mudroom door. She looked fresh, her cheeks pink from the warmth inside, but her clothes still looked as neat as they had that morning.

"I'm back," he said, and he gave her a hesitant smile.

"Dinner's ready." She held a dish towel in her hands and she fiddled with it, then turned and went back into the kitchen.

Jeb followed her, and he'd known it would look different in here, but he hadn't anticipated this much change.

The kitchen table was clear, as was one counter. The other counter was still cluttered. The floor was swept and mopped—he could smell the vinegar she'd used—and food waited on the table, covered with plates. The curtains had been removed from the kitchen windows, so everything looked brighter in here, exposing the wood that looked dusty and dry. He'd never bothered oiling it. That was on him.

"Where are the curtains?" he asked.

"Oh, I was going to wash them," she said. "The cooking oils get into the fabric, and it—"

She stopped. She was going to say that it smelled, wasn't she? Had he been living like a slob? Peter hadn't thought of these things either, if that counted in his favor.

"Oh," he said. "Well, I guess that's good, then."

"I made a beef roast," she said. "We'll have some for sandwiches tomorrow, then, for your lunch."

"Yah. Thanks."

Jeb slid into the chair at the head of the table. He didn't normally sit here, actually, but being the man of the house, he should probably claim it. She sat down in the chair next to his and pulled the plates off the bowls. Steam escaped, along with tantalizing aromas. There were potatoes, vegetables, some fresh rolls, and the meat. She had a separate dish of gravy to the side, and he eyed it hungrily.

Leah looked at him silently, expectantly.

Right.

"Uh." He bowed his head. "Lord, thank you for this food. And bless this home."

The last words caught in his throat, and instead of trying to say more, he raised his head. This home. Their home. He wasn't quite brave enough to call it "our home" yet. Leah reached for the spoon in the mashed potatoes and began to dish up his meal.

"This looks good," he said.

"I did try." She smiled, then added food to her own plate. He waited until she'd finished serving herself, as well, before he took his first bite. The food tasted as good as it had smelled, and he ate ravenously for a couple of minutes before he came up for air.

"I tried to clean up in here for you," he said. "I guess it wasn't enough, but—"

"It's fine, Jeb," she said, tearing a bite off her roll. "Leave the women's work to me."

Except all this had been his domain up until now, and it felt strange to just hand it over, even though it was right and proper that he do so. He felt like he should have at least handed it over in better shape.

"I didn't know about washing curtains," he said. "And I don't think Peter did either. With the two of us in here, we thought we did pretty well."

"It's okay," she said.

Jeb fell into silence, unsure whether he should plead his case further or simply let it go. Having anyone come inside and see how he lived was never easy for him. The only one who visited was his sister, Lynita, and she showed up when she pleased. He'd long since stopped worrying what she thought. But he kept other people out. Like when an elder came by to check up on him, he'd step outside and they'd talk on the step. He didn't bring people in to judge him.

"How was work today?" Leah asked after a moment of silence.

"Good," he said past a bite of food. "Your brother is a help. We delivered the marriage license to the lawyer, so that's started."

"Simon came by and told me about that. He said it will take a week?" she asked.

So, Simon had already informed his sister. That annoyed him slightly, because it was yet another break the younger man had taken when he should have been working.

"About a week, the lawyer figures." Jeb swallowed and reached for a glass of water that sat in front of his plate and took a sip. "I'm giving Simon work with me. That way he won't be alone. I might be scarred, but I'm big. I can defend him, if need be."

Leah looked nervous sitting there. She hadn't eaten much, and he watched her for a moment while he sopped up some gravy from his plate with one of the rolls.

"Are you okay?" he asked.

She nodded. "Yah."

"The food is good," he said again, hoping it might make her relax a little more to know he was appreciating the meal. She pushed back her chair.

"I forgot the butter for the rolls—"

"Leah, sit." It came out more gruffly than he'd intended, and she froze. "Please." He softened his tone. "I just mean, I don't need butter. This is delicious. And you don't seem to be eating. You deserve a good meal as much as I do."

Leah sank back into her seat, and she picked up her fork again. "If those Englishers find my brother—"

"I wasn't joking. They'd have to get through me. I *will* protect your brother, Leah."

Leah's gaze moved over him, her brown gaze slipping over his shoulders and chest and then down to his hands resting on the table. Her shoulders relaxed then, and some of the color came back into her face. Did that mean she felt safer with him standing between her brother and danger? He liked the thought of making her feel safe. He was a big man, but his injuries had never healed as well as they could have, though he was still strong. Here was hoping he would be enough to scare off some Englisher twits.

Leah took another bite, and for the first time she smiled more naturally.

"You're right," she said. "The cottage is probably safer anyway. It's farther from the road."

Looking at her sitting at his table, chewing a bite of food and cutting another piece of roast beef with her knife, she was oddly endearing. But she looked vulnerable, too. He was struck by just how petite she was next to him. If the Englishers scared her, it was for good reason.

"You're safe here, too," he added, his voice low.

She stopped chewing and looked up at him, her dark gaze locked on his face.

"Okay?" he said. "I might not be what you wanted. I might not be good-looking or good with words, or whatever. But I'm big, I'm tough, and I won't let anyone hurt you. Ever."

She stared at him, and he wasn't sure if she was going to answer him.

"So . . . you have that," he added.

Leah swallowed, and some color rose in her cheeks. "Okay."

And Jeb felt better. His own obstinate presence standing between her and danger was one thing he could offer. He'd been through a lot, and he didn't scare easily either. If he couldn't be an ideal husband, at least he'd be a useful one.

Chapter Seven

When dinner was done and Jeb had settled at the table with a pair of shoes and a tin of polish, Leah let the water out of the sink and wrung out the cloth. The clean dishes were stacked on the dish rack, and she eyed the cupboards. She'd already discovered that the dishes were arranged in the cupboards in a mishmash sort of way, the logic of it lost on her. As far as she could tell, Jeb's favorite dishes were all put into one cupboard where he could get at them easily, and everything else got stuck wherever there was space.

"I'm going to be rearranging the kitchen cupboards tomorrow," Leah said.

"Why?"

She looked over at Jeb to see if he was joking, but he looked up from the shoe, his expression bland.

"Uh—" She hesitated. "I'll be doing the cooking. I just have my ways I want it to be."

Jeb didn't answer, and he looked down again.

"Jeb, this is our home, right?" she said.

"Yah."

"And I'm the woman in this home, so the kitchen is . . . mine." Was she overstepping?

Jeb didn't move for a moment, then he nodded. "Yah, that's true."

"You aren't used to having a woman here, but you'll see. I'll make this place into a home."

Jeb put down the shoe and stood up. "It was a home already."

She'd overstepped. She could feel it. But she couldn't spend her time here on eggshells either. This was her home, too, now, and if she didn't clean this place up, not only would she go crazy in this dusty chaos, but people would talk.

"I don't mean to offend you," she said, softening her voice. "A woman's touch is . . . a woman's touch! Just trust me. I'll clean, I'll organize, I'll get a laundry schedule going, and you'll see how much more pleasant I'll make it for you. A well-run home is a woman's job, and you'll feel the difference. I promise."

"Have you been upstairs yet?" Jeb asked.

"No," she said. It had felt wrong somehow. Private, maybe. This house seemed steeped in testosterone—Jeb's presence in the very cracks. Her suitcase sat beside the stairs still. For all her eagerness to put her mark on this place, she hadn't been brave enough to climb the stairs.

"I might not have done much with the kitchen," Jeb said, "but I did put together a decent bedroom for you."

Leah looked over at him in surprise. "You did?"

"I wanted it to be . . . nice." He headed for the stairs and picked up her suitcase. "You can let me know if it's okay."

Jeb started up the stairs and Leah followed. The upstairs hallway was bare, slightly dusty, but there was no clutter. An open door revealed the tiles of a bathroom.

Jeb opened the next door and pushed it all the way open, allowing her to enter the room first. The room was east-facing, so she'd get the first morning light. There was a bed in the center of the room draped with a white coverlet. A small chest of drawers was next to the bed, serving as a bedside table, too, and a mirror stood next to the window. And on the other side there was a rocking chair with three folded towels piled on the seat. The thing that drew her eye, though, was a small vase of wildflowers sitting on the windowsill.

"You brought flowers," she said, and when she looked over at him, she was reminded that he'd been married before. He knew what women liked.

"I thought you might like them," he said, and he glanced away, embarrassed.

"I do like them."

It was a simple room, but clean. She could see some dust in the corners, but Jeb had obviously put some effort into cleaning the room out.

"It's a very nice room," she added. "I'll be very comfortable here."

"You can do what you want with it," he said. "It used to be Peter's room, but I cleaned everything out. He used to like being right next to the bathroom. There's a door here"—he tapped on a closed door with a hook lock on it—"that goes straight into the bathroom for you, so if you wanted a bath, you'd have . . ." He cleared his throat. "Uh, privacy, I guess."

"Thank you."

It seemed like he'd put some thought into her comfort with the flowers, the access to the bath . . .

"Where do you sleep?" she asked.

"Across the hall."

"Oh." She looked through the open door into the hallway. But his bedroom door was shut, and all she could see was darkness.

"I don't have much more in my own room," he said. "More mess, maybe." He smiled at his own joke. "I'll make an effort to clean up more, though."

He pulled a pack of matches out of a pocket and put them next to a lamp on her dresser, then put her suitcase next to the dresser. "I forgot those."

Leah looked around the room once more. She'd feel more at home once she unpacked her clothes and did a proper wash of this floor, but for the first time she was seeing some beauty in this place. Her bedroom would be lovely once she was done with it. And it would be hers . . .

"I don't want people to know about this," she said quietly. "Sleeping separately, I mean."

"I don't have people visit," he replied.

"I know, it's just—" And in a rush, she realized that if people did visit, there was a chance of them spotting this sleeping arrangement and their secret would be out. "If people knew, they'd talk."

"They already talk about me," he said dryly.

"You know what I mean," she said. "Look, we aren't married for love. We aren't fooling each other, at least. But we might as well get everything we can out of this marriage, and you know as well as I do that we both will gain a lot socially by being married. You'll be talked about less with me as your wife. People will stop bothering about the past so much if they have something new to chew over. And for me, I'm not the old maid anymore. But if people know about . . . this—"

Jeb nodded. "Yah. I get it."

"They'll be talking about us again," she said.

"And all we've gained will be lost," he concluded.

"Yah."

Jeb swallowed. "I wanted this farm, and that's why I did this, but you're right. I do stand to gain a lot more than just land with a wife like you."

Leah felt her cheeks warm. Did he see more than a ticket to an inheritance?

"Like me?" Was she really fishing for compliments? But she wanted to know how he saw her.

"Yah. A pretty woman, but also smart. You teach school, so you must be, right? And you're well-spoken. You sound . . . polished." He paused, then added gruffly, "And you're moral."

The last word gave her pause, especially because of how he said it. *Moral.* "I hope my brother's ways haven't reflected badly on me. I did my best in raising him, but I was doing it alone, and I think losing our parents was harder on him than any of us realized."

"I know you're a good woman," he said. "I might stick to myself, but even I hear things. Or Peter heard things, and he passed them along."

"Oh." She smiled feebly. "That's good."

"I just appreciate that."

"Thank you . . ."

"Whatever our sleeping arrangement, we have to be a team here behind closed doors, and out where people can see us."

"A team." Not a romantic view, but a pragmatic one. "We're on the same side."

An image of Rosmanda rose up in Leah's mind—Rosmanda with that sad look on her face when she tried to give her advice about her wedding night. Leah would have to make up for that and show Rosmanda a happy and united marriage, because right now, all Leah wanted was to erase any doubts her friend might have. She'd said too much on her wedding day, and she wouldn't make that mistake again. It used to be her reputation that mattered to her, but now it was theirs—their mutual reputation as a married couple. They reflected on each other.

"I'll let you unpack then," Jeb said, and moved to the doorway. "I'm glad you like it."

She listened as Jeb's footsteps creaked down the stairs

toward the kitchen once more, and then she exhaled a long sigh. Her wedding night was past, and now it was just a matter of settling in.

She went to the window and picked up the vase of flowers. They were like delicate, purple slippers, and she lifted them to her nose to smell them. Then she went to the door and looked across the hallway.

There was his closed bedroom door, the metal knob gleaming in the low light. Leah hardly knew him, and yet here they were. She hadn't seen him happy, or angry, or sad . . . so it wasn't as if she'd had a chance to see him at his worst or his best, and standing in the doorway of this little bedroom and seeing the few feet between her bedroom and his, she was reminded of just how large and muscular this man was. A woman might dream of a strong husband like that, but did she really know what she was getting herself into? A bedroom to herself had seemed like a bit of safety, a way to remove herself from the physical obligations of this marriage—whatever they might entail . . . she wasn't even sure. But this room wasn't quite the refuge she'd imagined either.

This was still a very small house. And his presence could be felt in every square inch of it.

Oh, God, let him be kind . . .

Jeb stoked the fire in the stove a little bit higher. He had a small pot of milk steaming nicely—enough for two. He made this amount out of habit, because he and his uncle used to drink their tea this way every night. It was boiled milk and three tea bags tossed in until the milk became a soft brown. This pot of milk wasn't ready for the tea yet, though, and he stirred it for a moment with a wooden spoon to keep it from scalding.

Before his uncle's death, Jeb used to talk with his uncle

in the evenings, catching up on whatever news or gossip his uncle had gleaned. Peter had been a social man—he went to town, attended service Sunday, visited neighbors, lended a hand. His uncle's heart attack had been a blow to more than Jeb.

Standing in the kitchen alone, a lump rose in his throat. If Peter were here, he'd be at the kitchen table with a copy of *The Budget* in front of him. He used to pore over the obituaries and wedding notices.

"At my age, my friends are either dying or their kids are getting married," he used to say. "Either one is life-changing."

Jeb glanced toward the table—wiped clean and empty of clutter. He pulled the envelope from his pocket again and pulled out the paper. It was already smudged with dirt around the edges from multiple readings while Jeb worked, and he looked down at the words again.

Peter always had liked a wedding. . . .

Footsteps on the stairs drew his gaze, and he saw Leah standing there. She was still dressed, but her feet were bare now, and she came down.

"What are you making?" she asked.

"Milky tea." Jeb tucked the envelope back into his pocket. "You want some? There's enough."

"Sure."

He might as well get used to having her around in the evenings, because this would be their life. The pot came to a boil, and Jeb pulled it off the heat, then tossed in the tea bags and stirred.

"What was in the envelope?" Leah asked.

Jeb looked up, surprised she'd ask. But then, she was his wife now, so maybe he should get used to a little curiosity on her part.

"It was from my uncle," he said. "He left it with the lawyer on the occasion of my wedding."

"Oh. What did he say?" she asked softly.

"He congratulated us," he replied.

The rest of it hadn't been meant for her. It had been for him. Leah nodded, and he continued to stir the pot as the milk grew steadily darker. Then he pulled out the tea bags, squeezing them against the side of the pot with a spoon, and reached for the sugar canister.

"I liked Peter," Leah said. "I didn't realize he was such a character, though. I mean, to include that kind of demand in his will . . ."

"He hid it well," Jeb replied wryly.

"He used to send me a letter after I sent him a check for our rent, and he told me little things about Simon. Like, how he saw him at Sunday service, and how he dropped off some apples for Simon from his tree. Little details that made me feel better." Her expression darkened. "He never warned me about the gambling, though."

"He wouldn't have known," Jeb replied. He filled two mugs and carried them to the table. He pulled out a chair for her, then one for himself. "It might be a good idea to sit down and get to know each other a little bit."

Leah slipped into the seat he'd proffered, and she took a sip of the tea. "It's funny we're doing this now."

"Yah. But better late than never."

"What do you want to know about me?" she asked quietly.

"Who are your best friends?" he asked. That was a detail he should know. Who would be coming over here to check on her?

"Rosmanda Lapp—obviously, because they hosted the wedding," she said. "But she and I have been friends for about three years now. What about you?"

Jeb dropped his gaze. "I don't have a lot of friends."

"Do you have . . . any?" she asked hesitantly.

"I had my uncle. I moved in with Peter and his family when I was a teen, and Menno and I were a lot closer back then. We were like brothers, instead of cousins. Even when I got married the first time, Menno and I bonded over that. We got married the same year, so . . . But . . . things changed."

"What changed?" she asked.

Jeb sighed. This had very quickly become about him, and he'd been hoping to hear more about her. But there was something about her soft brown eyes and the way she looked at him, half-hopeful, that made it hard not to answer.

"My uncle and I liked farming. Menno wanted to be a preacher, and he preferred woodwork. There was something about me and his father bonding that irked Menno. I don't know. Things changed."

"Jealousy," she said.

"Yah, I suppose."

"You can't be blamed for someone else's weak character," she said.

Leah had sided with him—he noticed that.

"Do you have any other friends?" she asked.

"I keep to myself," he said. "But you know that."

"Yah . . ." She nodded. "That's okay."

"It'll have to be," he said, but he shot her a smile to soften the words. "It's who I am. Anyway, what about you? I know your parents were killed in that buggy accident when you were a teenager."

"Yah. A really hard time. I did my best with Simon, but . . ."

"Why didn't you move in with extended family?" he asked.

"Because the only family I had was in another community, and they didn't have much money, so we'd be a burden.

I was already sixteen. I could work and take care of Simon myself. I decided to stay." She paused. "What about you? What about your *mamm*?"

Jeb had known she'd ask again, and he dropped his gaze.

"Why didn't she come to our wedding, Jeb?" she asked quietly. "Is it me? Am I not good enough for her, or—"

"She's in Rimstone," he said, cutting her off. "And no, the problem isn't you."

"Where I was teaching?" She eyed him curiously. "So close enough that she could have come . . ."

"It's a little complicated," he said, clearing his throat. "My *mamm* got pregnant as a teen with my sister. Mamm never would reveal who Lynita's father was. So, when she got pregnant again with me . . . I suppose it solidified her reputation. I don't have a *daet*. At least not one that acknowledges me."

Leah's expression blanked as she seemed to register that information, then she shook her head. "Your *mamm* was an Amish woman who . . ." She swallowed.

"Yah." Did they have to say it out loud? Whoever had fathered her two *kinner*, he had reason enough to keep himself hidden. "Mamm raised us as best she could in the community, but it was tough. She was always *that woman*, and no man would marry her. I don't know who our father is—or if we even have the same father. Mamm wouldn't breathe a word. So when it was time to find my sister a husband of her own, she asked my uncle if he could give me a fresh start, too."

"Do you see your *mamm* ever?" Leah asked.

"Sometimes. I take the bus out there every year or so and visit her. It can be hard to get away from the farm, though. I don't have anyone to cover now."

"Does she know . . . about me?"

"I didn't write her a letter yet to tell her," he said.

"Why?"

Because putting it down into words on paper had felt too much like hope. He said, "I didn't know if you'd go through with the wedding."

Leah was silent for a moment, then she nodded. "That's understandable. Now that the farm is yours, will you ask her to come live with us?"

"She wouldn't come," he said.

"Why not?"

"Too many questions. We'd have to lie if we wanted to make up a new story to make her acceptable to a new community, and she won't do that. So it's better for her to stay where she's known and she's already earned some forgiveness over the years than start fresh in a new place."

Leah sucked in a breath, and he watched her face. She didn't look at him. Instead, she stared into her mug. What would that mean to her—would he be even more of a liability than she thought?

"What's her name?" she asked softly.

"Ruth King."

"Ruth . . . I didn't hear about her in Rimstone," she murmured.

"Good. That means the rumor mill has set her aside for the time being." It was a good sign.

Jeb leaned his elbows on the table, and a moment of silence stretched between them. Abundance was his new life, and his *mamm* had prided herself on giving him that— something away from the shame of his parentage. How often had he wondered who his *daet* was? But his *mamm* wouldn't say.

"No one knows about my *mamm*," he said. "Except Lynita, of course. And her husband. So you don't have to worry about facing that in the community here."

"I should meet her, though," Leah said, lifting her gaze to meet his.

Did she really want to? He frowned slightly. "In time."

She nodded, then sucked in a breath. "More immediately, then, I want us to have friends."

"You can," he said. "I would never hold you back."

"You've been married before," she said. "You know how these things work. I can have friends on my own, yes, but now it's going to be about couples getting together and . . . and . . ."

"And?" He looked over at her, waiting for her to spell it out.

"As a married woman now, it would help me with those relationships if we could have friends together," she said, a little breathily.

"Leah . . ." He softened his tone. "I am who I am. I know this community means everything to you, and I can understand why even better now. It's all you have."

"It's all you have, too!" she countered.

"But I don't trust them." He heard the bitterness in his own tone.

Leah fell silent.

"You can go out," he added. "I'm not going to stop you. Have friends. Enjoy your new status."

"There's a game night tomorrow night," she said. "It's being hosted at Rosmanda and Levi's place."

"You should go," he said.

"It's a couples' night," she clarified. "And we're newly married. If I go without you, it will start questions."

Jeb sighed. "I'm not good in groups. You should know that."

"It won't be that many people," she said. "And we don't have to go if you don't want to, but I couldn't go without you either."

Jeb pressed his lips together. Leah wasn't asking for

much—just an evening out with her friends where she could show that she was married. He got the farm, her brother would get out of debt, and what would she have? A scarred and inhospitable husband. It was a little early to be disappointing her.

"Fine. We'll go."

"We will?" A smile came to her face, and he knew then exactly why he'd agreed to this. It was for that smile.

"I'm not charming," he qualified. "I don't make small talk. I'm not exactly the life of the party."

"You don't need to be," she said, picking up her mug. "I'm just happy we can go together. I'm quite easy to please, actually."

"Are you sure?" he asked with a low laugh. "I've yet to meet a woman who's easy to please."

She looked back at him, frowning slightly.

"I know why I'm here, Jeb, and I'm satisfied with that," she said, meeting his gaze. "I'll be happy to be known as a married woman. That's all. I'm not asking for more from you."

Was this the secret to happiness—limited expectations? He watched as she rinsed her mug in the sink, and he wondered what he would tell his mother.

She'd sent him and Lynita to Peter to give them a better life, and looking at how his life had turned out, he had to wonder if his *mamm* had ever regretted her decision, at least for him. Because he sure had. For all he'd loved his *mamm* and wanted to provide for her, he'd also resented her for having shipped him away. He'd been all of thirteen—not half so grown as he looked. And Lynita had been a fiercely loyal sister, but she couldn't be his *mamm*, too.

Let me stay with you, Mamm! he'd pleaded. *You need a man around here. What are you going to do alone?*

But the truth of the matter was, he didn't want to be

without her. He didn't want to go live with some aunt and uncle he'd never met. He didn't want to face his days without his *mamm* in them. And at the age of thirteen, staring at her with his heart in his throat and tears in his eyes, he'd never felt more desperate.

I'll be fine, son. And so will you. Besides, you'll have your sister with you.

Let me stay, Mamm . . .

No. You'll thank me for this later—you mark my words. Your life will be better. You'll write me letters, and you'll come to visit. But you'll never tell anyone who I am, all right?

Life would better—that's what she'd told them in her letters, too. She'd repeated it over and over again, and maybe she needed to believe that, because otherwise, she'd sent her children away for nothing. But then Lynita found a husband, and that seemed to be the proof his *mamm* needed that she'd been right that a life away from her was better for both of them.

But moving away from his mother all those years ago hadn't changed that he was very much her son—making brash choices and hoping for the best just like she had.

He'd have to write her a letter and tell her the latest news . . .

Dear Mamm,
*   I've gotten married again . . .*

She should have been at the wedding. Appearances be damned.

Chapter Eight

The next evening, outside Rosmanda and Levi's house, Leah stood in the summer dusk with a pie in her hands as she waited for Jeb to unhitch the horse from the buggy. She'd made the pie that morning—her contribution to the game night. Their contribution, she should say.

There was a time when she used to make her pies with such careful attention to detail, hoping that a young man would notice it. Now, she was married, and a pie took on new meaning. She was now a part of the community of adults, and this pie was her way of contributing as an equal. People would be eating, and they'd go through a lot of food. Rosmanda would need the contributions to keep people fed.

The pie wasn't perfect today. There was a dent in the center from where they'd gone over a bump in the buggy and she'd nearly dropped it. She was still disappointed. Even if this pie wasn't going to be used to find a man, it was a representation of her abilities as a wife, and she already felt like she was falling short.

"You can just go in," Jeb said as he unbuckled the traces.

"I'll wait," she replied, and she watched as he worked. He was quick and confident, but earlier, when they were getting ready to go, he'd been more reluctant. Part of her was worried that if she didn't step through the door with him, he wouldn't come in.

"How long since you've done something like this?" Leah asked.

"How long since you've seen me at a social event?" he countered.

"Never," she admitted. "But I was with the youth group, and then I had women friends . . . it was different."

She hadn't been in the same social circles, being an unmarried woman.

"It's been a long while," he said, patting the horse's neck as he came around to lead it toward the stable. Jeb paused, his dark gaze meeting hers. "I'm doing this for you tonight."

A smile flickered across his lips. He didn't seem quite so daunting out here in the soft, warm evening. His scars melted into the darkness, leaving just a tall, broad man with a deep voice and a certain tenderness in his gaze.

"Oh . . ." She smiled hesitantly. "Thank you."

"I told you before I'm not good with—" He glanced over her shoulder toward the house. "—groups."

"This is our community," she said. What were the Amish without their connection to one another?

"This is *your* community," he countered, then led the horse forward. "I'll just get the horse in a stall."

Leah stared after him, noting that unmistakable limp as he walked. From inside the house she could hear muted laughter and the murmur of voices. *Her* community? She was new to being a wife, and everything would be different. This would be like starting fresh in a lot of ways. It would be his community, too, in time. If she did nothing else, she was determined to bring him back. He couldn't stay living that lonely, distrustful life, could he? God worked in mysterious ways.

Jeb came back outside the stable, shutting the door behind him. He paused at her side and adjusted his straw hat.

"Okay," he said.

"You ready?" she asked.

"No." He sucked in a breath. "But let's do it anyway."

She smiled at that, and they made their way toward the side door. It was propped open, the screen door shut to keep the bugs outside. Leah went first, and she knocked on the screen frame, then opened it. They wouldn't wait on ceremony here.

"Hello?" Leah called. She could smell the scent of popcorn and some warm baking. There was a male shout of victory as someone won a game of some sort, and the sounds of friendly chatter tugged her inward.

Rosmanda poked her head into the mudroom, and a smile broke over her face. "You're here! I didn't expect to see you for a couple of weeks at least."

"Surprise," Leah said, and her friend shot a smile past Leah to Jeb.

"Welcome, Jeb. Come inside. We have games going and all sorts of food." Rosmanda accepted the pie from Leah. "This looks good—what is it? Blueberry?"

"That's right. Excuse the dent. I was saving it from a bump in the road."

"Dents are perfectly edible," Rosmanda said with a grin. "Come on in."

Leah glanced over her shoulder at Jeb, but the earlier openness in his gaze was gone, and Elizabeth, another young married woman, poked her head into the mudroom with a smile.

"You're here! How does it feel to be married?" Elizabeth asked.

How did it feel? Leah wasn't even sure yet. It felt like a strange dream where nothing felt quite like it should, but she couldn't wake up.

"It's . . . wonderful," Leah said. This was the appropriate

answer, and she looked over at Jeb to see what he would say, but he stayed silent.

Leah followed Elizabeth and Rosmanda into the kitchen. There was a game of Dutch Blitz happening around the table, and a group of kids could be heard running around upstairs. There was a thump, a wail, and Rosmanda paused, looking up toward the ceiling, but the cry stopped.

"Are you going to check on them?" Leah asked.

"That was one of my girls, I think, but it wasn't a hurt cry," Rosmanda said. "They're fine. Let's put out your pie."

The men at the table had fallen silent, and Rosmanda noticed their exchanged glances. After a couple of beats, one of the men, Malachi, Elizabeth's husband, scooted his chair over. He was one of the newly married men in their community, and his married beard looked sparse at best.

"Do you want to play this round, Jeb?" Malachi asked.

Jeb cleared his throat, then nodded. "Sure. It's been a while."

Jeb pulled up a stool and sat in the space two men made for him, and he lifted his gaze, meeting Leah's for a moment. He looked wary, uncertain. This was for her—she knew that. But if he only gave it a chance, maybe this could be more than a kind gesture the next time they came out. Jeb looked down to the cards being shuffled.

"So, how is married life?" Rosmanda asked with a smile.

"Fine." Leah smiled back, but she wondered how sincere she looked.

"You look spooked," Elizabeth said, coming up. She slipped her arm through Leah's.

"I'm not spooked," Leah said with a low laugh. "It's just . . . a lot to adjust to."

"At least you don't have to get used to doing all the housework alone," Elizabeth said. "You were already running your own home with your brother. When Malachi and I got married, I was used to having my *mamm* and three younger sisters sharing chores with me. Now, that was an adjustment to taking care of a home on my own!"

"Are you living in the farmhouse, then?" Rosmanda asked Leah.

Leah nodded. "I'm trying to sort out the kitchen to my liking."

"It must be nice to spread out a little bit," Rosmanda said.

"It is," Leah said. "But I'm still figuring out what's in the cupboards and what I'm missing, so I'm not appreciating the extra space yet."

Plus, there was all the clutter she'd had to wade through. But she couldn't mention that. Already, there was need for marital discretion.

"We should come help you," Elizabeth said. "With three or four of us sorting things out, we can get your cupboards in order in a couple of hours."

"No—" The word came out before Leah could even think better of it, but having others come over and sort through the kitchen with her wouldn't actually be helpful. "I'll invite you all over properly, but we're still—"

"Honeymooning?" Rosmanda supplied with a teasing smile.

Leah's cheeks heated and she didn't answer that. They'd all assume that was what was happening, but it wasn't.

"All she'll admit to is kitchen organizing," Elizabeth said, and she collapsed into giggles. "I'm sorry, Leah, but this was me two years ago, and it's nice to be able to tease someone else for a change."

"Poor thing," Miriam said with a good-humored smile. The older woman grabbed a dish cloth and wiped off a cutting board that had been used for slicing bread, then reached for a loaf of sweet bread. "Leah, don't let them tease you. But I do have a bit of advice for you."

"Oh?" Leah asked hopefully. Miriam was Rosmanda's mother-in-law, and she'd been married longer than Leah had even been alive.

"Make doing the dishes a pleasure," Miriam said meaningfully, then tapped the side of her nose.

"What?" Leah asked feebly.

"Make it . . . time together," Miriam said. "What I'm saying is, if he will stand there with you drying dishes, then reward him with sweet words and a little flirting. . . . Trust me on that. If you can start it now, the rest of your marriage he'll pitch in and help you dry dishes and won't even be sure why."

"I just thought that Stephen was a good husband that way," Rosmanda said.

"Did you?" Miriam raised her eyebrows innocently. "He's a very good man, dear, but I'm also a good wife."

Leah couldn't help but laugh at that. "You're a wise woman, Miriam."

"Oh, I stumbled into that by accident," Miriam replied. "All sorts of good things come out of the early days, and all that flirting that goes on between you. But it's worked well for me. Mind you, Stephen uses the same trick on me all the time. He'll bring me along with him when he checks on the new calves, and I'm sure he only wants me there for opening and shutting gates for him, but he treats me like the only woman in the world while we do it, and well . . . even at my age, I enjoy the attention."

Miriam looked across the room to where Stephen was standing, watching the game of Dutch Blitz. The older man looked up at the same time, and he gave his wife a small smile. Leah could see the familiarity and tenderness between the two. They still had the spark, this older couple, and Leah looked between them wistfully. Maybe she and Jeb could develop that kind of friendship over time—

helping each other with chores and that sort of thing. Except, she doubted the flirting would be much use to her.

Did all the marriage advice need to contain that teasing hint of the physical relationship? Leah looked over at Jeb, who was only half-heartedly playing the game, slapping down a card here and there while another young man whooped out his winning hand. Marriage was supposed to be about practical things. That's what married women told the younger ones coming up behind them. Marriage was about a man you could trust, about working together, building a family together, a business, and worshipping together. Marriage was about community.

And all those parts of the relationship that mattered most were developed before the wedding. When couples were dating, they were supposed to stay pure, but that friendship they cultivated would last a lifetime. That was what an Amish young woman was told over and over again. She hadn't expected this change in emphasis now that she was legally married. It felt intrusive, embarrassing.

"Marriage is long," Rosmanda murmured next to her. "Give it time . . ."

Were her thoughts so obvious? Leah dropped her gaze. Marriage *was* long. For better or for worse, with the Amish, it was for a lifetime. Perhaps she didn't need the advice of the other women quite so much as she'd thought. She'd longed for the time when the community of married women could be her support, but she hadn't anticipated hiding quite so much. And Leah didn't hide things very well, it would seem. The other women could see right through her. So perhaps she didn't need their advice so much as she needed their respect. She'd have to figure out the rest on her own.

* * *

Jeb watched as the other players slapped down their cards in the fast-paced game. Flick, flick, flick, then a whoop as another young man won.

He tossed his cards into the pile, then stood up.

"You're not going to play?" Malachi asked.

Jeb remembered Malachi as a rambunctious six-year-old at his first wedding. Malachi had very loudly come out with a bad word and found himself spanked by his father out by the buggies. Jeb remembered feeling bad for the kid. He'd been so embarrassed when he came back after a paddling—his young pride having been wounded more than his backside. And now Malachi was here, married and fully grown.

Matthew, the one Leah had been engaged to, would have been a kid back then, too, although Jeb didn't remember him. Just another kid. There were a lot of kids in any Amish community. Was Matthew even here tonight?

"Nah, I'm done," Jeb said, and he stood up, stepping back. "I'll watch."

It didn't feel like that much time had slipped away since he'd married Katie, or since her death. He'd just gone about his business and kept to himself. How could fifteen years slide by without him noticing? The kids from his wedding were married already, with *kinner* of their own on the way.

Jeb's gaze moved toward the women. Leah stood with her back to him, and the other women seemed to be teasing her by the good-natured laughing happening over by the sink. But his eyes were locked on his wife.

She was slender, but she had a definite shape to her that he liked. Her hair was carefully tucked up underneath her *kapp*, but there was a wispy tendril that had escaped at her hairline, and he found his gaze moving down the porcelain line of her neck to her dress. It had been a long time since he'd been around a woman, let alone shared a house with one, and he'd been noticing things about Leah—the shape of her body, the way she ran her hands down her hips when she thought she was straightening herself out.

Leah put her hand up to her neck, shaking her head and laughing along with the women. Leah's fingers were slim and pale, and he realized that he hadn't held her hand yet. Maybe he never would . . . but he wondered what those fingers would feel like in his palm. The things he'd noticed about her, the details he appreciated, had been from afar.

"A wife is a blessing," Stephen said.

"Yah." Jeb turned his attention to the older man who'd come up next to him. They had some history, and Jeb eyed the older man, wondering how much he'd acknowledge.

"I'm glad you've found happiness," Stephen said, his voice low. "I hope you stay that way."

There it was—the barb. He couldn't say he was surprised.

"That's a strange way of congratulating a man," Jeb said curtly.

"This isn't your first marriage," Stephen replied.

"No, it isn't." Jeb met Stephen's gaze, refusing to be cowed. "Are you trying to say something?"

"It takes two to make a marriage happy, son," Stephen said quietly.

"Agreed."

"You can't blame a woman if your home isn't peaceful," Stephen said. "Leah's a good woman. We care about her happiness, too."

"I've been married for two days," Jeb said curtly. "Have you already heard rumors?"

Stephen was talking about Katie and they both knew it, but Jeb refused to give him the satisfaction of acknowledging it. Jeb had been just as misled as Katie had been. The community that should have steered Jeb straight had let him down, too.

Jeb didn't wait for Stephen to reply. Stephen had been one of the older men to encourage him to marry Katie. Stephen had lied to his face, convinced a young man to marry a girl who'd never love him, and now blamed him to this day because Katie hadn't settled obediently into his arms? Anger simmered up inside him, but this was an old rage that had burned for years. He wouldn't get into an argument with Stephen tonight. There was no point. Katie was dead, and Stephen would believe whatever he wanted to believe.

"A word of advice," Stephen said. "Marriage is what the man makes of it. A happy wife is because a man knows how to treat her well."

"A happy wife has chosen to *be* a wife," he snapped. Not only had Katie been pushed into their marriage, but she'd been resentful for every moment of it. Could he blame her? Fifteen years after her death, he could still feel the bullying that had made their marriage happen.

"Jebadiah—" Stephen began, but Jeb raised a hand and stopped him.

"Enough," Jeb growled, and the older man fell silent.

It was then that Jeb noticed that the women had gone silent, too, and they all stood there staring at him, Leah in the center of them all. Her eyes were wide, and he could see the pleading in them.

All she wanted was a proper outing with other couples, and he was already ruining it.

"Excuse me," he said gruffly. Jeb turned and stalked out of the kitchen and into the hallway that led to the sitting room beyond. He stood there in the dim light provided from lamps in either room, and he realized he wasn't willing to go into the next room. He wanted solitude, quiet.

He wanted to get out of here, go out to the company of the horses . . . Anything but stay in this house.

Stephen still blamed him! And had Stephen and Miriam really known Katie's parents all that well? They'd moved into Abundance when Katie was a child still, and they had no relatives around here. But Stephen and Miriam had stood for that couple as if they'd known all their kin. They'd stood for Katie—been desperate to "rescue" her from the clutches of some Englisher boyfriend, because Heaven knew that the worst thing that could possibly happen was one Amish girl running off with her Englisher love. If she had, they all might have been a great deal happier, and Katie, while damned by her community, might still be alive.

It turned out that marriage didn't solve all those problems after all, and a girl's heart didn't let go of her lover quite so easily as they'd all anticipated.

"Jeb!" Stephen said, coming down the hall toward him.

"Your business with me is through," Jeb said, turning to face the older man. "I'm not a boy anymore. You told me to marry Katie, and I did. I tried to love her. I tried to be good to her, and God knows I tried to save her from that fire. What more do you want from me?"

"Don't use the name of God—"

"Like you did, you mean?" Jeb asked with a bitter smile. "I seem to remember you telling me exactly what *God* wanted. He wanted marriages that produced children. He wanted Amish to stay Amish. He wanted us to protect the women in our midst with our manly, fortifying presence. Something like that."

Stephen's face paled. "God puts the responsibility on a man's shoulders—"

"To force a wedding?" Jeb shook his head. "If Katie had any choice in the matter, if anyone had actually listened to her—including me, might I add—she'd probably still be alive."

"Kindness goes a long way with a woman," Stephen said, lowering his voice. "That's all I'm trying to say. In this marriage—to Leah. Gentleness. Patience. The fruits of the spirit. They go a long way in creating a happy home."

Stephen was worried about Leah now. He could see it in the older man's eyes—the trepidation. He wasn't sure what Jeb had become after all these years, and perhaps looking him in the face hadn't relieved any of those worries. But whatever Jeb had become was because of this community, and Stephen in particular.

"And you think I was some kind of monster in my first marriage, do you?" Jeb asked. "Is that it? You think behind closed doors I was some kind of raging beast?"

"I didn't say that. But—"

"Maybe I wanted too much?" Jeb went on bitterly. "You think it was too much to want my own wife to love me?"

"This marriage with Leah can be different," Stephen said slowly. "You can make better choices—"

"It already is different!" Jeb retorted. "And it isn't about my choices this time. For one, she chose this." Mostly. At least this time it was circumstances that had pushed her, not the community. "And I know what to expect this time around."

Stephen didn't answer. His gaze moved over Jeb's scarred face and moved down to his gnarled hand. Jeb clenched his hand into a fist, the skin tightening uncomfortably. His hip had started to ache again, and he straightened his leg, trying to push against the pain. Stephen was right— Jeb was no longer the strong, young man to do the community's dirty work. He was now a scarred hermit . . . and perhaps Stephen was wise to be a little nervous about Leah's choice in a husband. Jeb was no longer any woman's desire.

"We ruined Katie," Jeb said quietly. "You and me. And

everyone else who went along to make her marry me. Whatever she became . . . whatever I became . . . that was because of that wedding. All of it."

"Only the Lord knows why bad things happen—"

"—to good people?" Jeb finished the worn phrase for him. "Do you think I was a good person, marrying a woman who I knew didn't want to marry me? Do you think you were a good person helping her parents to pressure her into it? So maybe bad things happen to bad people, or maybe bad things just happen, Stephen, because you seem to have escaped the retribution that I've suffered."

From the sitting room, he could hear the sound of several couples playing a game of Uno. There was laughter, a groan as someone had to pick up four cards. Such an ordinary pastime. What was Jeb even doing here? He didn't belong.

"Leah's a sweet young woman," Stephen said quietly. "And I believe she'll make a good wife to you. I wanted to speak to you, man-to-man, to give you some advice. And I realize now that isn't welcome. But you chose this wife, Jebadiah. The rest of us had nothing to do with it."

"Yah, I did."

"Then as a man who has been married for much longer than you have, let me say one thing. You just have to . . . be patient."

"Patient for what?" Jeb demanded. He wanted to make Stephen say it out loud. Was he talking about their physical relationship? Had news about that already gotten out? He wouldn't even be surprised if it had. He knew how a tight community like theirs worked.

"Be patient as you wait for the easy times," Stephen replied. "Be patient for when it feels more natural between you. That takes time."

Jeb nodded. "I intend to."

"Good." Stephen sucked in a deep breath, and he pasted a smile on his face that didn't quite reach his eyes. "That's all I wanted to say, really. It's said. Now—will you play a game?"

"No." Jeb was tired of playing games. He was tired of pretending everything was fine when it wasn't. He'd pulled away from these people for good reason—they couldn't be trusted.

"Jeb?"

Leah came into the hallway, a plate of pie in her hands, and both men looked up. She smiled hesitantly. Stephen didn't say anything, but he headed back toward the kitchen, brushing past Leah as he went. She was a surprisingly welcome sight standing there with that plate in her hands and the fork glinting in the low light. She met his gaze uncertainly.

"I brought you some pie," Leah said.

"Thank you," he said gruffly.

"What happened?" she asked.

"Nothing."

"You seemed . . . angry," she said.

"We have some history," Jeb said. "Nothing to worry about."

"Should we leave?" she asked.

Yah, they should. And he had no desire to play some silly game, but he would do it after all. Leah wanted her couples' game night, and she would have it. He'd stand here and eat her blueberry pie, and then he'd sit in that room with the game of Uno and wait out the rest of the evening.

For her.

"No," he said. "It's fine. I'll play Uno."

Leah handed the plate over to him and he accepted it with a nod.

"Please be nice . . ." she whispered.

"I'm always nice," he said woodenly. Unless he was unfairly judged by the very community who had broken him. Then he was honest. They thought that by keeping their community intact, they were saving themselves from hellfire. No one seemed to take into account the kind of hell people could live in behind closed doors.

Leah met his gaze hopefully, and he forced a smile. He'd play nice, even if he didn't want to tonight. She turned and headed back toward the kitchen, looking at him over her shoulder once more before she disappeared again. Jeb stood there with that plate in his hand.

He felt it all coming full circle again—a brand-new marriage based on something other than love, the resentment beginning, the appearances to be maintained. Except this time, instead of the wife being the angry one who was filled with so much rage at the unfairness of the life ahead of her, it was him. Leah was the confused one with the best of intentions. Leah was the one who'd end up broken and confused as to what had happened here, because he knew exactly how it felt to be married to someone this angry.

It was heartbreak.

Chapter Nine

"I'm glad you came," Rosmanda said later that evening when they stood by the door, getting ready to leave. Leah leaned over to give her friend a hug. Rosmanda's belly pressed against Leah's, and she felt a tap as the baby kicked.

Leah shut her eyes against the wave of sadness. She always thought she was prepared for moments like this—steeled against the weight of her own longing. And then something as ordinary and sweet as the tap of a baby's foot inside his mother's belly could bring tears to her eyes.

"Oh!" Rosmanda laughed, rubbing her belly. "Did you feel that?"

"I guess I was crowding the little one," Leah said, but her throat thickened with emotion. "Thank you for having us, Rosie."

"Anytime," Rosmanda said. "You know that."

There were a few people still playing games at the table—this time it was Pictionary, and the women had joined in, so it was "the girls against the boys." Most of the food had been eaten, and people had turned to mugs of tea and coffee.

Outside, Jeb sat in the buggy waiting, and when he looked

over at her, his expression was steely and grim. She pushed open the screen door and headed out onto the step.

"Good night!" Leah called over her shoulder, and she let the screen door fall shut behind her as she made her way out to the buggy. She lifted her skirt, then pulled herself up. Jeb scooted over a little bit to make room for her, and once she was settled, he flicked the reins and the buggy started off.

The night was warm and the moon hung almost full in the dark sky. As they pulled out of the drive and onto the road, Leah put her hand down onto the seat to keep herself stable as they bumped up onto the pavement. She looked over at Jeb. His jaw was tensed, and his glittery gaze stayed fixed straight ahead.

"That was a nice evening," she said. Jeb didn't answer, and she watched him for a moment. "Wasn't it?"

"I'm glad you enjoyed yourself," he replied.

"You're rather good at Uno," she said.

She'd slipped into the Uno game later on that evening, and Jeb had beaten them all twice in a row. Admittedly, some of the people got a little testy after that, but then Lydia had won, and things smoothed over again.

"It's just luck," Jeb said. "You work with the cards you're dealt."

"I suppose," she agreed. "And it was fun."

Jeb didn't answer that, and his gaze stayed locked on the road. The clopping of the horse's hooves melded together with the soft squeak of one of the buggy's wheels. She could feel Jeb's tension emanating from him like heat from a coal.

"Are you angry at me?" she asked.

His gaze softened then, and he looked over at her. "It wasn't you."

"Then what?" she asked. "I know you and Stephen had

some words, but after that it seemed to be okay. And sure, some people weren't being good sports about losing—"

"About losing to me," he countered.

She'd noticed that, too. But people could be difficult sometimes. Being part of a community wasn't always easy.

"Maybe the next one will be better," she said. "They'll be more used to seeing you." His gaze flickered toward her again, this time more warily. Had that sounded like she'd been talking about his scars? She couldn't help but look at that puckered skin then, and she felt the heat rise in her face. She was making things worse.

"They'll also be more used to losing to you," she added, to qualify it.

"I'm not going to another one of these," he said.

"Oh, Jeb . . ." She forced out a laugh. "It was one night. I'm sure—"

"I'm serious," he said, cutting her off. "That was the last one."

The last time to go to a community event as a couple? Her heart sped up in her chest, and she felt the panic setting in.

"So you're never going to be sociable again?" she asked incredulously. It seemed ridiculous, except he'd been doing just that for years. "This marriage is supposed to help us socially. That was part of the agreement."

"I don't need more awkwardness and confrontation," he said.

"This marriage was supposed to help *me* socially," she amended. He was silent then, and Leah pushed forward. "Jeb, I know it was awkward. I could see that. But this is just the start. We're the newest couple and people will gossip. But the more they see us, the easier it will get. Then some other young couple will get married, and they'll be the newest ones and we'll be considered wise and experienced."

"Do you know what Stephen said to me?" Jeb asked, his voice low.

"No—"

"He's afraid for you." Jeb's lips twitched as he said the words, and she could feel his disgust at the thought.

"Afraid for me, how?" she asked.

"For your safety. For your happiness. I don't know exactly. He had counsel for me on being *kind*." He flicked the reins again as the horse started to slow.

"I didn't say anything to them to make them worry, if that's what you're thinking," she said.

"You wouldn't have to," he said woodenly. "They already think the worst of me."

"Maybe he didn't mean it the way it sounded . . ." The words trailed off when she glanced over at her. "They didn't stop our marriage, did they?" she asked. Because if they were truly so worried about her as to bring it up with her new husband, she thought they would have said something before now. Bringing anything up now seemed more like gossip and less like legitimate worry.

"No, they didn't do that, to their credit," he muttered.

And yet Stephen had said something to Jeb . . . She remembered the tender look that passed between Stephen and Miriam. Had the older man only meant it to be advice to a newly married man? Maybe it had been something more innocent than Jeb was assuming.

"I'm not a danger to you," Jeb added, his voice low. "I'd never hurt you. I'm not what they say. I know I'm not easy to look at anymore, but I've got a heart, and I didn't marry you to make you miserable. I'm not going to hurt you, or . . . or . . . make you unhappy."

"I think I know that," she said quietly.

They fell into silence, and Leah scooted a little closer to him along the seat, not quite close enough to touch him, but she could feel the heat of his body. Jeb leaned toward her, his arm pressing against hers as he looked down at her, his gaze softening.

"Thank you for coming tonight, all the same," she said.

"Yah." A smile twitched at the corners of his lips. "You're welcome."

Suddenly, there was a jolt as the wheel hit a pothole, and the buggy heaved heavily, and she felt her body fling forward. But even as she catapulted, Jeb's arm shot out and she collided with muscle. His hand clamped down on her leg, and she bounced off him and back into the seat.

"Oh—" she gasped.

"I didn't see that one," Jeb said, leaning forward for a better view of the road, but his hand stayed firmly on her upper thigh, as if he'd forgotten where his hand had landed. He was stronger than she'd even guessed he would be—his fingers alone keeping her pinned against the seat, his touch a little too intimate to be comfortable. She put her hand up on his arm, giving him a gentle nudge, and she felt the work-hardened muscle.

"Sorry." He leaned back against the seat and his arm settled across her body as he looked over at her, his touch lightening. "You okay?"

His reaction had been swift and strong, but also with a strange confidence. She'd never been touched like that before—as if this man had every right to have his hands on her body, no hint of an apology in his dark eyes, with his large hand covering her thigh and his thick arm emanating heat against her body. He smelled close, musky and warm.

Leah nodded. "Yah, I'm okay."

"Good." But he didn't move, and his dark gaze met hers. There was something in the way he was looking at her— something tender yet direct—and when his gaze moved down to her lips, her breath caught.

"You're beautiful, you know . . ." he breathed.

"Am I?" she whispered.

"Yah." He smiled ruefully, then pulled his hand off her leg, leaving a handprint of sensation where his fingers had pressed into her, and she felt chilled where his warm arm had pressed against her body. She sucked in a wavering breath.

The horse plodded on, and Leah tried to calm the pattering of her heartbeat. She smoothed her hand over that spot on her leg where his hand had been.

"Did I hurt you?" he asked. "I only meant to catch you."

"No," she said. "I just . . . If someone saw that—"

His response was a low laugh. "If someone saw that, then what, Leah?"

She realized how silly it was then, because what would they see? A married couple going over a pothole. Nothing more. A husband protecting his wife from the jolt. A compliment given.

"You're my wife," he said, and there was something almost possessive in the way he said it, and it made goose bumps rise on her arms.

"Yah. I'm still getting used to that."

They continued on, silvery moonlight illuminating their way as the buggy rattled over the pavement. Leah stole a look at him, his profile on the undamaged side of his face looking like any other Amish man. His beard was full and thick, dark as mahogany wood with a few gray strands shining silver, and she could see just how handsome he had once been.

And maybe he still was . . .

There was something about how she saw him that had changed over the last couple of days. He was large and intimidating still, but he was also kind, and when those muscles were used in her protection . . .

Had he meant what he said—that she was beautiful? A smile tickled the corners of her lips. Was that how he saw her?

It was nice to be married. And maybe he'd soften yet and they'd go to another outing together. There was always hope.

Jeb shut the door to his bedroom and heaved a sigh. He undid the buttons of his shirt and pulled it off. His bedroom window was propped open with a stick, cool evening air ruffling the curtain as it flowed inside, a welcome relief against his skin. He could hear the chirp of crickets and the croak of a lonely toad somewhere out there in the grass.

He hadn't meant to touch her, and the protective gesture in the buggy had been one of instinct. But once he'd touched her, he hadn't wanted to pull away either. He could still remember the softness of her under his hand, her heightened breathing after the surprise of the jolt. But then, she'd run her fingers over his arm . . .

He shut his eyes, then rubbed his hands over his face. It was a strange thing to heat a man's blood like this, but it had been a very long time since a woman had touched him . . . and his last wife had never touched him like *that*.

Leah's touch had been gentle, even a little exploratory. And it had taken every ounce of self-restraint not to pull her into his arms properly and feel her against him, run his hands around her waist, and lower his lips over hers. What was it about this woman that drew him to her?

He pushed back the image that rose in his mind. He shouldn't even be thinking these thoughts. He knew better. He wasn't about to push himself onto her and ask for more than they'd agreed upon. He'd been with a woman before who had put up with him while she pined for another man, and Jeb hadn't exactly improved over the years. Whatever attraction he felt for Leah wasn't the issue. She hadn't married him for that, and Jeb wouldn't try to change the rules of their marriage.

From the bathroom, water turned on—a soft trickle into the sink. He knew the sound.

Jeb sighed. He'd been curious if Matthew would show up to that game night tonight, but he hadn't. He wasn't sure what he'd even do if faced with the younger man. There was no competition . . . technically. Matthew was married with a baby on the way. And how could Jeb exactly compete with the younger man who'd held Leah's heart? Jeb was the husband Leah had taken on for her own practical reasons, but Matthew, she had loved.

Except, he'd have to face the man at some point—look him in the eye. He'd rather stay hermited away than do that, quite honestly.

Jeb wasn't ready to sleep. The water seemed to be stopped, which likely meant she was back in her bedroom, so he picked up his light and opened his bedroom door.

He stepped out into the hallway with the lantern in one hand, and he saw the pale ripple of a nightgown. He and Leah both froze. She wore a long-sleeved, cotton nightgown, her uncovered hair falling in a thick brown braid down her back. She stared at him, eyes wide, her lips parted.

"Hi," he said. He realized then that he was standing in the doorway without a shirt on, his pants hanging lower than usual without his suspenders. His entire chest was exposed—the length of puckered scars down his side. Her gaze moved down his torso, and he could see the horror in her eyes. He reached for his shirt.

"I was just—" She licked her lips and they grew pinker, looking away. "I was hungry."

"Me too," he said, and he pulled on his shirt, doing up the buttons. He wasn't living alone anymore, or with his uncle. He'd have to watch that. "I was thinking of peanut butter on bread."

The Amish peanut butter was sweet—a combination of corn syrup, honey, peanut butter . . . It was comforting—a sweet treat from his childhood, when things were still safe and warm.

"That would be good." She smiled hesitantly. "Unless you needed some time to yourself."

"It's okay. Come on."

She hesitated. "I should get dressed."

"Why?" He met her gaze. "I can't see anything through that, and we're married, Leah. What are you afraid of? Someone would see you in your nightgown in your own kitchen?"

He didn't wait to see what she chose, but he headed down the staircase, and he heard the soft squeak of her feet on the stairs behind him. He smiled to himself. This was one of the pleasures of a wife—a woman's presence, her smell, the soft flap of her nightgown around her ankles. He might not have anything else from her in this marriage, but he could enjoy the small things.

He hung the lamp on the hook above the table, the rocking, the swath of light teetering across the kitchen.

"I was thinking—" Jeb said, pulling out the bread. "About Matthew."

"Matthew?" She came up to the counter, and with her so close, he wondered if he'd see the signs if she lied to him. Would her face pale? Would she blush? Would she look away?

"Yah. Is it awkward between you?" he asked.

"A little," she said.

He hadn't expected her to admit to that, and it made him feel better that she did.

"They were at our wedding," she added.

"Yah, I saw them. Do you love him still?"

Leah blinked. "I don't think—"

"I just want to know," he said, softening his tone. "If I can't avoid seeing the man, I at least want to know what to expect. You didn't marry me for love, so I don't expect it. But . . . do you love *him*?"

"I'm not sure."

"You can say if you do."

She heaved a sigh. "I'm trying not to love him. It's been a year since we broke up. And I thought he was the one God had saved for me. I thought—"

Jeb pulled a tub of sweet peanut butter from the cupboard and pried open the lid. It used to be a honey container.

"So what happened?" he asked.

"I told him I couldn't have *kinner*," she said. "And that was all it took. He just . . . it was like snuffing out a candle. Whatever he felt for me vanished, and he turned it all onto Rebecca. So yah, I loved him dearly, but I question what he felt for me."

Jeb nodded. "And what he feels for his wife, I imagine."

"What he feels for her isn't for me to judge," she said tightly.

"I'm sorry about that," he said. "You deserved better treatment."

"It is what it is," she said. "I can't give birth. He knew what he wanted."

And Leah would be faced with Matthew's pregnant wife—the babies, the family Leah hadn't been able to provide. Jeb smoothed the peanut butter onto a thick slice of bread and passed it over to her.

"What about you?" she asked, accepting the plate. "What is it that I don't know about Katie?"

Jeb looked up at her and found her dark gaze locked on him. He normally hated scrutiny, but she wasn't looking at his scars this time. Her gaze met his.

"She hated me," he said quietly, and as the words came

out, he realized he hadn't meant to say it. Not so bluntly at least.

"Why?"

"Because she loved an Englisher boy, and I wasn't him," Jeb said. "Her parents and several prominent members of the community were very concerned about her relationship with that Englisher. He'd been asking her to leave her family and run away with him. Their solution was to arrange a marriage for her."

"Why did you agree?" Leah asked.

"Because—" Jeb paused, his mind going back to those naïve, hopeful days. Did he want to reveal so much? "Because she was beautiful and I'd been halfway in love with her for a long time. All of us boys were. And the community had chosen me. I was stupid enough to think that after we were married, she'd love me back."

"But she didn't . . ." Leah sounded like she understood how a young woman's heart worked.

"No, she didn't," he admitted. "And this is why I resent the community so much. They assured me she would. They told me that as married men they understood women better than I did, and any hesitation I felt was natural, but unfounded. I could trust them, they said. And they knew for a fact that she'd settle into married life and start having babies."

Leah winced at the last word. Right. He hadn't meant to rub that in her face.

"Was it very bad?" she asked softly.

"Terrible." He cleared his throat. "She never did forgive me."

He could remember the icy silence in their home that could last for days, interspersed with her sharp tongue where she could find the one thing he was most sensitive about and stab at it with her words. She'd learned how to insult the things that made him a man. She knew how to pick away at his sense of self-worth. She'd been very good at tearing a man down.

"Is that why you're asking about Matthew?" Leah asked.

Jeb picked up his own plate of bread with peanut butter, but he didn't take a bite. He sighed, putting it back on the counter.

"Maybe." He pressed his palm against the counter, feeling his scarred flesh go tight.

"You think I'll hate you?" she whispered. "Because you aren't Matthew?"

"I hope you won't." Jeb looked up.

"I'm glad you aren't him," she said. "Because he could change his affections as quickly as I could change a dress."

"And you can't change your feelings like that," he concluded.

"No, I can't."

He was saying too much. Was it that she was a beautiful woman, too, and that was his weakness, or was he just this lonely for someone to unburden himself to? He shouldn't be telling her so much, but there was something about her that drew him to her. The lamp hanging from the hook above the table sputtered twice and then went out.

"Blast," he muttered. "I didn't refill it."

He'd been a little preoccupied the last few days, and his normal routine—the refilling of lamps, the cleaning of boots—had fallen by the wayside. It took a moment for his eyes to adjust, but moonlight from outside illumined parts of the kitchen. Leah's nightgown shone in a rectangle of moonlight, her bare feet looking pale against the wooden floor.

"I think she blamed the wrong person," Leah said softly.

"What's that?" He frowned slightly.

"Your wife," she said. "She blamed you. She had a whole lot of other people she could have blamed."

"I suppose I was more convenient," he murmured.

Jeb smiled at his own dark humor, and before he could think better of it, he stepped closer to her. Leah didn't move away, and when he reached out with his good hand, she didn't flinch when he ran his fingers down her forearm, stopping at her wrist. She was beautiful in the moonlight, her face almost as pale as the moon itself, and her dark eyes shining in the darkness. From where he stood, he could see the flutter of her heartbeat in the tender hollow where her neck met her collarbone.

"I don't like to talk about that," he admitted softly.

"We should be friends, Jeb," she said.

"Yah?" Friends. Look at her—standing there in her bare feet, smelling faintly of soap and something else that was sweeter, he wouldn't exactly describe her as a friend. He didn't feel friendly toward her. Not in that way, at least. When he looked down at her, he saw a woman—the softness of her figure, the roundness of her body beneath that nightgown . . . He swallowed.

"In the dark, you look different," she said quietly.

"How so?" He ran his hand down her arm again, and this time he caught her hand in his. This was his good hand—the smooth, strong hand that hadn't been burned down to a claw.

"You look—" She hesitated.

"Like a normal man?" he provided. "It's okay. You can say it."

"I don't really mean that," she said. But she did. He knew it. There had been times he'd stared at himself in his bedroom mirror by the light of the moon and he'd noticed the same thing—the forgiving nature of night's shadows.

"Under all these scars, I'm just a man, you know," he said, and his gaze locked onto hers. He didn't know what he meant to do, but she didn't look away like he expected her to. She met his gaze easily enough, and those plump lips parted as she sucked in a breath.

And maybe it was that he wanted to prove his point—
that he was a man after all—but he stepped nearer, closing
those last few inches between them. The fabric of her
nightgown brushed against his pants, and he dipped his
head down, his mouth hovering over hers. He waited for
her to pull away, to shove him, to laugh—he wasn't sure
what. He waited for some show of scorn or disgust, but it
didn't come. Leah stayed there, motionless, her soft hand
in his. And then she tipped her face subtly upward, and he
lowered his mouth over hers.

Her lips were soft and yielding, and for a moment he
could hear his own heartbeat thudding in his head. He
wanted to pull her closer—but he didn't dare.

It was like holding a butterfly, knowing that if you did
more than let it light on your finger, you'd crush it. And
he'd crush this moment if he let go of the careful rein he
maintained on his desires.

Leah was the first to pull back, and he shut his eyes and
pressed his lips together. He opened his eyes again as her
hand tugged free of his. She backed up two steps, and for
the first time he saw wariness in her eyes.

"I should go to bed," she whispered.

"Leah—" He wasn't sure what he wanted to say, but his
voice didn't stop her. She left her plate untouched on the
counter, and the staircase creaked as she went up and disappeared.

It was so quick that he almost questioned whether he'd
kissed her at all.

Jeb stood there, his heart hammering in his chest. That
had been a mistake. He knew it. They'd agreed not to cross
these lines, and he'd already gone and kissed her.

When would he learn?

Leah wasn't so different from Katie. She'd loved another
man and she did not love Jeb. What he was doing here was
courting heartbreak. He'd been down this road already.

Chapter Ten

Leah shut her bedroom door with a click and dropped the hook to lock the door from the inside. Her heart was pounding, and she touched her lips with her fingers.

He'd kissed her. There had been something about the moonlight that had softened him, and while she'd been nervous of his muscular frame, somehow he'd seemed gentler down there in the kitchen, and his worry that she'd hate him like Katie had nearly broken her heart. There he was, just a man who'd married the wrong woman, afraid he'd court the same spite from *her*.

Leah might be many things—infertile, childless, heartbroken, resentful at the man who'd cast her aside, and possibly still in love with the same cad—but she was not cruel enough to blame her own unhappiness on the man she'd married.

And Leah hadn't meant to even get that close to him. But in that low light, she hadn't been able to make out the scars so easily, and he'd seemed . . . like a man. Just a man. Nothing more intimidating than that. But even thinking of the feeling of his lips moving over hers brought goose bumps to her skin. She rubbed her arms.

Now that she'd kissed him back, was he going to want more? That was the thought that had sent her back up the stairs so quickly. That kiss hadn't been planned, but it didn't change anything either. She wouldn't have *kinner*, no matter what sort of relationship she had with her husband, and she didn't want to share that man's bed. Besides, with his injuries, he likely couldn't have *kinner* either. This bedroom—this precious space—was only a formality. Their relationship would never include those physical intimacies.

And yet that kiss . . . it made her question what she thought she knew.

Leah pulled back her sheet and blanket and crawled into her own bed. She'd been at fault down there—she wasn't exactly an innocent. She was a woman of thirty who'd already been engaged once. She'd been kissed before, and she knew what a man's desire felt like. She'd known what he was thinking when he looked down at her like that, his dark gaze growing intense. But even if his injuries would hold him back, it didn't mean he wouldn't want some sort of intimacy with her, and she should have stopped him earlier if she wasn't willing to give it. What did he think of her now?

And yet, as Leah closed her eyes, she could still feel the touch of his lips meeting hers. . . .

The next morning, Leah awoke at dawn, as she always did in the summer months. The night had cooled off her bedroom, and she shivered a little as she pulled off her nightgown and reached for a fresh dress. Outside her bedroom window, the sun glowed over the horizon, the sky a bright pink, flooding her room in rosy light.

She pulled out her pin box and pinned her dress into place, holding the pins between her lips as she worked. Her fingers could almost do this in the dark. It didn't take her long to finish dressing, and once her hair was combed and wrapped up in a bun underneath a fresh *kapp*, she left her room and paused in the hallway.

Jeb's bedroom door was open a crack, but she couldn't hear any movement. She headed down the stairs to the kitchen and saw that his boots were gone, so he was out doing chores already. She exhaled a shaky sigh.

Would things be different now after that kiss?

Leah started a fire in the belly of the stove, and for the next hour she cooked breakfast and put together a lunch basket for the men to eat later on in the day. When she finally heard Jeb's boots on the step and the side door opened, it wasn't just Jeb who came inside, but Simon, too.

"Simon!" It was a relief to see him—to have him here as a buffer between herself and Jeb.

"Hi," Simon said with a slightly bashful smile. "I thought I'd give you some space, but Jeb said—"

"Yes, of course," she said. "You're working with Jeb. Of course you're eating with him, too. Consider the honeymoon over."

Jeb's gaze flickered toward her, and she felt the heat rise in her cheeks. Perhaps she'd meant that for Jeb as well. Whatever they'd started last night—it was over. She wasn't willing to change the terms of their agreement.

"What's for breakfast?" Simon asked.

"I've got corn bread in the oven," she said, "and eggs and sausage. I don't have any canned applesauce for the corn bread like usual, though."

That was how Simon liked his corn bread best. She'd have to buy some other woman's preserves at the market in Abundance until autumn came and she could jar her own. Jeb would have the many benefits of a wife—a cook, a housekeeper, a gardener, a laundress. He could be grateful for all she was willing to put into this home. Was that some guilt talking? Probably. It was also a wife's duty to share her husband's bed.

The men sat down at the table, and Leah fetched another plate and more cutlery for her brother, then brought the food. She'd missed Simon, she realized as she watched him dig up a square of corn bread. She nudged the plate of eggs toward him, too.

Jeb's leg touched hers under the table, and she glanced in her husband's direction. His gaze was locked on her, and she smiled hesitantly, then took the spatula from her brother and dished up Jeb a piece of corn bread, too.

"How's the farm?" she asked.

"Good," Jeb said. His tone was low, gruff, and it didn't quite match the way his eyes moved over her.

"I'm going to work on the garden today," she said. "It's a bit overgrown."

"I couldn't do it all," Jeb replied. "We focused on the farm mostly, and tried to keep up with the garden in the evenings."

"I know. I just wanted you to know that I'm going to work on it. What do you want for dinner tonight?" she asked.

"Whatever you feel like cooking. I'm easier to please than you think." A smile quirked up the side of his mouth, and his gaze softened. There was something in that softened look that warmed her a little.

Leah dropped her gaze. This was all in front of her brother.

"Simon, will you be joining us?" Leah asked, turning toward him.

"No, I'm going into town to meet some friends," her brother replied.

Leah frowned, and Simon shifted in his seat.

"I'm telling the one I owe money to when I'm paying him," Simon amended.

"When is that?" Leah asked.

"Tomorrow," Jeb cut in. "The money will be in my

account then, and I'll go get a money order made. It'll be taken care of."

Leah nodded. It would be done—the whole reason she'd married Jeb. And Simon would be safe again.

"You be careful with that Englisher," she said, spitting the word out like a curse. "You can't trust him."

"I know that," Simon replied, but when she met her brother's gaze, she wasn't satisfied that he did.

"They're already thugs," she said. "They want money, and if they think they can get more—"

"Leah, I'm not some newborn kitten," Simon said. "I'll handle it."

She looked over at Jeb, but his gaze was focused on Simon, and his expression was grim. She'd simply have to trust the men to take care of this. She had no control over it, and that was a worse feeling.

When they'd finished eating, Leah took the plates and headed for the sink.

"Simon, meet me at the cow barn," Jeb said. "You can start feeding that calf."

Simon nodded. "Okay." Her brother's gaze moved toward her. "Sure."

Leah forced a smile. "Come by whenever you're hungry, Simon."

Jeb didn't say anything, and there was some awkward silence until Simon had his boots on and he tramped out the door.

"Are you avoiding me?" Jeb asked.

"I'm just making sure my brother is eating," she said.

"It's not going to be easy for us to talk if he's always here," Jeb said.

Leah looked over her shoulder. "You're the one who brought him to breakfast."

"Yah, but you're bringing him back for snacks," he said with a small smile.

Leah didn't answer, and she didn't return his smile.

"You're angry," Jeb said. "About last night."

"I'm not!" She sighed and turned away again. She hadn't nailed down exactly what she was feeling yet.

"You sure?" he asked. "Because I'm angry."

"At me?" she demanded. "You're blaming *me* for that kiss?"

"I'm not mad at you," he retorted. "I'm mad at myself. There was something about the moonlight and having a beautiful woman in my kitchen. I shouldn't have kissed you. That's not what we agreed on."

"I'm not angry at you," she said. "I'm just—"

She was scared he'd want more and she wouldn't be willing to give it. She was afraid the rules were changing and she'd only have herself to blame.

"I promised myself I wouldn't do that," Jeb said, lowering his voice. "We both know why we got married, and I promised that I wouldn't try to seduce my own wife."

"You wanted to take me to bed, then?" she asked, turning.

"No." He cleared his throat. "I'll lay it out for you. I don't want to sleep with you. And that's not because I'm not attracted to you, or I don't think you're beautiful. On a purely physical level, I'd love nothing more than to take you to bed, but I can't do it."

"Why not?" she whispered. The scars . . . that was the thought that leaped to mind. How severe had his injuries been?

"Because I know who I am," Jeb said. "I know what I want. I won't sleep with a woman I don't love, and once I have made love to her, I have expectations of my own."

Leah licked her lips. "Like what?"

"Like . . . talking—really talking." Jeb looked away. "The deep kind of love that gets underneath all the other trappings. If I can't have the real thing, I don't settle very well for halfway. I'm just that kind of man. I can blame Katie for the downfall of our happiness, but I was to blame, too. I wanted more than she could give, and I couldn't be happy without it. I told myself I'd never do that to a woman again."

And yet, he'd married her. And they didn't love each other . . .

"And living . . . like we plan to?" she asked warily.

"I think I can do that." He cleared his throat. "I know why you're here, and I respect it. But I'm not going to toy with anything else. I won't be kissing you again. If that makes you feel any better."

Leah should be relieved, but something inside her twinged at those words. Because she could still remember the feeling of his mouth on hers. She could remember the tremble of his self-control. . . .

Jeb went to the door and plunged his feet into his rubber boots.

"Jeb—" She picked up the lunch basket she had waiting and brought it over.

"Thank you." He accepted the basket, but carefully didn't touch her fingers as he took it. Then he opened the door and stepped out in the cool morning air, the door shutting firmly behind him.

Leah stood in the doorway to the mudroom and looked back at the dishes stacked in a crooked pile on the counter, and smelled the scent of breakfast still hanging in the air. He wouldn't kiss her again. He wouldn't ask for more.

That was what she wanted . . . wasn't it?

Jeb passed by the house a few times as the day crept by, and the last time he passed, he saw Leah in the garden on her knees, weeding. She looked up and saw him, and he raised his hand in a wave. She waved back. Funny—put fifty yards between them and the tension seemed to dissipate.

He'd been thinking about her all day, though. As if he could help that. Their careful rules were supposed to make this easier, but all he could think of was how she'd looked in the moonlight with her eyes shining and her lips parted just before he'd covered them with his own. Stunning. She was heart-stoppingly beautiful. And he'd have to stop indulging himself with her. She was his . . . but only so far.

As Jeb trudged back toward the house that evening, he saw a new buggy parked by the stables, and a man was just coming out of the low building. He looked in Jeb's direction, then raised his hand in a wave. It was Isaiah, his brother-in-law.

Jeb sighed. Most people got offended when Jeb disappeared from public and stopped joining in on the social activities. His sister, Lynita, was different, though. He stopped asking her over, but she didn't stop coming by. She and her husband dropped by at least once a month, and she'd make herself busy in the kitchen, whipping up a meal for all of them to eat. Peter had liked her immensely.

And it looked like Lynita and her husband had decided to drop in . . . within the first week of their marriage. Lynita was many things, including fiercely protective of her younger brother, but she wasn't always delicate. So much for privacy.

Would Leah mind? Or would she be glad for some company that wasn't him?

When Jeb came inside, he pulled off his boots and washed his hands in the mudroom sink. He could hear the murmur of women's voices, and when he came into the kitchen, he nodded to Isaiah, who sat at the table with a glass of lemonade in front of him.

Lynita stood at the counter, her sleeves rolled up as she patted flat a piece of dough.

"You're back," Lynita said with a smile.

Leah was at the stove, and she smiled in Jeb's direction, too.

"I wouldn't stop you from kissing the man," Lynita said, casting Leah a teasing look. Would she rise to the bait? Her cheeks flushed, but she didn't move from her spot by the stove.

"You popped by, did you?" Jeb asked.

"We're here to wish you well, and you know I can't wait for an invitation," she said. "Besides, someone has to look in on you."

"I have a wife for that now," he retorted.

"Maybe someone needs to look in on her, too," Lynita replied. "And I like her, for the record."

Leah smiled at that. The women seemed to be getting along, although it looked to him like Lynita had taken over the kitchen. Jeb went to the cupboard for a glass of his own, and he paused next to Leah. She smelled nice. As he edged past her, he allowed one hand to skim her back.

He might not kiss her again, but he could at least touch her. He grabbed a glass and headed back to the table, where a pitcher waited.

"How come you didn't bring the kids?" Jeb asked.

"There was something we needed to talk to you about," Isaiah said. "And it was best done without the *kinner* around."

That sounded ominous. Jeb poured himself a glass of lemonade and took a sip. It tasted good, especially after all that sweating he'd done out there.

"Yah?" Jeb said, eyeing his brother-in-law.

Isaiah shot his wife a look, then sighed. "It's Menno."

"Our cousin? What about him?"

"He's been saying some things, and word is getting around," Lynita said. As she talked, she continued to work—

using a cookie cutter to press out perfect biscuits. She slid them onto a pan.

"Menno is like that," Jeb said.

"He's saying you pressured his father into giving you the farm," Isaiah said.

The words took a moment to sink in. He'd known Menno would be jealous—even Peter had known that—but this was a serious accusation.

"If that will was my idea, why would I make it so that I had to get married to get the money, then?" Jeb demanded. "That's ridiculous. I did no such thing."

"He's saying that the stipulation that you marry came from his father's desire to leave the money to his real son," Lynita said.

Jeb gritted his teeth. So that was what Menno was saying behind his back? Did he bother telling people that he'd had little respect for his own father and barely ever visited him? And all because Peter had punished Menno when he was a hardheaded kid. Menno had never forgiven his father for that. Did he bother telling people that he'd barely put a week's worth of work into this farm since his marriage, and that Jeb had worked this land tirelessly?

"So let him talk," Jeb said. "He's lying."

"People don't know that," Lynita replied.

"Then you tell them he's lying," Jeb retorted. "You know I didn't strong-arm Peter into anything. He told me years ago he intended to leave the land to me as appreciation for helping him out when his own son wouldn't. How could he have run this farm alone?"

There was silence from his sister, and Isaiah looked down into his glass.

"This could be brought to the bishop," Leah said quietly, but in the silence, her voice carried.

"No." Jeb sighed. "I'm not sure I trust the bishop to be on my side of this. Menno might be a lazy man who refused to help his own *daet*, but he knows how to polish his own image for the bishop and elders."

Leah had been thinking about how to fix this for him, though, and he appreciated that. She just might have his back, after all. He looked up to find Leah looking at him, her expression worried.

"It'll be okay, Leah," he said. "Quit worrying her, Lynita."

"Maybe she should be worried," Lynita replied. "I mean . . . you need to look at the bigger picture, Jeb. He's talking to the community and making it look like you are a liar and a cheat. I know you aren't, but Menno is respected, and—"

"I'm not," he finished for her.

"You know how it is, Jeb." Lynita shot him a meaningful look. "Besides, Peter wasn't our father, he was Menno's. If this is about money—"

"It is, partly," Jeb admitted. "I worked this land for barely anything. I could have been building up my own home, working somewhere that paid properly. That inheritance was my payment. And what little I made, I was supporting Mamm."

"I know . . ." Lynita's gaze softened at the mention of their mother.

"What are people saying exactly?" Leah asked.

Jeb wasn't sure he even wanted to know, let alone have Leah know. "It doesn't matter."

"It does!" Leah countered. "People's good opinion matters."

"They're saying that Jeb took advantage of a frail and sick old man to make him leave his land to him," Isaiah said. "And they're linking it to the fire."

Those words were like a punch to the gut.

"How?" Jeb demanded. "How could that possibly be linked to Katie?"

"It's been suggested that the fire wasn't so accidental," Isaiah replied.

Jeb saw the blood drain from Leah's face, and she put her hands on the counter to steady herself. He didn't care so much about public opinion, but he cared a whole lot about *her* opinion. Blast it, why did his sister have to come and blather about all this in front of his wife?

"Leah, that isn't true," Jeb said, and he shot his brother-in-law a glare. "I can promise you that. If it wasn't an accident, why would I have run into that fire after her?"

Leah nodded. "That's true."

"I told you before that Menno and I never really got along. He's jealous of the relationship I had with his *daet*, and obviously right now he's jealous of that inheritance. He thought he'd get the farm anyway—even with how distant he was with Peter. So he's . . . just barking at a tree."

"It might be a bit more than barking," Lynita said. "He's bending the ear of anyone who will listen."

"And what would you have me do about that?" Jeb demanded.

"Give it back to him!" Lynita shot back. "Just hand it over!"

"I'm not doing that!"

"Then give him half. Peter was his *daet*, after all. Menno's the only son in the family," Lynita said. "This is becoming a big embarrassment, and being respected and trusted in a community is important, Jeb. You of all people know that. I know you've written off the community's good opinion, but I haven't!"

He knew his sister's fears. They'd come from a sordid past, at least in Amish estimation. And while the Amish didn't blame children for their parents' mistakes, they sure did watch for a similar sinful streak in those children. Lynita had started fresh with Isaiah, and she had *kinner* who were nearly grown, but a reputation could still be sullied. A bad enough mar could affect her own *kinners'* ability to find quality spouses.

Except he'd asked Leah to marry him for this land, and if he gave it away, this marriage of convenience, this life-long commitment that was supposed to be worth it for the money and the land, was a waste. He couldn't do that to Leah. They got married for a farm, and he *would* keep it.

"That would make all this for nothing," Jeb breathed.

"All what? Your marriage?" Lynita shook her head. "It wouldn't be for nothing, Jeb. It would be for love, I thought. You've found a beautiful woman who loves you. A good wife is a blessing. Land is just—"

"Land is a future, land is security," he said. "Land is a life, Lynita!"

Color tinted his sister's cheeks and she looked over her shoulder toward Leah. Did she assume Leah's feelings would be hurt?

"Lynita, Leah understands this," he said with a sigh. "I promised her a farm. We hurried up this wedding for the land. I think it's obvious to pretty much everyone. I'm not giving up this farm and that's final."

Lynita turned to Leah, and Leah dropped her gaze.

"My husband is the one who takes care of business in our home," Leah said demurely, and Jeb smiled ruefully. She'd wanted this land and the money that came with it as much as he did.

"We can talk about it again another time." Lynita sighed, then turned to Leah. "These biscuits are ready for the oven."

Jeb looked over at Isaiah, who sat staring into his half-finished glass of lemonade, his lips pursed.

"You think I'm so crazy?" Jeb asked.

Isaiah shook his head. "I see your point, Jeb. I'm just not sure it will help you in the end."

Because the community would side with Menno. The

bishop and the elders would put pressure on him to "do the right thing" or else be shunned. And Jeb was bitter enough that he'd keep the land and accept a shunning. But Leah's priorities might be different from his. Leah had married him for the money, and it was the one thing he could provide for her.

He wasn't giving up yet.

Chapter Eleven

Leah licked her lips and looked over at the men at the table. They were talking in low voices—she couldn't make out what they were saying—but Jeb looked grim. What would happen if Menno got this farm and the money that came with it?

Anxiety bubbled inside her. The will was clear—if Jeb married, he inherited. But somehow, she'd never considered the possibility of the community pressuring Jeb to do anything differently. Jeb might not care about the community's opinion overly much, but Leah did. She'd hoped to gain some acceptance as a married woman, not find herself cut out of things because her husband had insulted people's sense of fairness and honesty.

"I didn't mean to upset you," Lynita said quietly. "But I don't believe a wife should be left in the dark either."

"No, I agree with that," Leah murmured. She certainly wanted to know what was happening, and it was a sign of respect that Lynita had spoken to her brother in front of her. She could have taken Jeb aside, and Leah wouldn't have known any of this.

"You should talk to him," Lynita said. "When he gets stubborn like this, he won't listen to me."

"I don't have the influence you think I do," Leah said woodenly. "He's the man. He'll decide."

"You're the wife," Lynita countered. "You have influence. Trust me. Besides, he cares what you think."

Did he? Leah wasn't so convinced. Besides, did she really want her husband to give away her brother's chance at paying off those Englishers and her own chance at a comfortable life?

"Menno is wrong in this," Leah said, her voice low.

"Partly," Lynita said. "But I understand his anger, too. Just think it over yourself, okay? That's all I'm asking. I'm glad Jeb has you. It's not just him now. Before he married you, he didn't care what the community thought of him at all."

"He still doesn't," Leah said.

"He's changing," Lynita said. "And for the better. There was a time he swore he'd never marry again, period."

"Why?" Leah asked.

"Why?" Lynita's eyebrows went up. "You don't know?"

"Well, I know about Katie, but—"

"She broke his heart," Lynita said softly. "She might have loved another man, but he loved *her*. I don't know what happened behind closed doors, but she managed to crush him."

Across the room, Jeb sat in his seat at the head of the table. She couldn't see his scars from this angle, and he looked tired.

"Was it just that she didn't love him back?" Leah asked.

"Whatever it was, it left him scared of marriage," Lynita replied. "And there were a few old maids who would have married him still, after that accident. But he wasn't interested anymore—in marriage, or the community either. He just—gave up. Until you, of course. So I know you're special."

Less special than convenient, but she couldn't say that

out loud. It did explain why he was equally unwilling to open himself up to more in their marriage.

"I'm going to pray that Menno backs down," Leah said after a moment of silence.

"You pray for miracles," Lynita said. "I'm just trying to deal with facts. Sometimes it's wiser to pray for those miracles but be prepared for things as they are. God doesn't always knock down the city's walls, you know? Not every city is a Jericho."

"You're probably right," Leah said. It seemed easier to just agree with Lynita.

Lynita looked mollified at that response, and she reached for a jar of sour cherries.

"I hope you don't mind me bringing along a few preserves," Lynita said. "But I know you were away all year teaching, and I know the kitchen you married." Lynita laughed at her own little joke.

"That's appreciated," Leah said, laughing as well. "I'm going to be busy this summer and fall just stocking the pantry. I've got to focus on that garden, too. I'm tempted to keep both gardens going—here and at the cottage with Simon. It'll give me more to harvest."

"I'll lend a hand, if you need it—" Lynita twisted the lid, then used a butter knife to pry the lid top off the canning jar. "And we have these cherry trees that give us more cherries than I can even jar. If you want to help me harvest them, I'll send you home with buckets of cherries." As it came loose, the juice inside came out in a slosh. "Oh!"

The dark red juice soaked into the sleeve of Lynita's dress, some spots spattering across her white apron.

"That'll stain," Leah said with a wince. "I'm sorry."

"Oh, I did it to myself," Lynita said. "But I'd better try to clean it up in the bathroom."

"You know where it is?" Leah asked. "There is some stain remover under the sink."

Lynita smiled and headed for the stairs, then said over her shoulder, "And you don't mind lending me a fresh apron, do you? I'll have to soak this one before the stain sets in."

Lynita didn't wait for a reply and headed up the staircase. Leah's stomach dropped. She knew exactly where Lynita would be looking for a fresh apron, and she wouldn't find one there.

Leah wiped her hands on a cloth and hurried up the staircase after her guest, but when she got to the top of the stairs, she saw Jeb's bedroom door open, and Lynita was nowhere to be seen.

Please, God! she silently prayed, and when she got to Jeb's door, she saw his sister standing in front of the dresser with a frown.

"I'll get it for you," Leah said, forcing a smile. "Go on into the bathroom—"

"Where are your clothes?" Lynita asked, looking around. "This bedroom hasn't changed since—" Her expression froze.

"Uh—" Leah wasn't sure she could answer that question.

"A woman doesn't move in without a trace," Lynita said quietly, and she turned her gaze onto Leah with trepidation. "Did you not move in?"

"Yes, I moved in," Leah said. "Of course!"

"Then where are your things?" Lynita repeated. "Is my brother mistreating you?"

"Your brother is fine," Leah said firmly.

Lynita left Jeb's room, and she followed Leah into the bathroom. Leah breathed a sigh of relief. This was better— get Lynita cleaned up and safely downstairs, and hopefully she wouldn't ask any more questions about where Leah kept her things. Maybe she'd need to hang a dress in Jeb's room, just for times like these.

Leah had put some laundry soap under the bathroom

sink for her own spot removing, and she bent down, opening the cupboard, but then she heard the squeak of the doorknob, and her heart skipped a beat.

Lynita pulled open the door that led between Leah's bedroom and the bathroom, and she stood there with a wooden expression on her face.

"Lynita . . ." Leah breathed, slowly rising to her feet once more.

"I see your things now," Lynita said quietly.

"Yah, I just keep them—" But Leah didn't have the breath to finish her lie. Lynita turned toward her, her eyes misting with tears. They stood there, neither speaking for a couple of beats.

"You don't share a room?" Lynita whispered at last.

How could she explain? Leah felt her cheeks heat with embarrassment. His own family—they'd hate her now. They'd think she was no better than the Katie who had crushed Jeb before her.

"I—" Leah sucked in a breath. "I hardly know him. He's almost a stranger, and—"

"But you *married* him," Lynita said. "You had to expect—"

"I know!" Leah cut her off. "It's just . . . the wedding was really quick. There was no courting time—at all! We don't really know each other, even. This was a mutual agreement. I'm not fighting with him, and he's not upset with me. You can ask him yourself."

"He wouldn't tell me if he were," Lynita breathed. "He's a man who likes his privacy. But I have to admit, I'm worried."

"Like you said before, you can't know what's going on behind closed doors, and you shouldn't even know this," Leah said.

"I'm sorry." But she didn't sound terribly sorry. She sounded like she was thinking this through.

"Lynita, I have to ask you to keep this a secret," Leah pleaded. "This is private business between a husband and a wife, and no one should know about it. If you told people—"

"Do you take me for a gossip?" she asked. "I'm not that, I can promise you. Of course I'll keep this to myself."

Could Leah trust her? She wasn't sure, but she didn't have much choice at this point.

"Leah, can I give you some advice?" Lynita asked.

"Yah." Leah swallowed hard.

"I know what it's like to be a new wife. I was nineteen when I married Isaiah, and I was terrified. I hardly knew him, and I wanted to be married, but . . . There is a whole lot more to marriage than I ever realized."

"I'm not a young thing anymore," Leah said. "I'm thirty, not nineteen."

"No, but you've never been married before either," Lynita countered. "And it can be overwhelming."

"I don't need advice about . . . that," Leah said curtly. "I have a friend who's told me plenty."

"I'm not giving advice about *that*," Lynita said, her cheeks flushing momentarily. "My advice is this—get to know him. He's older than you, he's gone through a lot, and those scars must be intimidating at best. I get it. But if you take some time and get to know your husband, I'm sure things will take care of themselves between you."

"I'm sure it will," Leah said quickly. "I just need some time."

"Yah, it will take time," Lynita replied. "A lifetime, actually. But that's what makes for a sweet and happy marriage—truly understanding how each other think and work. Just . . . get to know him a little more."

Leah nodded. It was better advice than Rosmanda's right now. But then, Lynita knew a little more than Rosmanda did at the moment, too. What did Lynita think of her now?

Leah moved toward the bathroom door. "I'll get back to the food. Feel free to grab an apron—they're in my top drawer."

Lynita nodded. "Thank you."

As Leah pulled the bathroom door shut behind her, she rubbed a hand over her face. If word got out, their reputation wouldn't recover, and her continued childlessness would only keep them at the top of the gossip pool.

Leah came down the stairs, and Jeb looked up.

"You okay?" he asked.

"Fine." Leah forced a smile. "Lynita spilled something on herself. It's all sorted out."

She went to the kitchen sink and washed her hands, then turned back to the meal preparation.

There was more to marriage than the making of babies and birthing them. But this marriage was based on some very real needs on both sides. Her brother needed that money, Jeb needed this land, and she needed to fit into the community as a respectable married woman. But no one else would understand how they found their balance behind these closed doors, and the thought of her private life being bandied about by her community stung.

She glanced toward the staircase again.

It was no longer Menno's gossip that worried her most, it was Lynita's.

Dinner was delicious—it always was when women got into the kitchen and Jeb didn't have to fend for himself. Leah seemed somewhat tense, but Jeb wasn't sure he blamed her after all the discussion of Menno and the farm. Lynita let it drop after that, but it still hung in the air. After a meal, some tea, and some pie, Isaiah suggested it was time they leave.

"I'll help with the dishes first," Lynita said.

"No, I'll help my wife," Jeb said with a smile. "You two go on home. I'm glad you came, though."

As nice as it was that his sister took it upon herself to maintain a relationship with him, he'd had enough chitchat. Lynita's reason for coming here wasn't just out of familial duty, and he needed some quiet so he could think . . . maybe even talk it through with Leah. She was the one who had a stake in this, after all. But give up this farm? That was asking a lot of him.

So Jeb shook Isaiah's hand at the door, then bent down and gave his sister a one-armed hug.

"Thanks for coming by," he said.

"You'll think it over?" his sister asked him seriously. She didn't have to clarify what she was talking about.

"I'm not giving up this farm," Jeb said. "I'm sorry about that, Lynita. But Menno is wrong."

"You could share it," she said softly. "Wrong or not, he's married to the bishop's daughter."

"You think Menno wants to share?" Jeb shook his head. "Thanks for coming by, Lynita. But I don't need you to be my *mamm*, okay? I'm a grown man, and I have a feeling my wife has a few opinions on the matter, too."

In fact, he was more than certain she'd have an opinion. This farm had factored into her decision to marry him.

Lynita sighed but didn't say anything else. Jeb went with Isaiah to help him hitch up, and when Isaiah and Lynita's buggy was crunching over the gravel drive toward the main road, he headed back inside.

Leah had the water running into the sink, and she looked up as he came in.

"She drops by," Jeb said. "It's her way."

"Yah, I noticed. I don't mind, though."

"If you do, I could ask her not to," Jeb said. "She's been doing that ever since Katie's death. It was good then, because otherwise I probably wouldn't have made the effort."

"I don't mind," she repeated. "It's nice to have family."

Jeb picked up some dishes from the table and carried them over to the counter. Leah turned off the water and started washing. Was she upset? He couldn't tell.

"About Menno," he said. "Legally, he doesn't have any right to this land. My uncle's will was clear. If I married within the time frame, then the land was mine. And he left me that letter, explaining it all."

"Why didn't you tell your sister about it?" she asked.

"I like to keep my business to myself," he said. "I'd hate to have Lynita tell people I have the letter and give my cousin time to spin an explanation for that, too."

Leah nodded. "But Menno has connections."

"Those connections don't change Pennsylvania law," he countered.

"They might sway the Amish community's opinion about you," she said. "And that's the one that affects us."

"The community already has an opinion about me," he said. "They've whispered about me for fifteen years. What should it matter if they have more to whisper about?"

She rinsed a plate, and he reached for it and grabbed a dish towel. He might as well help her out. When it was just him and Peter, they'd often do the dishes together. It went faster with two.

"It matters because your reputation is now mine," she said.

"Wait—" He put the dried plate on the counter. "Are you saying you want me to give up this farm? Give up the money?"

"No." She shook her head. "Not altogether. But your sister has a point about sharing the land."

"Half a farm won't be enough to keep us fed, Leah," he replied. "This isn't a big farm. It's on the small side, and if we chop it in half—"

"Maybe you could work it with Menno," she said.

"He doesn't want to work with me!" Jeb laughed bitterly. "It's a very nice thought, but he has a carpentry business he works with his brother-in-law. He's never liked farming, and he's never liked me. He won't want to farm with me. I can guarantee that. He'll want to sell it."

"Could you buy him out?" she asked.

"So now I've gone from owning a farm free and clear to a hefty mortgage?" he asked with a shake of his head. "All for what—to hand some cash to my cousin to make him happy? What if I don't care about his feelings right now?"

Leah sucked in a breath. "As long as my brother's debt is paid, that's what I care about."

"And that happens tomorrow," he said.

"Really?" Her gaze whipped over to meet his.

"Yah. I'm taking Simon with me. We'll go to the lawyer's office and the bank, and then I'm going with Simon to pay off that Englisher."

"You'll go with him?" Tears misted her eyes.

"He'll need a witness that he paid it. And I'm not just handing over that kind of money to a gambler and hoping for the best," he retorted.

"Thank you," she said.

"It will be all right, Leah," he said, softening his tone. "It's almost done. Don't worry about Menno. It's just gossip."

Leah was silent for a moment, then she winced. "It might be a little more than that. Your sister went upstairs."

He eyed her silently.

"And into your bedroom," she added.

His stomach sank. He knew Lynita and her curiosity. She was also deeply protective of him, and if she suspected he was being taken advantage of . . . "And eventually into yours, I presume?" he asked quietly.

"Yah." She sighed. "She knows."

"Blast!" he muttered under his breath, and he rubbed at his scarred shoulder with the heel of his good hand. "What did you tell her?"

"I said that I hardly know you and that . . . it's taking time to get comfortable." Her cheeks grew pink.

"And you hate lying?" he asked uncertainly.

"Yah, I hate lying, but I also hate having someone know about this!" she said, turning from the sink. She grabbed another towel and dried off her hands. "You think people will talk about Menno's gossip? Wait until they hear your sister's!"

"She won't say anything," Jeb said.

"Are you sure about that? You didn't trust her not to tell anyone about the letter!" she shot back.

Leah had a point there, but his sister cared more about the family's reputation than he did. She had good reason to keep her mouth shut. Leah's cheeks glowed pink, and she turned back to the sink more quickly than necessary.

"You're embarrassed," he concluded.

"Aren't you?" she asked, not turning. There was the rattle of cutlery on the bottom of the sink. "Having people know we sleep in separate bedrooms—"

"But they won't know," he said.

"It's still embarrassing."

Their life, this marriage they'd agreed upon, was embarrassing for her. He understood. The men wouldn't let that little fact rest either, if they knew about it. But he wasn't embarrassed by her.

"What do you want to do?" he asked. "Do you want to sleep in the same room, then?"

"No," she said. "I don't."

"Okay . . ." He picked up another plate to dry. "Leah,

you'll have to trust Lynita. She's family, and she cares. I can promise you that."

"Okay." She rinsed another plate and put it in the dish rack.

But Lynita knew . . . and he didn't exactly like the fact that she'd know something intimate about his marriage like that. Leah had been the one to care what people thought, but it turned out that he did, too, in this situation.

"What did my sister say exactly?" he asked.

Leah rinsed some utensils and put them in the rack. "She suggested I get to know you better. She said that marriage isn't only about the physical, and that if we knew each other better it would make for a happier marriage."

"Are you happy right now?" he asked cautiously.

Leah looked up at him. "Yah. But friends and community—they matter to me. You and I can sort out our own marriage our own way, so long as we keep it private and I can have the respect of the people I care about."

It sounded so fair, so honest. He nodded. "Yah. Okay, then."

"I'd like to try this again, actually," she said. "Once Simon's debt is paid, it will be just the two of us again."

"Try what?" he asked.

"Having another couple over," she said. "My friend Rosmanda. You know her husband, don't you?"

Guests. As if his sister tramping into their home wasn't enough. This was her solution, to drag more people into this home?

"And you aren't afraid of them seeing as much as Lynita did?" he asked incredulously.

"I have a plan for that," she replied. "I want to keep some dresses hanging in your bedroom. And some *kapps*—maybe on top of your dresser. It would make it look more like I slept there. And if someone saw my room, we could just say it's a guest room."

"A guest room," he said, mulling over her idea in his mind. Having her dresses in his room, a *kapp* or two . . . Would they smell sweet and floral like her? It might not be quite so comfortable for him staring at her things in his bedroom. He was supposed to be controlling his desire for her, not stoking it.

"I think it would work," she said. "So, we let them see what they expect to see, and then our business stays private."

He smiled wanly. "I can appreciate your ability to keep some secrets."

She shrugged. "It benefits me, too. So, what do you think? Can I invite my friends for a dinner?"

No. That was what he wanted to say. Absolutely not. Keep people out. If she wanted privacy, then he knew exactly how to get it. He'd had privacy the last fifteen years.

"I'm not good with people," he said.

"I know."

Leah met his gaze hopefully, and there it was—the sweetness in her gaze, the hope in her expression. How could he turn her down?

"All right," he said. "But don't expect me to be good at this. I like my privacy, and I had gotten used to my sister coming by, but—"

He wasn't sure what he was trying to warn her of exactly. Disappointment?

"It'll be fine," she said with a shake of her head.

"I'm not charming," he said at last.

"I don't think they'll mind at all," Leah said, and this time when she smiled, it warmed her eyes and lit up her face. His heart stammered in his chest.

She was gorgeous . . . Did she know that? How much was he already doing for her—taking Simon under his wing, helping the young idiot get his debt paid off, handing over fifty thousand dollars . . . and now he was bringing her friends into their house.

"Okay, well . . ." He picked up some cutlery. "I guess it's okay, then."

Every fiber in his being longed to say no, but after that smile, he couldn't do it. He'd made her happy, and it warmed a place in his heart that hadn't been touched in many, many years.

Chapter Twelve

The next day Leah left the house right after breakfast to go up to the cottage and weed the garden there. If they were going to be self-sufficient that winter, she'd need to can as many fruits and vegetables as possible, and she was feeling optimistic again.

She'd seen Jeb and Simon off as they headed to town, and even Simon seemed happier, and they could put all of this behind them. And then if Menno tried to get some money out of them, at least this most dangerous debt would already be paid. Simon would be safe again. They could shut out the Englishers and focus on a good Amish life.

God, let this go smoothly . . . she prayed in her heart. It was so close to being over. Simon was *so* close to being free.

Teaching in Rimstone, she'd never imagined what Simon was up to. It almost seemed like blissful ignorance now. When she was finishing up the school year with the *kinner*, she'd been thinking about the garden mostly. She'd assumed her brother was doing just fine, just as his letters assured her. Her worry had been that she didn't trust Simon to plant the way she'd instructed him to do it.

All the same, she missed the *kinner* at the little Amish school in Rimstone. They'd filled her days for an entire school year, watched them grow and helped them learn.

There was one little boy, Benjamin, who had kept her on her toes. He'd struggled with the schoolwork, and he'd been a constant distraction to his classmates. He was the youngest child in his family, and there was quite a gap between him and his next older sister, much like the gap between herself and Simon. He reminded her of Simon at that age—the impish little smile, the glittering eyes. He was bound for trouble, but he was oh, so charming as he broke every single rule, and it was hard to be angry with him. But being the youngest by so many years meant that Benjie's *mamm* could focus on him. Unlike Simon, he did have parents . . . and hopefully his parents could get him in line better than she'd managed with her little brother. Because being endearing wasn't going to help Benjie. And the adults in his life softening to that dimpled smile wasn't going to keep him out of trouble. If she'd known this last school year what she knew now about her own brother, she might have been harder on the boy.

When Leah was finished with the garden she let herself into the side door to replace the gardening tools. She'd weeded, hoed, and watered the rows of vegetables. There were cabbage, peas, green beans, cauliflower—those were all doing well despite a bit of neglect. The broccoli didn't seem to be flourishing, though. That row looked stunted, even a little shriveled.

Leah washed her hands in the mudroom sink and peeked into the kitchen. There were dirty dishes in the sink, a loaf of bread left out on the counter to get stale. She grimaced. She paused for a moment, wondering if she could walk away and pretend she hadn't seen the mess. But she had . . .

She came inside and grabbed a plastic bag for the bread, then swiped up a cloth to wash down the counters and the table. There were crumbs everywhere.

Leah muttered to herself irritably as she wiped down

the table with brisk strokes. Then she started the water for the dishes and grabbed the broom from the cupboard. Had he ever touched this broom since her wedding?

Another hour passed as she cleaned up her brother's home, and then she headed back out again, locking the door behind her, and started down the gravel road toward the house she shared with Jeb. It was still hard to call it her own, but she was starting to feel more comfortable there.

The sun was high, and as Leah approached the house, she saw the buggy coming up the drive. Jeb had the reins and Simon sat next to him—all in one piece. The bruises from his earlier beating had faded, and there seemed to be no new damage that Leah could see, and she felt a surge of relief. She picked up her pace as she headed toward the buggy barn where they'd stop.

"Is it done, then?" she called as the horses plodded up. Jeb reined them in.

"Yah," Jeb said. "It's done."

"You've paid them?" she pressed.

"They're paid, Leah," Simon said. "It's done."

But Leah didn't feel entirely at ease just yet. "Did they give you anything—something that you can prove you paid them?"

"They don't give receipts," Simon said with a low laugh.

"It's done, Leah," Jeb said, and he met her gaze evenly. "I took care of this one."

His tone was confident, and his gaze didn't waver. It was nice to have a husband she could trust with things like this.

"Okay," she said. "Thank you."

"We've got a lot of work to catch up on," Jeb said, turning to Simon. "I'll unhitch and muck out the stables. You head up to the barn. There's that calf that needs feeding, and the stalls need mucking out there, too."

"Yah, sure," Simon said. "And thanks again."

Jeb gave Simon a nod.

Both men got down, and as Jeb got started unhitching the horses, Simon came over to where Leah stood.

"I've never seen that much money in one place," Simon said, shaking his head.

"And hopefully you never will again," she said.

"Yah. I know. It's just—" Simon smiled wanly. "It was a lot of money."

"Money that belonged to Jeb," she said. "You know what I did for you."

"I'm not making light of it, Leah," Simon said. "Okay? I'm just—Life goes on, right?"

And for Simon, it was probably as simple as that. The trouble had been taken care of, and his life would carry on as it always had. Except *her* life had been irrevocably changed.

"I cleaned your kitchen," she said curtly. "I can't believe you leave it like that. Clean up after yourself or you'll end up getting sick."

"I didn't ask you to do that," Simon countered, but when he saw her expression, he shot her one of his boyish grins. "You're the best sister, and I'm sorry. I'll do better. I'll be neat as a pin."

They both knew he wouldn't be, but that smile worked the charm it always did, and she found herself smiling back.

"New starts, Simon," she said. "Right?"

"Of course." He flicked up his hat at a jaunty angle and headed down the road toward the cow barn, his boots crunching merrily against the gravel.

When she turned back Jeb had already unhitched the horses, and the buggy sat under the rain shed. He appeared outside again, and he picked up the handles of a wheelbarrow.

Leah had work of her own to do—their garden to weed, their own house to clean—but standing there looking at the man who had just successfully aided her brother in his time of need, she remembered Lynita's advice to get to know her husband a little bit better. And maybe there was wisdom in those words, because for better or for worse, she'd bound herself to this man.

"You okay?" Jeb asked, and she realized she'd been standing there staring at him.

"Do you need help?" she asked.

"What?" Jeb shook his head. "It's men's work."

"But you were gone all morning," she said. "You said you were behind."

Leah headed toward the stable doors, and Jeb looked at her skeptically. She could feel his eyes moving over her, and she brushed past him into the dim stables. The horses were all outside, and the smell of hay and manure made her nose tingle.

Jeb followed her in with that wheelbarrow, and she looked back at him again.

"Your sister suggested I get to know you better," she said. "Remember?"

"Ah." He smiled faintly. "So that's what this is."

"I'm trying," she said. "Can I help?"

Jeb handed her the shovel. "If you insist."

She thought she saw a teasing glitter in his eye, but she took the shovel anyway and headed to the first stall.

"Do you think Simon is safe now?" she asked as she began to shovel the soiled hay into a pile.

"If he changes his ways, yah," Jeb replied. "You'd know better than I would if he intends to do that."

"I'm sure he will," she said, but it was mostly loyalty that made her say it.

"Then he'll be fine." There was something in his voice, and she looked over at him again to find his gaze locked on her. He didn't look so certain either.

"Will you keep him working with you now?" she asked.

"I need the extra hand. As long as he keeps working hard," Jeb replied. "It's better to have family here than some nosy kid who will go home and tell tales."

Leah turned to the stall and continued shoveling. She heard Jeb bring the wheelbarrow up behind her, and she began shoveling the heavy hay into the barrow. Leah grimaced as she hoisted a shovelful.

"Let me do it," he said, his voice low.

"I'm fine." She slid the shovel under another pile and lifted again. "I'm going to be canning fruits and vegetables this fall. I need to know your favorites."

"I like apples," he said.

"Okay. Applesauce? Canned apple slices?"

"Slices," he said. "And I like pickles."

"Me too." She banged the shovel against the metal wheelbarrow, shaking free some dirt. "I make a good dill pickle."

"Yah?" Jeb hoisted a bale of fresh hay from a pile in an empty stall. His muscles strained as he carried it, and she noticed that his scarred arm seemed to support less weight. She watched him for a moment, and he dropped the bale within reach.

"What?" he asked, and he crossed the distance between them, stopping close enough that she had to tip up her head to look him in the face. "You're staring."

His tone was slightly flirtatious, and she dropped her gaze. "Sorry."

"You want to know how bad my burns are, don't you?" he said quietly.

"It's the sort of thing a wife should know, isn't it?" And maybe she should have asked before, but she'd started to wonder with that kiss—was her husband as maimed in that regard as she thought?

Jeb looked down at her, his dark gaze moving over her slowly, then he sighed. "It's my whole left side. The burns were bad." He tugged at his shirt, exposing more of his neck. "It goes down my side, my hip, down my leg—" He lifted his shirt to expose his torso.

"You said it doesn't hurt?" she asked uncertainly.

"The actual scar doesn't hurt," he said. "But the tendons shrunk, and they can be painful. My hip gets sore. I keep working on my joints, though, trying to keep them as limber as I can."

She nodded, then licked her lips. "You know that I cannot have *kinner*, but . . ." She wasn't sure how to ask this delicately. "Can you?"

A small smile tickled the corners of his lips, and he raised an eyebrow. She felt her face heat, but she refused to drop her gaze.

"Are you asking if the injury extends . . . that far?" he asked, his voice low.

"I don't know," she whispered. It sounded crude to even ask these questions, but she'd married him with one assumption, and she needed to have it confirmed or denied. "Perhaps I'm asking how much you've given up in marrying me."

"And you'd make that up to me with your fine dill pickles?" he asked teasingly.

"I'd—" Was he making fun of her now? She wasn't sure, but he seemed to see something in her face that sobered him.

"First of all, I know you can't have *kinner* of your own," he said softly. "And I don't care."

"Are you sure?" she asked.

"Isn't it a little late for me to decide I wasn't?" he asked pointedly.

Leah sucked in a breath, and Jeb reached out and took the shovel from her hands. The movement was gentle, and he started to scoop the last of the soiled hay—the work much easier for him. He clanked the shovel on the side of the barrow, then handed the shovel back and hoisted the load.

"But in answer to your question," Jeb said, glancing over at her, "yah, I can have *kinner*, sure enough. The making of them isn't a problem for me . . . if that was what you were asking."

So, he could . . . The realization was like a jolt. She'd thought he couldn't . . . the rumors had suggested . . . But then, maybe she'd been foolish to put so much stock in other people's whispers. Or maybe she'd just hoped that he couldn't have *kinner* either—that the blame would be on both of them. Her heart pounded hard in her chest. How much *had* he given up in marrying her?

"You thought I couldn't . . . perform the husbandly act?" he asked, turning toward her incredulously.

"I—" She felt her breath seep out of her. "I realized I'd never asked."

"And now you have."

Leah tried to hide her embarrassment by looking away, and Jeb wheeled the load of hay toward the side door. He paused when he pushed it open and looked back.

"I said I didn't care about having *kinner*, Leah," he said firmly. "If there is one thing about me, you can trust what I say. I don't play games. And I knew you couldn't have babies when I married you. I knew what that meant for our future. I'm not going to resent you for that."

Then he disappeared out into the sunlight, leaving her alone with the dust motes dancing in the air.

He wouldn't resent her. Her throat thickened with emotion. That was possibly the kindest thing a man had ever said to her in a very long time.

But he was capable of having children of his own . . . that stark fact was still foremost in her mind. She had vastly underestimated him, it seemed. So, if he wasn't pushing to share a bed with her . . . what did that mean?

Did Leah actually think he was a eunuch? Jeb dumped the manure onto the pile that would be carted out to the fields every so often and gave it a clanging shake.

A *eunuch*? He couldn't help but be irritated at that thought. Did he look like a eunuch to her? Sure, he had a limp, but he was every inch a man in every other way. Was that why she'd agreed to a marriage of convenience—she thought he couldn't make any claims on her physically?

That was a sobering thought. Perhaps she hadn't been giving him enough credit for his self-control around her, because she was a beautiful woman in his home, a soft presence in the room across the hall, leaving her delicate fragrance in the bathroom after she showered . . . and when she stood there in her nightgown, while it was modest enough, covering her from collarbone to ankle, he couldn't help but think about what was under it. He was only human, after all, and while he was a moral man, she *was* his wife.

And maybe it showed his own vanity, but he wanted her to recognize the man in him. He wasn't some scarred weakling in need of female care. He was a man—and his choice to keep himself from crossing those lines was just that, a choice.

He hoisted the empty wheelbarrow and headed back into the stable. Leah was shoveling out another stall, the shovel scraping against the cement floor as she pulled the hay into a pile.

She was slim, and while she didn't have the strength of a man, she did throw herself into the work, and he felt mildly bad about that. She had enough to do in the house without helping him out here. He wasn't exactly helpless. Add to that, he'd overheard part of her conversation with her brother . . . and she'd been cleaning up after him? He liked that even less. She wasn't "the woman" to clean up after every man within reach, brother or not.

Jeb pulled a knife out of his pocket and cut the twine on the bale. The hay sprung free, and Jeb grabbed a pitchfork from a hook on the wall and spread fresh hay on the floor of the stall. He eyed Leah for a moment, watching her struggle with another shovelful of muck. This was enough. She might want to help, but he wasn't going to let her do man's work. He reached for Leah's shovel and she looked up.

"You don't need to do this," he said.

"I'm following your sister's advice," she said, stepping outside the stall and grabbing the pitchfork. "And she was right. You're my husband, and I should understand you."

Understand him . . . Did she really want to do that? Under his grouchy veneer was a man with a lot of pain and very little trust. There was a reason why he kept to himself. But she didn't seem like she was going to be dissuaded either.

"Understand what exactly?" he asked.

She met his gaze, then shrugged. "Why you are the way you are, I suppose."

"And how am I?"

She blinked at him, and he smiled, showing her he was just being difficult.

"Fine," he said, and he started shoveling once more. "Did you actually think I was some sort of eunuch? Did I give you that impression?"

"It's the scars," she said. "I know you were hurt very badly in that fire, and people said—"

"Do I seem . . . less of a man somehow?" He fixed

her with a stare. He wasn't wanting to demand the right answer, but he did want to see if she was lying. Did he give off the impression of a man who'd lost his ability in that arena?

"No, you seem . . ." She sucked in a breath.

"Yah?"

"A little frightening."

He blinked at that. "Wait—I scare you?"

"A little bit," she said quietly, and she looked down at the hay, breaking off the eye contact. "I'm sorry. I don't mean to be insulting, it's just that—"

"The scars," he concluded.

"You're used to them and I'm not, I suppose. But you're also very big, and rather muscular," she said.

"That's not normally something a woman complains about," he countered.

"And . . . gruff."

Yah. She had him there. He knew he wasn't the gentlest beast around, but he'd been doing his best to soften himself around her. Apparently it hadn't been enough. He didn't like the idea of scaring her.

"Do you think I'd hurt you?" he asked hesitantly.

"I've never seen you angry," she replied.

So, she wasn't sure. He clenched his teeth. "I'm not that kind of man, Leah. I'd never raise a hand to you, or make you do something you didn't want to do. I believe a wife is a partner, and that God will judge a man by how he treats her."

"Oh . . ." She nodded. "That's good."

"You probably should have asked me this before you married me, you know," he added.

"I suppose I thought separate bedrooms would take care of it," she said.

"And you changed your mind on that?" he asked with a small smile.

He'd have to be gentler with her than he'd been, apparently. He hadn't meant to scare her. It had been such a long time since he'd been around people . . . been around a woman . . .

"I suppose it was just—" Her gaze flickered up toward him, then away again. "I know that women who can't have children don't appeal to men. I suppose it's natural."

"What?" He squinted at her. "You actually think that?"

She sucked in a breath. "I'm not some naïve young thing. And Matthew did love me. I can't explain it any other way. The minute he realized I couldn't have *kinner*, he . . . changed."

"And you think that's because a woman who can't give birth is somehow less appealing. Less attractive," he said.

"Jeb, we agreed that our relationship—" she began.

"And you think that's because I'm *not* attracted to you?" he burst out. Could she really think she could stand in his kitchen in a nightgown and not get his full and undivided attention?

She blinked at him. "Yah."

Jeb laughed softly. It was ridiculous, but then, she'd been through a lot. He stepped closer to her, so close that if he leaned in just a little, he could cover her lips with his . . . but he wouldn't. Instead, he stared down at her.

"That's not true at all. Look at you. You're gorgeous. I've thought so for years. You've got this way about you that draws a man in. I notice you—your eyes, the way your lips purse when you're deep in thought . . . this part of your neck—right here—" He ran his finger over the soft flesh just above her collarbone. "I can see your heartbeat there . . . I can't explain Matthew. He's an idiot. I can pretty much guarantee you he didn't love you as much as he claimed if he could just change course like that, but that wasn't because you aren't a beautiful woman."

She opened her mouth to speak, then slowly closed it.

"I'm attracted, okay?" he said, and he lowered his voice. "*Very* attracted. I see you in my home, in my kitchen . . . and I feel a whole lot. So never think our arrangement is because you aren't beautiful enough."

She needed to know that, and he hoped it didn't scare her. Maybe it would if she ever sensed the things he'd been thinking about in connection to her lately. . . .

"Then why haven't you—insisted?" she whispered.

"Do you want me to?" he asked. He caught her gaze, holding it. He wasn't sure what he'd do if she said yes—but he might do it right here and now. He could very easily consummate this relationship if she wanted him in that way. And in the dimness of this stable, with his beautiful wife staring up at him, that flutter of her pulse at the base of her neck tugging him closer . . . with some fresh hay just across the aisle, he could very easily make good on that . . . and regret it later, when he started wanting a whole lot more emotionally from their relationship than she cared to give. But physically—he was very, very capable.

Leah shook her head, and he carefully reined it all back in again. She didn't want him that way, and he wasn't about to press the issue. She was allowed to say no.

"Then, there you go," Jeb said quietly, and he stepped away from her again.

Leah licked her lips, her gaze still locked on him, and he sucked in a slow, deep breath. What did she think of him? He still wasn't sure. She was softening toward him. She'd never once said something cruel or biting. But he could still see that wariness in her eyes.

"Can I ask you something, though?" Jeb said, picking up the shovel again. "How come you cleaned your brother's kitchen?" She blinked at him. "I overheard you talking to him," he explained.

"Because it was filthy," she replied.

"For the record, I don't think a woman should be worked to the bone either. And taking care of one home is quite enough. You don't need to clean up after Simon," he said.

"I was just helping him a little bit," she replied. "He can be a bit of a slob."

"My wife isn't going to be worked like that," he said. "By any man."

"He's my little brother," she said with a smile tickling her lips.

"I'm not going to have people talking about how hard you have to work with me," he said.

"They won't."

"You really think that?" He turned back to the shoveling, heaving the soiled hay into the waiting wheelbarrow.

Besides, Jeb had noticed that Simon tended to lean on his older sister a little too readily, and he didn't like the thought of Leah's affection being taken advantage of. And Simon, while he obviously loved his sister a great deal, had been more than willing to offer her up in a marriage for his own convenience. So maybe Jeb was feeling protective of Leah right now. She had the right to say no to him, and to her brother's wishes, too.

"He's not a little boy anymore," Jeb replied. "Just remember that."

She met his gaze, then nodded.

"Leah, you wanted to understand me a bit better," he said. "So I'll tell you this much. I don't like being taken advantage of, and I don't like my wife being taken advantage of either. Your life should be better because you married me, not harder. You shouldn't have double the work." He cleared his throat. "Whatever we are, whatever our agreement about this marriage, I want you to think you made the right choice in taking me on."

He didn't know how else to say what he was feeling— the depth of his responsibility toward her, how seriously he took those marriage vows. She was his wife, and it was his job to provide for her, keep her safe, and ensure her happiness . . . even if that happiness was dependent on him keeping his distance.

Chapter Thirteen

Leah came back into the house, and the screen door bounced shut behind her. She stood there in the cool of the kitchen, her heart pattering in her chest.

Jeb was attracted to her—very attracted. All her assumptions about Jeb had been wrong. He'd called her beautiful. And when he looked down at her, she'd seen that desire blazing in the depth of his eyes. Only today had she realized that he was capable of following through on it.

And yet he hadn't.

She took off her boots and headed to the kitchen sink to wash her hands. Even Matthew had never told her about his feelings for her quite that clearly. He'd been more poetic. He'd likened her eyes to velvet and her fingers to the whitest of eggs. He'd told her that he longed to call her his own, and that nothing could change his feelings for her. But he'd never been quite so specific as Jeb had been.

She put her hand over the spot in her neck that he'd touched, and she could feel the tremble of her pulse under her fingers. He'd noticed that . . .

Do you want me to?

Jeb's voice had been so deep when he'd said that, and she couldn't but wonder what would have happened if she'd said yes. If she closed her eyes, she could imagine he was another man—younger perhaps, less battered by life. But she'd heard the very real offer in those words, and she felt the tingle of goose bumps.

Except she'd been honest when she said no. He might be her husband, but she still didn't really know him, and when she lay in bed at night, it wasn't Jeb that filled her thoughts. She still thought of Matthew, sorting through his words, wondering how he'd moved on to Rebecca so quickly. Had he been interested in her at the same time he was courting Leah? Because Matthew and Leah were going to get married that fall, and a wedding still happened—except Leah was no longer the bride. Matthew had moved on to Rebecca so swiftly it had left Leah spinning. It did make her wonder if there had been some overlap there . . .

But Matthew had moved on, and Leah had determined to do the same. She'd even gotten married! However, when a woman was lied to, it was harder to move on until she could make emotional sense of it. Maybe that was just self-punishment.

Leah dried her hands on a kitchen towel and looked around the kitchen. She pulled open a drawer—the farthest one from the drawers she'd already explored—and pulled out some serving spoons, a potato peeler, and a pair of oven mitts that looked like they'd been overly used and then shoved into a drawer. There were some recipe cards, and she pulled them out—one for a tuna salad, one for a shoofly pie, and another for a macaroni salad. There was another card at the bottom of the drawer, and she pulled it out.

But this wasn't a recipe card after all. It was a folded piece of paper, and on the outside of it was written in bold letters, *Jebadiah*.

It wasn't for her—obviously—but the page was only folded once and it had been crumpled on one end so that it hung open, the beginning of the letter already in view. The paper had been folded for a long time, and it crackled a little as she opened it up.

Dear Jeb,

You'll realize that I'm gone. I can't do this anymore, and I'm sorry that I even accepted your proposal. It was stupid of me to go through with it, but I honestly thought I'd forget Aiden.

I haven't. I love him, and I always have. My parents said I'd forget him, but how could I? He's the one man I've ever loved, and he's asked me to run away with him.

Please, don't tell anyone for a few days. I know you aren't any happier in our marriage than I am, but if they come after me and try to make me come back, I won't come. It will be uglier that way. I'm sure you can appreciate that.

So goodbye. I'm sorry it has to be this way, and I'm sorry I couldn't be the wife you wanted. I wasn't kind, or pleasant. I didn't want to be, but please know that I'm not like that all the time. Not with Aiden. I won't even ask you to forgive me. You don't need to. I'm going English, and I'm not coming back.

Katie

Leah stood with the letter in her hand for a moment, the words sinking in. Katie had meant to go English? When had Jeb gotten this letter? Because Katie most definitely died in that fire . . . Leah had been at the funeral. The whole community had been there.

Had Jeb known this?

The side door opened, and as the sound of Jeb's boots

on the wooden floor thumped through the mudroom, she hurriedly tried to refold the letter and smooth down the crumpled end of the paper. Then he appeared in the doorway.

"I just came for a glass of—" His gaze fell to the letter in her hands. "—water."

She stopped fumbling and looked down at the paper in her hands. "I'm sorry, Jeb. I was going through kitchen drawers and I came across it."

"What is it?" he asked, then his gaze focused on the paper and the color drained from his face. "So, you read my letters now?"

His dark eyes flashed, and he strode across the kitchen and took it out of her hand, then shoved it into his pocket.

"It was wrong of me," she stammered. "I'm sorry."

"This was private!" he snapped.

"It was in a kitchen drawer!" she retorted. "And it wasn't in an envelope. It was just there with a mess of recipe cards! If you want to keep something private, I'd think you'd go to more bother than that."

Jeb stood there, motionless. The crumpled paper poked up out of his pocket, and he seemed undecided about what to do exactly. Leah went to the tap and got him a tall glass of water, then brought it back to him.

Jeb accepted the glass, his dark gaze fixed on her.

"I didn't know," he said after a long moment.

"That she was going English?" Leah asked, shaking her head.

"I didn't know . . ." he repeated, but he sounded hollow, and he cast her a look of such deep sadness that her heart skipped a beat in response.

"What happened?" she whispered.

"I only found it afterward," he said. "She wasn't there for dinner, and Peter had gone out to visit someone, so it was supposed to be an evening with just the two of us. I thought we'd have dinner . . . alone. But there was nothing prepared, and this letter must have blown off the counter, because it was on the floor and I didn't see it. I was wandering around the house, looking to see if she was doing laundry, or maybe if she'd gone out to the garden, when I smelled smoke, and I looked out the window, and saw the barn, and—" His voice trembled. "She had a cell phone out in the barn. I'd found it the day before and we'd fought. I told her that it was against the community rules, and . . . and I knew why she had it. She was calling *him*. And yes, I was jealous. What husband wouldn't be?"

"Why was she in the barn?" Leah asked.

"She must have been calling him again. At least that's what I assume, looking back on it. Maybe she was getting him to come pick her up. I don't know. But when I got to the barn, there were already flames, and I could hear her screaming, and I tried to get in there. I went inside again and again, but I couldn't get to her. I was close . . . I know I was close! I heard her coughing, but I couldn't get to her. I collapsed in the smoke. A firefighter pulled me out. They didn't find Katie alive."

"What caused the fire?" she whispered.

"A frayed wire on her cell phone charger. That's what the fire investigator said, at least." He shrugged weakly. "I'd seen the charger, but I didn't know it was a fire hazard. I guess I knew that confronting her on it wouldn't fix anything. She hated me, and I wasn't the one she loved. But if I had, she might still be alive." His voice caught. "Peter showed me the letter when I got back from the hospital. I don't know why he didn't show me earlier. Maybe he was afraid I'd be implicated in her death. But while I knew she was in love with another man, I had no idea she was leaving me that day. I'm glad I didn't know. There was no hesitation on my part. I did everything I could to save her. It just wasn't enough."

Katie had been leaving him . . . walking out to be with her Englisher lover. And while everyone was worrying about Jeb's role in her death, no one knew this.

"Why didn't you tell anyone?" she asked.

"You mean, why not try to set them straight?" he asked bitterly.

"She wasn't the sweet girl they all thought," Leah said. "She was cheating on you, Jeb."

"Yah, she was," he agreed. "And that fact would have made me look even more guilty—Englisher cops would think I wanted revenge. Which I didn't. We were both caught in this misery. And I was perfectly willing to live out my life as a single man if she left."

"I still think you should tell the bishop at least," she said. "They're judging you more harshly than they should, Jeb. They think you were some cruel husband and she was just a sweet girl. They have no idea she was being unfaithful and was going to go English. If anyone deserved some sympathy, it was you."

"I don't need sympathy." He caught her gaze and held it. "This is my *private* business. You understand that? I don't want anyone to know. If I did, I would have told them years ago."

Leah stared at him. Didn't he care what they said behind his back? Because she did. As his wife, she wanted them to know that he was a good man. She hadn't married some monster, preying on the hopes and wishes of sweet women. He'd been used, too.

"Leah?" he prodded.

"Yah," she said. "It's your business."

"Thank you." He drained the glass of water. "There's a lot of work left to be done. I've already lost daylight today."

Leah nodded, and he headed for the door again, his

limp slightly more pronounced than it had been earlier. He was sore.

He didn't turn around again. The door opened and shut, and Leah was left alone in the kitchen.

Katie had left him . . . and he'd nearly died going after her in that blaze. And yet somehow, the most heart-wrenching part of the whole story was Jeb coming home to that empty kitchen, no food ready, wondering where his wife had gone.

The young, defiant, vibrant Katie had died, and that was a terrible loss felt to the very core of their community. But Katie had also broken him . . . and maybe, in a way, the whole community had, too, because Katie hadn't seemed to have much choice in that marriage either. All he'd wanted was to be loved, and in that, Leah could sympathize. It was all she'd wanted, too. Rejection had a way of eating away at a person's heart. There were too many questions, the chief of which seemed to be, *why wasn't I enough?*

That evening Leah sat at the kitchen table, one of her dresses in front of her. It needed to be hemmed up another inch—the fabric was starting to wear. She'd already eaten her own dinner, but she had the meal on the table still, chicken potpie, boiled vegetables, and baked potatoes, all sitting in covered casserole dishes to keep them warm.

The sun had set, and she had a lantern hanging from the hook above the table. The lump of butter was melting onto the plate in the heat of the day. The kitchen window was propped open, and a faint breeze came through the room, exiting again through the screen door.

She heard Jeb's approaching footsteps, and she could make out the hitch in his step, the limp that held him back. He came up the steps, then inside. She put aside her sewing and started taking the lids off the dishes.

"That smells really good," Jeb said as he came into the kitchen. He pulled off his hat and rubbed a handkerchief over his forehead. "I thought you might be in bed already."

"Why?" she asked.

"It's late." He shrugged.

"Jeb, you're my husband. I make you your dinner and I will sit with you while you eat it."

One part of Jeb's story had been playing through her mind that evening—how he'd come back for dinner with his wife and found an empty house and no food on the table. Her heart ached for the young man he used to be— hoping for love, even for a meal, and never quite getting it.

"Yah?" He smiled faintly. "That's nice."

He came to the table and sat down, then he started dishing himself up.

"You deserve a meal, you know," she said.

He plopped a baked potato into his plate, then met her gaze. "What's this about?"

Leah stood up, reached for the pitcher of lemonade, and poured him a glass.

"You came home to no meal. I know that wasn't the thing I should have been fixating on in your story, but . . . You shouldn't have come back to no food."

Jeb reached out and caught her hand and she froze, his fingers moving slowly over hers. His hand was callused and hard, but his touch was gentle. She sucked in a wavering breath.

"It's in the past," he said quietly.

"I only just heard about it," she said, trying to smile but not quite managing it.

"I'm not the same man I was back then," he said.

"Why not?" she whispered.

"I don't expect the same things," he said, but he hadn't

released her hand. His touch moved up to her wrist, and she tugged her hand free. He let her go. Then he bowed his head, murmured a blessing, and started to eat.

Jeb didn't take long to eat, and while he did, she washed up the last of the dishes. When Jeb had finished eating, he handed her his plate and then reached for the cloth.

"I can do it," she said.

"Let me wash the table," he replied. "That's the least *I* can do."

She handed over the cloth and dipped his plate in the sudsy water. She looked over at him, watching him stretch with his good arm to reach as he cleaned the tabletop. He came back and handed her the cloth. She washed the dish, put it in the rack, and then pulled the plug on the dishwater.

"I like having you here," he said quietly.

"Yah?" she said.

"I'm not easy to get used to, and I might be stubborn as an old mule, but I do appreciate what you're doing for me, Leah."

She smiled at that, uncertain of how to respond. It was nice to know that he'd grown to like her contributions around here.

He nodded toward the stairs. "It's late."

Jeb headed over to the lamp above the table and reached up, turning it off and leaving them in darkness. After a moment her eyes adjusted to the dim light of the kitchen, and she followed Jeb up the stairs. The hallway was darker still, and she could feel Jeb in the warm stillness with her, but she could hardly see him.

"Jeb—" she started, but as she turned, she collided with him. Strong hands caught her around the waist, and she let out a breathy laugh. "I couldn't see you properly."

There wasn't much light up there, except for the moonlight from the kitchen that pooled at the bottom of the stairs, but where they stood in the space between the bedrooms, they were in darkness, and she couldn't make out his face. And somehow in the dark, having him hold her like this wasn't quite so daunting. And the strength in those hands . . .

"What do you need?" he murmured.

"What?" she breathed.

"You said my name."

"I don't remember," she whispered, then laughed softly.

What was it about the velvety darkness that made everything feel so different? His hand moved up her side, then she felt his fingers on her cheek.

"Thank you for waiting up . . ." he said, his voice a low rumble. "I didn't expect it."

"Maybe you should start to," she whispered. "A meal isn't too much to ask, Jeb. Neither is your wife's company at the table."

"I don't like to ask for too much," he murmured.

And maybe she didn't either. It was easier than being turned down, being rejected.

"You'll always get a meal from me," she whispered. "You can count on it."

Leah felt him lean toward her, the tickle of his breath against her lips, and then his warm lips covered hers, and this time when he kissed her, he pulled her against him. The gesture was tender, gentle, but she would have had to push back hard to counter him. He was a strong man— yet she sensed that if she pulled back, he'd release her. Her hands went easily to his sides, and she could feel the difference through his shirt—the soft, supple skin of one side versus the bumpy scars of the other.

His lips moved slowly over hers, as if exploring her in the darkness just as she was doing with her fingers over his torso. His hands moved up her back, then down again, stopping at the small of her back where Jeb let out a low moan, and he pulled back, his breath ragged.

"I have to stop . . ." he breathed.

"Oh . . ." She wasn't sure what to say to that, and she dropped her hands.

"I'm a man after all," he said, and she could hear the wry smile in his voice. "And I already told you how you make me feel. It's been a long time since I've held a woman, and if I don't stop now, I'll ask for things we'll both likely regret."

Things like what? Somehow, in the darkness, it didn't seem quite so scandalous to wonder that . . .

"Okay."

He stepped away, and she felt the coolness of the evening air rush between them. It was likely better that he did stop, because something inside her was softening under his touch . . . and back in the brazen daylight, she might very well wish she hadn't explored him like this in the darkness.

A little curiosity about a man could lead to a whole lot more demands . . . expectations . . . and that was her reasoning, wasn't it?

Except it was hard to remember, and she stepped back toward her own room, her eyes now better adjusted to the darkness so she could make out the doorknob.

"Good night, Leah," Jeb said quietly.

Leah opened the door into her bedroom, which shone brighter because of the open curtains and the starlight. "Good night, Jeb."

She'd been afraid of this marriage, but maybe it wasn't quite so terrifying after all.

Leah shut her door and leaned against it, shutting her eyes. She could still remember the feeling of his lips, his hands, the brush of his beard against her face . . . He seemed so confident in the way he touched her, and she had found herself responding in the darkness. No man had ever touched her like that before, and he seemed to know what he wanted and how to go about getting it.

Would it be so terrible to give in?

She'd know in the morning, when sunlight could burn away these secret feelings of longing that seemed to be growing inside her. Because she did wonder what would have happened if he hadn't stopped himself. What came next? She wasn't sure. She knew the logistics of the act, but . . . not the dance. Even now, in the darkness, where all she could hear was the thumping of her own wayward heart, she knew that she couldn't just give this a try. Because once she went to his bed, if she didn't want to do it again, there would be hard feelings. This tender friendship that was blossoming between them would be dead.

If she went to his bed with him, it would be a watershed moment, and all the protection she'd negotiated for herself would be over.

No . . . it was better to go to bed alone.

For now.

Jeb rose earlier than usual the next day and poured his frustration into his work. He wasn't sorry for that kiss, even though he was afraid of facing her now. She was his wife and he'd found her in his arms. So he'd kissed her. It was that simple.

But it was also what she'd said about him being worthy of a meal. He could count on her for a meal . . . that's what she'd said, and it was such a sweet thought that she'd wait up for him to make sure he ate. It was more thoughtfulness than he'd experienced in all his adult years.

When he'd kissed Leah, she could have pulled back or stopped him. She hadn't.

He wasn't wrong here! That was the sentiment he'd been repeating to himself ever since he got up that morning and marched out into the sunrise. She was his wife, and he'd kissed her.

So why did it feel wrong? But maybe "wrong" wasn't quite what he felt. It was intimidating. He was scared, if he had to truly face it. Every time he let down his guard and kissed that woman, his heart tugged toward her just a little bit more. It didn't help that he'd been noticing her for the last few years. She was beautiful, but not in the more blatant ways of some women. Her beauty was a low simmer, something he could tumble into and halfway drown in if he weren't careful. And he was tired of drowning for women who didn't want him.

Leah was kinder than Katie had been, she was a better woman than Katie, but she'd been equally pressured into marrying him, even if those pressures came from different sources. And here he was letting himself feel things he wasn't going to get reciprocated to him.

If he wasn't careful, he was going to fall in love with his wife, and then it would be the same old misery all over again. It was better to feel firm friendship for her, to appreciate her, to learn to trust her with the details of their shared life . . . but love? That got messy. Especially where his heart was concerned, because when he fell in love, he fell hard.

So, while he wasn't sorry for that kiss, if he were smarter, he'd regret it. Because he had bigger problems right now, like a cousin who was trying to ruin him with gossip. Lynita had been right that he couldn't just let that go, but handing over half the farm? He couldn't do that either. He'd thought he could just let his cousin hate him, but he couldn't sit still and let his cousin ruin their standing in the Amish community. This mattered too much to Leah for him to allow that to happen.

Jeb finished the morning chores in record time and had most of the work done before Simon even arrived, later than usual. The young man looked bleary, but at least he was here.

"I have to go on an errand," Jeb said. "I'll need you to do the horse barn while I'm gone."

"Yah," Simon said with a nod. "Sure."

"I think your sister is making a pie," Jeb added.

"Oh, yah?" Simon brightened.

Jeb sighed. Simon wouldn't be working hard, but at least he was helping out. Jeb left Simon to his chores, and he hitched up the buggy.

Jeb didn't just have a sense of responsibility toward Leah's happiness anymore either. He wanted her to be happy because she deserved it. And because she thought he deserved a little kindness in return. She'd married him to help her brother, not herself. The least he could do was try to smooth things over with his cousin, if he could. Maybe a conversation between men could iron this out. He owed it to his wife and his sister to try, and all he could do was pray that God would soften his cousin's heart.

Menno's carpentry shop was located in the town of Abundance. Menno and his brother-in-law ran the place together. They made solid Amish furniture for the Englishers who'd drive miles and miles to purchase their wares. They did well, and Menno, Jeb had to admit, was a skilled craftsman. He was particularly known for his cabinets.

When Jeb arrived at the shop he wondered if this was a good idea. He needed to smooth things over with his cousin, but from what he'd heard, Menno had nothing good to say about him behind his back. Would this even help, or would it give him more fuel?

He pulled open the front door and came inside to find an Englisher couple ahead of him, and Menno standing with his arms crossed. His cousin glanced up at him as he came in, and his expression froze as he recognized him, then turned back to the couple.

"The delivery isn't included in that price. There is another company that will carry it from our shop to your home.

These are their rates—if you want installation, you can speak to them about that."

"Would you arrange that for us?" the woman asked. "And if you could take off some of the price, because we thought—"

"No," Menno said. "The full bedroom suite will take a lot of my time to complete, and I can't lower the price any further. You are already getting a very competitive rate."

"If we went elsewhere . . ." the man hinted.

"You won't get solid wood and Amish craftsmanship," Menno replied, meeting their gaze evenly.

The man sighed. "Right. Right. Okay, well, we'll think it over and get back to you. You have a phone, right?"

"It's all on my card," Menno said, pulling a business card out of his pocket. "But keep in mind, the work will take twelve weeks. There are no rush jobs."

As the couple left the shop, Jeb watched them go, murmuring together over the price, apparently. But they'd be back. Jeb had seen the look in the wife's eye. She wanted that furniture.

Menno eyed him silently, his arms still crossed over his broad chest, waiting for Jeb to speak first.

"Good morning," Jeb said.

"What are you doing here?" Menno asked. "I doubt you're ordering furniture."

He could be—he was newly married, after all. But Jeb didn't see the point in playing games today. Jeb looked around at the empty shop. There were a few cabinets lining the walls, a headboard, some wood samples, and there was the smell of shaved wood that permeated the air from the workshop in the back.

"I was hoping we could talk privately," Jeb replied.

Menno pursed his lips, then headed for a door. He said something to whoever was in the back, then propped the door open with a wedge.

"I'll give you fifteen minutes," Menno said. "We can talk outside."

Menno led the way out a side door. It led to an alley between buildings, and it smelled mildly of garbage. Jeb glanced around once they emerged into the alley, and he wrinkled his nose.

"It's private," Menno said curtly. "And it's the best I can do right now. What do you want?"

"I've heard that you're complaining," Jeb said.

"Yah. I am," Menno replied. "You're taking the land that should be coming to me."

"Your *daet* left it to me," Jeb replied. "It's in the will, plain as day."

"My *daet*—" Menno's voice broke, and he stopped, swallowing hard. "My *daet* might not have cared terribly about my ambitions, but I know that in his heart, I was still *his only son*."

"This isn't a competition," Jeb said.

"No? It sure looked that way to me," Menno said.

"Menno—" Jeb sighed. "You've been telling people that I defrauded you. That's criminal. You're accusing me of something very serious."

Menno didn't answer, and he looked away, his jaw clenched. But it wasn't the old stubborn anger he saw in his cousin's bearded face, it was grief. The other man's eyes misted, and he blinked back his emotion.

"My *daet* loved me," Menno said gruffly.

"Yah," Jeb agreed. "And you loved him. But you never could get along."

"Because of you!" Menno shot back. "If you weren't in the middle of everything, I might have been able to build a relationship with him! But he had the perfect replacement sleeping the bedroom next to mine. The son he always wanted." Menno's voice dripped disdain. "And you're living in the house I grew up in. What does that say to you?"

"I liked to farm," Jeb said simply. "And I worked almost for free ever since I was a teen. He told me that he'd pay me back for my labor when he died. And I was willing to do the work."

"Why?" Menno demanded. "Why work for free? Because you were angling for the whole thing!"

"No, because I loved him, too!" Jeb barked back. "Peter was like a *daet* to me. And I never had that in my life. Where was I going to go? Who did I belong to, if I didn't belong with him?"

"You've got a *mamm* somewhere," Menno said, a bitter glint coming to his eyes. "You traded her in for my *daet*. You traded your real *mamm* for a family you liked better."

Anger boiled up inside him, and Jeb clenched his hands into fists at his sides. He'd traded her in? He'd done nothing of the sort. He'd been working to build a decent life for himself, the very thing she urged him to do in the letters she sent.

Work hard, son. Keep moving forward. I can't give you a proper life, but your uncle can. It can be lost all too easily. Don't be stupid. Don't be rash. Hold your temper and your passion. A moment's relief is not worth a lifetime of pain. Take that from a woman who knows.

"You know nothing about her," Jeb said, warning crystalizing on the edge of his words.

"Yah. Because you walked away." Menno spread his hands.

Menno was trying to goad him. He'd always been particularly good at that in their growing-up years. How many times had Menno poked at him, and when he retaliated, gone off and shown his bloody nose to his father? Jeb shut his eyes for a moment, willing the anger to subside, his mother's advice still in mind.

"What do you want from me?" Jeb asked.

"I want my inheritance," Menno snapped.

"Are you willing to farm with me?" Jeb asked.

Menno clenched his teeth. "It's mine, Jeb. You know it. Do the right thing. You took my *daet* away from me years ago, and now you take the family farm. Is that who you've become?"

It was an old argument—one Jeb couldn't win, because Menno would never see things differently. Jeb was the usurper. And maybe his cousin was right—if Jeb hadn't been on the scene, would Peter have had a warmer relationship with him?

Inside the store, both men heard the dingle of the bell above the door.

"Give me a sign of good faith," Menno said, his tone softening. "My *daet* had a working account. He had at least thirty thousand in there. Give me that money to start. We can discuss the rest later."

It hadn't been thirty. It had been fifty. And the money was gone now that Simon's debts had been repaid.

"What do you need it for?" Jeb asked.

"Does it even matter?" Menno demanded. "You took it all, Jeb! And you'll make me beg for even that?"

"It matters to me," Jeb said curtly.

"Fine. We want to expand, open a new shop," Menno said. "We'd each run one location—it would give me some elbow room. I'm sure you can appreciate that."

"So that's what you want your inheritance for—you'd sell it," Jeb said slowly. "And you'd continue to build this business here."

"What do you care?" Menno shook his head. "It should

be mine to do what I want with. I'm my father's only son. I deserve to grow my own business!"

So, he was right. If Jeb handed over half that land, Menno would sell it for the cash. A workable farm would be chopped up until it was too small to support a family, and all those years of working for his uncle would have been for nothing.

"Will you give me that?" Menno asked. He paused. "Please."

Jeb wasn't holding out for his cousin to beg. He no longer had the money, but that was his own private family business. Leah wouldn't want people to know about that.

"I can't do that," Jeb said woodenly.

Menno stared at him, disbelief flooding his face. "Are you serious? You'd hold back even that?"

"I'm sorry, Menno. I would if I could . . ."

His cousin shook his head in disbelief, then turned toward the door to the shop. He didn't look back, and Jeb felt the sting of his cousin's reproach.

"Menno—" he started.

The door slammed shut.

It would be easier if Menno were simply an angry man bent on revenge. But he wasn't. Menno was a grieving son who thought he should have at least part of his father's legacy.

But Menno's inheritance would mean chopping an already small property into a parcel so small it was all but worthless to farm. And with the amount of farmable land being eaten up these last few decades, Jeb wouldn't be able to just sell his half and start fresh elsewhere. It wasn't so simple anymore.

And he *was* sorry. If Jeb could see a solution here, he'd be happy to share with his cousin. But he'd already drained that account, and the rest of the inheritance was the land itself.

Jeb stood for a moment in the hot, smelly alley, and then he headed back toward the sidewalk and the buggy parking lot, his left leg feeling tighter and more painful than usual. He wanted to smooth things over with his cousin, but he'd already rescued one gambling fool. He had nothing left with which to do the right thing.

Chapter Fourteen

The next morning Leah stood back from the pan as the fat spattered. The bacon sizzled on her iron skillet, the edges just starting to crinkle. She'd made corn bread this morning, and it already sat in the center of the table, steam curling up into the air. There was honey to drizzle on top, a pot of oatmeal sitting with the lid clamped on, and she was currently frying the bacon to complete breakfast.

Outside the kitchen window the birds twittered as the new day began. Dew clung to the grass, shining like pearls in the rosy light of dawn. This was what happiness was supposed to feel like—a married woman in her own kitchen.

The day before had been a strange one. She and Jeb didn't talk about that kiss this time around. Maybe it was harder to talk about when they both knew they'd gone against their earlier promises to stop that. She noticed that Jeb was warming toward her, though. He seemed more willing to please her in small ways. Ironically, Rosmanda's mother-in-law would probably pat her on the back for that—kiss the man and make him more pliable. That sort of thing.

But Leah didn't like that thought. She wasn't interested in manipulating a man into doing things she wanted him to do. An honest agreement with an honest man was better . . . and yet she felt a little more eager to please him, too, after that kiss. And that made her feel nervous. Their marriage was changing, and the very thing they said they wouldn't do was edging closer.

But perhaps doing what they never thought wasn't all bad, because Jeb had made some serious declarations about limiting their contact with the community, and she could only hope that if he could change his mind about their physical relationship, maybe he could change his mind about their relationship to the Amish community, too. Maybe he would soften, see the beauty in friendship and community. Because they had guests coming tonight . . . She hadn't had a chance to invite Rosmanda and Levi, but it seemed that God was working in mysterious ways again.

The side door opened, and Jeb came in.

"Smells good," he called, and there was a muffled thump from the mudroom as his boots came off.

Leah flipped the bacon with a fork, one strip at a time, listening to the sound of water running as he washed up in the mudroom sink.

"The bacon is almost perfect," she said, and he appeared in the doorway with a towel in hand. He headed straight for his place at the table.

"I meant to tell you yesterday," Leah said. "Rosmanda and Levi are coming over for dinner tonight."

"When did that happen?" He reached for the spatula and levered up a slice of corn bread. He put it onto her plate, and then served himself a slice, too.

"Well . . ." She pulled the bacon out of the pan, letting it drip before putting it onto the plate. "Actually when Simon went to town yesterday, he saw Rosmanda there. She . . . invited themselves over."

"Simon went to town?" Jeb frowned. "When?"

"Around noon?" She frowned. "I thought you knew."

"No."

"I'm sure he wasn't shirking his work—" she started.

"I'm not convinced of that," Jeb said. "But whatever. So . . . people do this? They just invite themselves over? I thought that was just my sister."

"Rosmanda's my best friend," Leah said. "You agreed we'd have them over—remember? Besides, if she's inviting herself, they're bringing most of the food, so there is no worry about them being a burden." Leah came to the table and put the bacon down in front of Jeb. "And . . . I miss her."

Jeb looked up at her, then shrugged. "Yah. I can understand that. You miss . . . people."

"I do," she agreed.

"I don't." He sighed, then nodded to her chair. "Let's eat."

Leah sat down, eyeing Jeb uncertainly. Would he change his mind now? Jeb said a brief blessing over the meal, then reached for the honey.

"If you really don't want them to come, I could—" she began.

"It's fine," he said, softening his tone. "I did agree to this."

Leah did miss Rosmanda and her little girls. And Levi was a nice man. He wasn't quite so staunch and serious as other Amish men, and that might be ideal for Jeb. This was a chance to show people that they were a normal, happy couple. And gossip being what it was, they needed this.

"Rosmanda makes a delicious blackberry pie," Leah said. "Her pies are better than mine. It's the crust—she's got this way with it—"

"I don't want another woman's pie." Jeb's expression remained grim, but when he glanced up at her, she couldn't help but smile.

"That's nice of you to say, Jeb."

"It's the truth."

"It'll be fun, Jeb. You'll see."

That evening, Rosmanda, Levi, and the girls arrived at five, with plenty of time to spare for cooking. Levi carried an overflowing basket—bread, two pies, a bag of new potatoes, three bushy heads of lettuce, and a freshly plucked chicken. Leah had known her friend wouldn't come empty-handed. Rosmanda didn't carry anything, and her belly looked even larger than it had the last time Leah saw her.

"This looks wonderful, Rosie," Leah said, and she bent down to give each of the twins a squeeze, then straightened to hug Rosmanda.

"I didn't think you'd mind a bit of company," Rosmanda said, and accepted a side hug as she smoothed a hand over her domed stomach. "Is Jeb still doing chores?"

"Yah. He'll be in soon, though," Leah said. "You sit. I'll take care of this."

"Don't be silly!" Rosmanda laughed.

"Then peel potatoes," Leah said. "Sit down!"

Rosmanda didn't protest again, and she sank into a kitchen chair. Leah handed her a peeler, a pot, and a bucket for the peelings. Then the side door opened, and everyone silenced. Jeb's boots echoed on the floor, and Leah sucked in a breath.

"He's back," she said with forced cheer, and she crossed the kitchen and looked in to the mudroom. Jeb deposited his boots on the mat, gave her an indecipherable look, and then turned to wash his hands. Leah came into the room.

"They're here," she whispered.

"Yah, I noticed," he said. He lathered his hands with soap, then rinsed them.

"Jeb . . ." She wasn't sure what she was asking. She wanted some normal, if that wasn't too much. She wanted people to see them and feel happy for them instead of uneasy. She wanted to have fun tonight—to enjoy some time with Rosmanda.

"I'll be nice," Jeb murmured, and he smiled. "Okay?"

"Okay." Was she worrying for nothing? The girls had brought their dolls with them, and they had set them up on their father's lap. Levi smiled down at the girls indulgently, then looked up as Jeb came into the kitchen.

"Jeb," Levi said, gathering the dolls in one hand and standing to shake hands. "Congratulations."

"Thank you," Jeb said, and he looked down at Leah hesitantly. The twins stood with mouths gaping open, staring at Jeb.

"We're very happy," Leah said, putting a hand on Jeb's arm. It didn't feel natural—not here with people around. Jeb seemed different around others—pent up, uncomfortable. The man in the dark, the man when they sat alone in this kitchen—he was different. But other people couldn't see that. She looked down at the girls again.

"Go to your *mamm*," Levi ordered, and when the girls didn't move, he tapped them on their shoulders, turned them toward their mother, and gave them both a nudge. "Go on."

"It's a little surprising," Leah said feebly.

"It's okay," Jeb said quietly, and when she looked over at Jeb, she found his gaze following the little girls sadly. How did it feel to frighten children?

"I don't think we've ever had a chance to talk," Levi said, clearing his throat. "And our farm isn't far from here. We should help each other out at harvest."

"Yah. Yah . . ." There was something in Jeb's voice

that didn't sound in full agreement, though. Leah let her hand drop from his arm.

Rosmanda bent down as far as she could in her condition and was whispering quietly to the girls. They looked over their shoulders once toward Jeb, then back to their mother. Leah moved toward the kitchen, and she overhead the last of Rosmanda's little lecture.

". . . it hurts people's feelings. And we don't want to do that, do we?" Rosmanda pointed to a spot on the floor closer to the counter. "Go play there."

Hannah and Susanna did as their mother asked, but their little eyes kept moving across the room toward the men.

Rosmanda followed Leah into the kitchen. "I'm sorry about that," she said. "Maybe I should have warned them before. I was hoping that being so young, they wouldn't question a difference like that, and . . . Anyway, I'm sorry."

"It's okay," Leah said. "There was no harm meant. It's fine."

She hoped it was at least. Jeb had kept himself away from curious eyes and prying questions for years now, and she'd seen the look on his face.

"Are you sure?" Rosmanda asked.

"It's fine," Leah repeated. "Scars can be alarming for little ones. When they get to know him, they'll feel a lot more comfortable."

If they got to know him. Jeb looked so stiff over there talking with Levi. He was being awkward enough with adults, let alone inquisitive *kinner*.

"There is a strawberry ice cream gathering next Saturday at the Smucker farm," Rosmanda said, changing the subject. "And you know Sarah Smucker's fresh-churned ice cream."

"It's awfully good," Leah agreed, but her gaze swept

back to where Jeb stood. He was rubbing his scarred arm absently.

"You should come," Rosmanda said. "Drag your husband out to make nice with the community. He might even have fun."

"I don't know about that. . . ." Leah forced a breathy laugh. "He has his ways."

"And you'll have your ways as a married couple," Rosmanda countered. "You'll do things differently together. He'll have to change, Leah. That's part of marriage."

"I'm not sure he knows that." Leah sighed, and reached for a roasting pan. "Thank you for inviting yourself over, by the way."

"You're very welcome." Rosmanda smiled warmly. "It'll take the whole community to soften that man up, but we'll get there. Don't you worry. I'm not about to abandon you to some lonesome existence all by yourself out here."

"I'm glad of that . . ." Leah reached out and grasped her friend's hand. "It's *so* good to see you."

"Is he kind?" Rosmanda asked, lowering her voice.

"Yah." Leah pulled her hand back and started arranging the chicken in the roasting pan for the oven. "Why would you ask?"

"At the games night, things seemed rather tense, that's all. And people started to talk—"

"He's a kind man," Leah replied. "He's just . . . He doesn't trust the community, and he's not like this." She nodded toward the men. "The stiffness, and . . . unfriendliness. Not when it's just us at least. He has a tender side to him."

"Obviously," Rosmanda said with a low laugh. "You fell for him, didn't you?"

"Yah, of course." Just for a moment she'd forgotten that she needed to keep up their image. "It's not easy for him. He's been done wrong by a good many people."

"Oh?" Rosmanda raised her eyebrows.

"And it's private," Leah conceded. "All I mean to say is that if you give him time, he'll be more natural."

Rosmanda nodded. "Of course. It's private. As long as he's good to you, Leah."

"He's very good." And Leah wasn't covering things over or trying to make a good impression when she said it. Jeb was kind. He didn't push himself onto her. He appreciated her cooking . . . There was a more tender version of this man underneath that gruff, impossible exterior, and she'd witnessed it.

The women both looked toward the men again. Levi glanced around uncomfortably, then seemed to think of something else to say, but the men's voices were too low for them to hear.

"Let me get you the spices," Rosmanda said. "Where do you keep them?"

"The top cupboard behind us," Leah said.

Jeb looked over just then, and his dark gaze met hers. Her breath caught. It wasn't tenderness in his gaze that she saw, it was misery. He hated this—she could almost feel it in her own body, it emanated off him so strongly. He looked like a wounded animal, begging to be released from his pain.

"Why don't we start with a little bit of pie?" Leah asked, raising her voice. "The meal will still be an hour, so I don't think a little slice of pie should completely ruin appetites, do you?"

Pie—it was a diversion at least. It was something she could offer. What was wrong with him? Why was sitting here with a perfectly nice couple who wanted to spend an evening with them such punishment?

Because she needed this—desperately. She needed friends and contact with the outside world. She needed gossip and commiseration and joking. Somehow it was hard to feel like a proper wife without a community around her to make her feel like she was married.

"Yah!" Levi said with a smile. "I would love a slice of pie myself."

Jeb didn't answer, and Leah went to the cupboard for the dessert plates.

"What kind of pie did you make?" Leah asked. "I made shoofly pie myself."

"Blackberry," Rosmanda said. "We have some bushes that are producing the biggest, plumpest berries. The twins have been eating every berry within reach, of course, but they don't know enough to move the brambles. Thank goodness! But I managed to get enough for a pie yesterday, and . . ."

And as Rosmanda chatted on about her blackberry bushes, Leah felt the tension in the room start to lift. For her at least. She knew that Jeb hated this, but life couldn't be cocooned away on a farm away from the Amish community, away from the gatherings, the friendships, and the moral support. Life couldn't be wrapped up in this casing of solitude and caution . . . Leah had to be able to *breathe.*

As Leah began bringing dishes to the table, Jeb got up and took them from her, carrying them the rest of the way. When the last of the food had been brought to the table, Leah brought some extra stools to the table for the little girls, and everyone got settled in their chairs. He felt Leah's fingers brush against his knee under the table, and he looked over at her. She gave him an almost imperceptible nod.

"Let's bow our heads," Jeb said. Everyone did so, including the twin girls . . . except for one who peeked up at him with wide, uncertain eyes. "We thank you, Lord, for this meal and for the hands that have prepared it. Amen."

He raised his head, and for a moment there was silence.

"Uh—" Jeb cleared his throat. "Go ahead. Serve yourself."

Rosmanda reached for a platter of chicken, and Leah picked up a bowl of potatoes. She turned to the little girl next to her. "Do you want some, sweetie?"

This was his table, his home. Yet he'd never felt quite so out of place in a very long time. He didn't know these people. In fact, they likely knew more about him than he knew about them.

And yet, sitting at this table, he could feel their warmth and friendship for one another. Leah was laughing at something her friend had said, and she passed the potatoes on to Levi. Jeb could sense how easy they were when they laughed at something. It had been too long since he'd felt that way in a group of people, and this didn't seem natural to him at all.

His mind wasn't on their conversation, though. He had other, more pressing things on his mind, like Menno's request and his guilt over not being able to do one small thing for his cousin. If he were alone, he'd be able to sort out his feelings about it, but with the chatter and laughter around him, he was just left with the misgiving rising up inside him.

Levi handed a platter of roasted chicken to Jeb, and he accepted it with a nod. He selected a piece of breast meat and dropped it onto his plate.

"Did you hear about the strawberry and ice cream social next Saturday?" Levi asked.

"What's that?" Jeb focused back on the other man. Levi was looking at him expectantly.

"Next Saturday. There's a strawberry and ice cream social," Levi repeated. "Had you heard?"

"When would I have heard?" Jeb asked.

"I, uh—" Levi smiled uncomfortably. "Well, consider this an invitation, then. It's being held at the Smucker farm. It starts at three."

Jeb nodded silently and passed the platter on to Leah. She was looking at him hopefully.

"Will we go?" she asked with a smile that looked just a little too bright.

"We'll see," he said. There was an ice cream churn around here somewhere. If Leah wanted ice cream, he could make that happen.

"I think it sounds like fun," Leah said, putting some chicken onto her own plate and setting it down on the table. "There are so many people I haven't seen in ages—"

It wasn't about the ice cream, and he knew his annoyance wasn't fair, but he was feeling closed in, like the whole house was shrinking in on him.

"You should go, then," he said.

What did Leah want from him? To start eating strawberries and ice cream with neighbors? To act like this was fun? He didn't know these people anymore. When he was a part of this community, her friends were barely teenagers. And he'd been away from everyone for too long. He wasn't going to chat and laugh with men ten years his junior who'd never tasted the bitterness of life, and he wasn't going to be acceptable to the more experienced men either. He was an outsider. And this evening wasn't going to change that.

"Maybe we'll talk about it in private," Leah said, and her smile slipped. She licked her lips. "Rosmanda, have you been quilting much lately? I was thinking of starting a new one."

The conversation turned as quickly as that, and the little girls started putting their fingers in their mashed potatoes, which got Levi to give them a stern look. This was community, and this couple who'd come to visit with Leah would go back and report everything they'd seen and heard. What would they notice—the steps that needed repair? The stable that needed paint? Or would it be more focused on him and his awkwardness around them?

Jeb pushed back his chair, and no one seemed to notice. He rose to his feet, and the table silenced. Everyone turned, looking at him.

"I'm just going to step outside for a minute," Jeb said.

Leah looked up at him uncertainly. "Are you okay, Jeb?"

"I'm fine. Keep eating." He sounded gruffer than he'd intended. She hadn't done anything wrong, and he didn't mean to take this out on her. But he needed out of there—away from this table, away from the small talk, the chatter and the wide, staring eyes of those little girls.

Jeb headed for the side door, feeling his limp a little more acutely with all those eyes locked on him. He let out a breath of relief when he got into the mudroom, and he plunged his feet into his boots. He pushed open the screen door and let it bang shut behind him.

The air was warm and fresh, and he immediately felt better. He could hear their conversation resume—not the words, but the tone. The voices were questioning, concerned, worried. They didn't need to bother. He was fine—or he would be once they'd left his home and gotten out of his space again. He headed down the steps and toward the barn. It was habit, mostly. There was a calf that could use some milk, and he might get a head start on some of the work. It wasn't like there wasn't a constant list of things that needed doing.

Jeb looked back at the house. . . . They'd expect him

back soon, but the thought of going back into that kitchen with the small talk, the smiles, the eruptions of laughter— he wasn't the jerk he must seem like in their eyes. He just couldn't do this. . . .

He'd told Leah he was no good at this stuff, hadn't he?

And Jeb was many things, but he wasn't a liar.

Jeb dropped a bale of hay from his perch at the top of the pile. He needed some hay easier to reach for chores the next morning, and he'd already cleaned out two empty stalls, fed the bottle-baby calf, and fixed a broken gate on a stall. He reached for another bale, grunting with effort as his bad arm screamed in pain. But he didn't listen to that—he never did. If he stopped when it hurt, he'd never do anything.

He dropped the bale, and it landed on the cement floor, the twine flexing but not snapping. That would be enough for a couple of days. He eased his bad leg down first, then climbed down the ladder to the ground.

"They're gone."

Jeb startled at the sound of Leah's voice, and he turned to see her standing there. Her hands were on her hips and she stared up at him, dark eyes flashing fire. He wasn't sure what she wanted him to say. There were a few beats of silence.

"They seem nice," he said at last.

"Do they?" She raised an eyebrow. "Because they don't know what you think of them now. You walked out at the beginning of a meal and just didn't come back."

"I'm sorry about that," he said.

"Do you know what that was like for me?" she demanded. "I served them their meal, I served them dessert, and I had to smile the whole time and pretend that everything was fine—making up a hundred excuses for you!"

"Then don't make up excuses!" he retorted. "They were *your* friends."

"And you're my husband!" Tears misted her eyes, and she looked away, blinking them back. "You embarrassed me!"

Remorse flooded through him at the sight of her tears. But while he felt badly for hurting her, he wasn't sure he could change things. It was the kisses—crossing that line. It made them both start hoping for things that hadn't been part of their deal. He wanted the physical connection and she wanted him to be a friendly Amish farmer. He couldn't change who he was, and sitting with a family in his kitchen, virtual strangers, and expecting him to chat and smile and laugh—it wasn't going to happen.

"I can't do it, Leah," he said, his voice low.

"Sit and eat a meal?" she said.

"I'm not the man you're hoping I'll become," he said. "You think I'll go from being a virtual hermit to a friendly man. You knew what I was when you agreed to this."

"Are you saying that having guests over is asking too much?" she breathed.

"Right now," he said. "My sister comes—"

"She's your family, not mine," Leah replied. "Rosmanda is my best friend in this world—"

"Then see her!" he said. "I'm not holding you back!"

"I'm married!" she said. "Do you understand what that means? My best friend has been married for years, and I've been waiting. Well, I finally have a husband and a home of my own, and while I won't ever have *kinner* of my own, I do have a husband. So forgive me for wanting to join the ranks of married women!"

"They know you're married," he said woodenly.

"Yah . . ." She shook her head. "But they don't know if I'm happy."

"Leah, I can't be that man," he said. "I won't become like Levi or Matthew, or—"

"I don't need you to be Matthew," she said. "I just need you to be friendly."

"I told you from the start—I'm no good with making nice. You can't change me."

"Rosmanda says that changing together is a part of marriage."

"Then maybe you should change a few expectations of your own," he countered. "I don't trust them. They're going back to discuss us at length—you realize that, right? And she'll whisper something to one person, and he'll confide something to another, and our business is going to be plastered all over the community in a matter of days."

"What will they say?" she said. "They'll say you walked out and never returned. If you'd stayed—"

"If I'd stayed, I would have choked!"

Couldn't she see that? He didn't keep people away because he was some kind of jerk—he couldn't handle them. Their gossip, their advice, their suffocating presence . . . He'd already experienced being in the center of a supportive community and look where it got him. He didn't care if they liked him—he wanted his space.

Leah stared at him, and he couldn't help but notice just how beautiful she was when she stared him in the face, no veils between them. She licked her lips. "Okay."

"Okay, what?" he said, his voice still rougher than he was intending.

"You can't do it." Her voice sounded heavy and sad. "I accept that."

"I'm not going to some strawberry thing either," he said. "Go alone. You'll see your friends. You'll have your community. They'll understand that your husband is peculiar. It'll be fine."

"Understood."

As easy as that? Except he could see that he'd let her down—embarrassed her—and he couldn't even tell her it wouldn't happen again. This was simply who he was and how much he could take. The community she counted on to buoy her up was the one that had ruined his life.

"Leah—" He reached out and caught her hand. "I'm sorry. I am."

She tugged her fingers free. "I have to clean up the kitchen. They couldn't get out fast enough. They thought they weren't welcome here."

He was isolating her, and that had never been his intention. But he could see it happening, and he didn't want to be the man who drained the life out of her. He'd sucked the happiness out of one woman already for not being the right man, and he was very likely doing it again. He wasn't Katie's Englisher, and he wasn't Leah's Matthew either. Leah was his wife, and he wanted to be her answer, her rescue, but right now, he was only disappointing her.

He was just a man with scars that went soul-deep who didn't know how to be any different.

And he didn't know how to make it up to her either.

Chapter Fifteen

Leah stood at the top of the drive, the midmorning sunlight soaking into her shoulders. She opened the mailbox—a rickety metal box with a dent on one side—and pulled out an envelope. It was addressed to her, but the cottage and the main house shared the same address, and for as long as she had rented that cottage for herself and Simon, Peter had simply hand-delivered their mail.

Leah tore open the envelope as she headed back down the drive toward the house, the gravel crunching beneath her shoes. The handwritten letter was from the Amish school board at Rimstone, and it was an invitation to come back and teach again come September. But it was more than that—if she'd come back earlier than September, they had some *kinner* who needed some extra help, little Benjie being one of them. And if she was willing to come sooner, they'd pay her for tutoring before she started the school year properly.

The words flowed over her, and she reread the letter three times while she slowly walked back toward the house.

The school board had no idea she was married, she realized in a rush. If they did, she'd never be offered the position. Married women belonged at home where they were needed, and there was no doubt she was needed here at the farm. There were two gardens to tend, fruit and vegetables to jar for winter, meals to make, a house to clean, laundry to do . . . She was needed here, but there was a part of her heart that still yearned for the life she'd had in Rimstone.

Leah was needed in Rimstone in a different way. The *kinner* needed her guidance and her enthusiasm. She could see their little faces light up when she encouraged them to keep trying and they finally mastered something. The parents needed her advice on how to help their *kinner* read better or her insight into their behavior when their parents weren't there watching. She was welcomed into homes in Rimstone, invited to events, and a few even tried to set her up with single uncles or older widowers . . . which she obviously couldn't allow anymore. But she had friends there—women who would enjoy her company and invite her over to cook together. She had a community life in Rimstone. She hadn't appreciated it quite so much as she should have.

Was it ridiculous of her to miss it now that it was in the past?

The sound of wheels drew her attention, and she turned to see a buggy coming into the drive behind her. Matthew held the reins, and Leah's heart sped up in her chest. This wasn't appropriate—unless he'd come to see her husband about some business or other.

Matthew pulled the buggy up beside her. "I'm glad I found you—"

Leah shook her head. "Is something wrong?"

"Your brother—" Matthew grimaced. "He's going to be furious I told you, but he's at another Englisher card game."

"He's—what?" Leah shook her head. "No, he wouldn't be—"

After all he'd been through, after the beatings, the deep

debt . . . after her marriage to save his *hintern* from those Englishers—he was gambling again?

"How do you know?" she demanded.

"I saw him going in—they always meet in the same place. It's in the back room of the pool hall in town. I was running some errands. I talked to him for a couple of minutes—I tried stopping him. He told me to mind my own business."

"The back room of the pool hall, you say?" she clarified.

"Yah."

"Good. Thank you. I'll take care of it," she said.

"Do you want a ride?" Matthew asked, and his glittering blue gaze met hers. Did he know how he could still make her feel? A smile turned up his lips. "I'll bring you back. It's not a problem."

For him, maybe. Except it was a problem. The last year shouldn't evaporate like this. He shouldn't be able to look in her eye like that and give her that tempting half-smile of his that had always been the one to draw her forward.

"That wouldn't be right," she said. "We're both married."

Matthew huffed out a breath. "These are extenuating circumstances."

"Yah," she agreed. "And I'd rather not have to explain them to your wife."

Matthew blinked at her, and whatever it had been in his demeanor that seemed to be stretching toward her dropped away. They could no longer have any special friendship between them—those days were done.

"Do me a favor, though," Leah said. "Hitch up our buggy."

She started forward again, not waiting for his reply. Matthew had come this far, and she wasn't asking him to do this for her exactly. She was asking him to do it to help Simon. She broke into a jog, tugging her skirt up higher to let her legs move freely.

"Where are you going?" Matthew called after her.

"To get my husband!" she shouted back.

Matthew wasn't the solution here, and he never would be again. He should save his moral support and tempting smiles for his pregnant wife. And as Leah ran, she sent up a prayer that God would keep her brother from losing anything more.

Leah found her husband coming toward the cow barn, and she waved her arms, then stopped running, leaning forward as her breath came in gasps. Jeb turned his steps toward her.

"What's going on?" he called, closing the distance between them.

"We have a problem," she said, her chest still heaving. "It's Simon—"

Jeb looked around, then jogged toward her. His expression clouded.

"Simon's in the far field watering the cows," Jeb said.

"No, he's not," Leah countered. "Matthew—" She sucked in a breath, still panting. "He just got here. He saw Simon in Abundance. He's at a card game again."

"He's—" The clouded look on Jeb's face turned downright stormy, and for a moment she wasn't sure if that rage was directed at Simon or Matthew.

"Matthew is hitching up our buggy for us," she said.

"Is he now?" That grim expression hadn't changed.

"I'll go alone to fetch Simon if I have to," Leah said.

"Go by yourself to deal with an Englisher gambling ring?" Jeb shot her an incredulous look.

"I'd rather you came with me, though," she said hopefully. "I obviously don't know what I'm doing here, but I'm not leaving Simon to that pack of wolves either."

Jeb muttered something under his breath that sounded a whole lot like a curse, then started back toward the stable, one hand on his bad hip as he limped along.

"Does that mean you're coming with me?" she asked, hurrying to catch up.

"Of course I'm coming with you," he retorted. "Let's go."

A wave of relief crashed over her. She wasn't alone in this anymore—and frankly, if it came to facing down some violent Englishers, she felt a whole lot safer with the beefy, irritated Jeb by her side than Matthew, with his coaxing smile.

As they came back toward the stable, Matthew's buggy sat unattended, and Matthew was under the buggy shelter, working with the straps that hitched a horse to the shafts. Jeb wordlessly headed in that direction.

"Thank you," Jeb said gruffly. "I can take it from here."

"Yah. Right." Matthew stepped back, and he shot Leah a questioning look. "I came by to tell you that I saw Simon—"

"Leah told me," Jeb said.

"Well, so . . ." Matthew didn't seem to know quite what to say. "I suppose I'll leave it to you, then."

"That would be good," Jeb said, looking up and shooting Matthew an irritated look. "This is family business now. I thank you for letting us know. Feel free to get on with your own business."

The command in Jeb's tone was unmistakable, and Matthew's cheeks flushed under his downy beard. Matthew crossed the scrub grass toward her.

"Is he always like this?" Matthew asked, lowering his voice.

"Yah, I am!" Jeb called, straightening. "I might be ugly, but I'm not deaf. Head on home to your wife, Matthew. I appreciate the gesture, but I'd be real glad to see you off my property."

Matthew strode back to his buggy and hoisted himself back up into it. He muttered something under his breath, then flicked the reins and tugged them hard so that the horse pulled the buggy in a tight arc. Leah stared after Matthew, then back at Jeb. Was this really how he treated his guests? Jeb gave an exaggerated shrug, then took the horse's bridle and led him around. The buggy was hitched.

If Leah wasn't mistaken, some sort of male communication had just happened between Matthew and Jeb. Jeb had just staked his turf.

"Let's go." Jeb's voice softened, and he held out a hand to her.

She put her fingers in his rough grasp, and he helped her up into the buggy seat. His grip was firm and strong, and she settled herself as he headed around the buggy and got up on the other side.

"He was helping us," Leah said.

"Agreed," Jeb said. "He was also doing it for you. Personally. He was checking up on you."

Leah frowned. Was he? Maybe. It was hard to completely erase a romance. And maybe that was a bit of a relief for her—Matthew's feelings might not have been completely fake if he still felt some tenderness for her. . . . Was it wrong to appreciate that?

"I didn't encourage that," she said. "I'm not that kind of woman, Jeb. I don't toy with other's women's husbands, and I certainly don't flirt."

She wanted him to know that—truly know it. It was more than her reputation. It was her ability to take some pride in her own life.

"I know," Jeb said.

"So, you didn't need to scare him," Leah said

Jeb flicked the reins and they started forward. His flinty gaze flickered in her direction.

"Scare him?" Jeb chuckled, and this time he actually sounded amused. "Leah, if that was enough to scare him, he's not much of a man. All the same, I'd rather keep him off my property."

They came up to the main road, and Jeb flicked the reins again, hurrying the horse into a trot. Leah settled back into the seat. And maybe her husband wasn't neighborly, but today that terrible attitude would be more beneficial to Simon than all the friendliness in Abundance.

She could only hope that by the time they got to Simon, they'd find that he had sense enough to pull himself out of the game. Because with Jeb's current mood, she wasn't sure what her husband would do.

The drive into Abundance wasn't a long one, but no matter at what speed the horse trotted, Jeb felt like they were moving at a crawl. He glanced over at his wife. Her face was pale, making her dark eyes look bigger as she stared straight ahead. She looked scared.

"I'll take care of it," Jeb said.

Leah looked over at him. "He might not be gambling, you know."

And arguing with her about that wasn't going to help matters, so he kept his mouth shut and reached over and took her hand. Her fingers were cold, but she squeezed his hand in return.

Leah needed support right now, and the fact that Matthew had tried to nose in at a vulnerable time irritated Jeb. The fact that he'd tried to nose into their private business at all was annoying. Matthew was married with a wife of his own—and maybe it was that he knew Leah had truly loved Matthew that made him feel pricklier. . . . It certainly made the younger man's presence all the more annoying. Funny how a little detail like that could make all the difference—who a woman had loved. Here he was, the big, muscle-bound lug who wasn't enough. And up until now, he'd thought he was okay with that. They both knew what they stood to gain from this marriage. Except Jeb had started giving in to whatever this was he was feeling for her . . . and he'd started doing the very thing he was trying to protect himself from: wanting more.

Blast it. He wasn't supposed to do this. His own deep desires were his downfall. If could find some sort of contentment with less, that was better. It was attainable.

Leah's hand felt good in his, and the contact was probably more comforting for him than it was to her right now. But when they got into the town limits, he let go of her hand and focused more directly on the road. He knew where he was going, and while there wasn't designated buggy parking, there was a grassy area where he could leave the buggy for a few minutes. Here was hoping he wouldn't be there long enough to get a ticket.

Abundance was a picturesque town, the summer sunlight softened by dappled shade. Large trees spread their limbs over the streets, and tourists stood on the sidewalks with their phones outstretched, taking videos of his passing buggy, no doubt. This kind of thing annoyed him at the best of times, but he didn't have the time to bother with it today.

"It's just up there—" Jeb reined the horse in at a four-way stop and let the cars opposite him go. Then he flicked the reins and guided his horse around the corner. "You stay in the buggy."

"I'm not staying," Leah said, and Jeb looked over at her.

"This is a seedy establishment," he said. "It's no place for a woman."

"Then it's no place for a decent man either," she shot back. "I'm getting my brother."

Jeb gritted his teeth. She was so stubborn! But he didn't have a lot of time to argue with her. If she was going in there, she'd have him at her side, if nothing else. He urged his reluctant horse into the car parking lot, reining in as a vehicle backed out.

"This isn't buggy parking!" the driver called out, rolling down his window.

Jeb ignored him.

"Hey, buddy!" the man repeated.

"Keep driving," Jeb barked. They always thought they meant well, but the Englishers treated the Amish like they were a step below—charming but not too smart. The driver shook his head, rolled up his window, and drove on.

Jeb guided their horse over to the grassy area and managed to get most of the buggy up on the sod. It would have to do. He hopped down, grabbed the horse's bridle, and tied it to the low-hanging limb of a tree. Leah climbed down, and she shot him a worried look. At least she had the good sense to be wary.

"Come on, then," he said, and he led the way toward the front door.

The pool hall was part of a strip mall that included a restaurant, a drug store, and a laundromat. It was on the corner and had darkened windows that had some bubbles showing where the plastic hadn't been applied smoothly. The front door showed the business hours, and it was too early to be open, but when he tugged on the door, it wasn't locked. So he strode inside.

Most people didn't mess with him if he walked purposefully enough, not that he frequented establishments like this. He held open the door for Leah, and when she stepped inside, she slipped her cool fingers into his palm. He closed his hand around hers, tugging her close against him.

"Leave the talking to me," he said. "I'm more intimidating."

She didn't argue with that, and he wound his way around the green-felted tables toward the back of the room. An Englisher wearing black jeans and a T-shirt with some strange-looking musician on the front sat beside a back door. The man wasn't very old, and he sported a wispy mustache but no beard.

"Place is closed, man," the Englisher said.

"I'm here to see someone," Jeb replied.

"Family outing?" the Englisher said, barking out a raspy laugh. "Get lost."

"A friend of mine is in there," Jeb said. "Simon Riehl. Amish fellow. He'll stand out. He's terrible at cards."

The Englisher smirked, then shrugged. "All right."

Jeb's first instinct was to tell Leah to stand here and wait for him, but he wasn't keen on leaving her alone with this fellow either, so when the Englisher stepped aside, he opened the door and tugged Leah into the room after him.

The back room was bigger than he'd anticipated. It looked more like a small warehouse, with some shelves along the walls loaded with boxes and restaurant-size bottles of condiments. On one side a table was set up, and it was surrounded by Englishers with cards in their hands and Simon—the only Amish man there. He held his cards fanned out in front of him, and his gaze flickered up when Jeb came in, then he froze.

"Let's go, Simon," Jeb said quietly, and his voice carried.

Simon didn't answer, but his gaze whipped over to an Englisher who looked up, annoyed. He wasn't a large man, but he exuded a confidence that labeled him the boss here.

"What's going on?" the man barked. "Who are you?"

"His family," Jeb replied. "We need him at home."

"Jeb, with all due respect, I'm busy here," Simon said.

And that was all it took. Because Simon was not only skipping out on work that he would have accepted payment for, he was sitting here gambling. And Jeb didn't care how he looked in front of these Englisher fools. He dropped Leah's hand and limped swiftly toward the younger man. Simon looked up in alarm, and Jeb shot out a hand, caught him by the back of the neck, and hauled him, scrambling to his feet.

"You're supposed to be at work," Jeb muttered. "Let's go."

There was a smattering of laughter from the men around the table.

"I was winning!" Simon blustered.

Jeb looked back at the Englisher who appeared to be the boss of the place, and the man shrugged.

"He's ahead," he confirmed.

"Consider it a life lesson, Simon," Jeb said. "Simon has just forfeited his winnings. Have a good day, gentlemen."

A smile spread over the boss's face, and he swept the pile of chips away from Simon's now empty place.

"What are you doing?" Simon hissed once he got his footing. He tried to jerk out of Jeb's grasp, but he couldn't.

"Shut up," Jeb grunted, and he propelled Simon toward the door. Leah opened it and they carried on out. The Englisher at the door eyed them as they left, and Jeb felt like he could feel the eyes on the back of him. These were not good men, and if there had been money owing, he doubted they'd have let Simon walk away, so they could just thank the good Lord for Simon's momentary luck.

Leah opened the front door, and only when they were outside in the fresh air again did Jeb drop his hand.

"What is wrong with you?" Simon demanded, pulling away and whirling around. "Who do you think you are anyway?"

"I'm the idiot who paid your debt!" Jeb retorted. "Get in the buggy!"

"I'm not going anywhere!"

"Get in the buggy," Jeb repeated, lowering his voice. "You think we wanted to come out here?"

"So what, Matthew came and tattled on me like a little boy?" Simon asked with a bitter laugh.

"Something like that," Jeb agreed. "You think those men won't beat you within an inch of your life if you step wrong?"

"I can handle myself," Simon retorted.

"You came to me for help," Jeb snapped. "Remember how scared you were? I'm the one who picked you up off the side of the road and got you home. And once you figured out just how much trouble you were in, you came to *me*! And now you risk yourself again? You're going to get yourself killed, and for what? For some money? For a thrill? You're an idiot, Simon. I can tell you straight. You're not smart, and you'll end up dead."

"Simon—" Leah's soft voice pierced the anger, and Simon turned toward his sister. "Tell me you don't owe anything."

"I was ahead!" Simon retorted.

"Thank God." She rubbed her hands over her face. "Okay. Then no harm done. I don't care if you lost money. I've had enough of this. What were you even doing in there?"

"I have a talent, Leah," Simon said. "Believe it or not, I'm good at that game! I was about two thousand dollars ahead when your husband here gave it all away."

Leah blinked at him, and for a moment Jeb thought she might be impressed. Then she shook her head.

"You were fifty thousand dollars behind last time," she said.

Jeb couldn't help but smile at his wife. She was smart—he liked that. Simon wasn't going to sweet-talk her into anything stupid. And she said it like she saw it. That was another trait he could appreciate.

"Get in the buggy," Leah said quietly. "We're going home."

Simon looked like he might argue that, but Jeb was out of patience.

"You're getting in that buggy, one way or an another," Jeb said, and he meant it. Those Englishers might beat him, but Jeb wasn't beyond hog-tying him if forced.

Simon seemed to take the warning in Jeb's tone to heart, because he sighed and headed toward the back of the buggy.

"I'm not bailing him out again, Leah," Jeb said quietly.

"You don't have to. He was ahead," she replied. And this time around, she was right. But it wouldn't be the last. Jeb was sure of it. Whatever it was that drew him out today, the lure wasn't gone. Whatever Simon thought he could get, whatever payoff seemed worth the risk . . .

"No, I mean if he does this again and isn't so lucky," Jeb said. It didn't matter what Jeb felt for Leah . . . "I'm serious. I don't have the money. I'm not selling land for him. If this happens again, we won't *be able* to pay it."

Leah's face paled, and she nodded. "No, I wouldn't expect you to sell land."

But she looked toward the buggy, where her brother hoisted himself up, and he saw the worry and sadness in those dark eyes. For all of Simon's weaknesses and stupid choices, Leah loved her little brother. Did Simon know what a treasure it was to be held in a woman's heart like that? But maybe he and Simon had more in common than he liked to admit, because he had a sister who never gave up on him either. And he didn't reciprocate to her as much as she deserved.

Looking at Simon, it was easy to think of him as a young idiot. He still thought he had "talent" when it came to games of chance, and he had no idea what it was like to face the world alone.

Jeb did.

Chapter Sixteen

That evening Leah poured the boiling water into a teapot and added three tea bags. She was used to making tea for a houseful of people since her time in Rimstone, and looking down into the pot, she knew she had made too much.

She put on the lid, waiting for it to steep.

When they got back that afternoon and Simon had gone back to work with Jeb, her brother had looked angry—that simmer in his gaze that told her that he hadn't forgiven them for the embarrassment of being dragged out of the card game like a kicking child.

And perhaps she didn't blame him for his anger. Not fully. But what else were they to do? At what point was she supposed to just step back and let him learn his lesson? Except with these Englishers, learning his lesson the hard way might very well get him killed. She should have stepped back earlier, when the stakes weren't quite so high.

Leah got down a mug, spooned two spoonfuls of sugar into it, and then filled it with steaming tea. She carried it through to the sitting room, where Jeb sat on the couch next to a kerosene lamp, his Bible open on his lap. He glanced up as she came in.

"I made you tea," she said quietly.

"Thank you." He accepted the mug.

It was a small gesture, but a genuine one. He'd dragged her brother out of a gambling den by the scruff of his neck, and for that he was her hero.

"With sugar, the way you like it," she said.

Jeb took a sip. "To be completely honest, I actually prefer it black."

Leah frowned. "But for days now I've been giving it to you with sugar. Why didn't you say anything earlier?"

"I guess I'm just grateful for tea." He smiled faintly. "Who knows? Maybe it'll grow on me."

Leah sank onto the couch next to him. "I didn't realize that. You don't have to get used to it. Next time I'll leave out the sugar."

Jeb took another sip and put the mug on the table next to him. "But this is the way you like your tea, isn't it? With sugar?"

She nodded. "Yah."

Leah was giving him the tea the way she liked it, and she was trying to give him support the way she would like it, too. But it was hard to tell if her attempts meant the same thing to him. In so many ways, this man was still a stranger to her.

"My wife's tea preferences—a good thing for a husband to know, I suppose," Jeb said.

She smiled at that. "I suppose."

"How's Simon?"

Her mind went back to earlier that evening. She'd stopped by the cottage, and he'd told her to go home to her husband. It had been harsh, and she'd felt small and stupid walking away again.

"He's not talking to me," she said.

"Hmm."

"Why would he go back to the gambling?" she asked quietly. "I don't get it."

"Addiction, most likely," Jeb replied. "I've seen it before with some other Amish men. There's a thrill in winning. They say it feels like God's favor. And they keep going back for more."

"It isn't His favor," she said. "It's an Englisher trap."

"Definitely," he agreed. "But they don't see it. They feel it. Those are two different things."

"Will he hate me forever?" Leah wasn't really asking Jeb, because how could he know? She was thinking aloud. Her brother—her sweet, dear little brother with those big, mischievous eyes—had always been able to hold a grudge. It was why she'd stopped spanking him by the age of nine. She'd said he was too old for a smack on his bottom, and maybe he was. But it was the resentful look in his eye that had stopped her. She wanted to guide him to better choices, not drive him away.

"It's possible to be the bad guy in someone's eyes," Jeb said quietly. "And you can't even argue it. You see how they see you. You know why they resent you. But you can still know that you're a good person."

"There's right and wrong," she murmured.

"Right for who?" Jeb asked.

"We were not wrong in pulling him out of that game!" she retorted. "He'll get himself killed if he keeps going!"

"Yah, yah . . ." Jeb sighed. "I'm not arguing that, I'm—" He looked over at her, chewed on the side of his cheek. "I went to see Menno."

Leah froze. Even the mention of his cousin's name made her feel nervous. Was Jeb going to give up the farm after all? Would he let his vindictive cousin pressure him out of it?

"Is it better between you now?" she asked. She didn't expect it to be, but there was still a little wriggle of hope inside her. Maybe God would work a miracle. Maybe Menno would feel a flood of familial affection. It wasn't that she wanted an inheritance that didn't belong to them, but marrying Jeb had come with a few expectations for comfort. A house of their own. A kitchen that belonged to her . . .

And yet she felt the isolating selfishness of those thoughts, too. Because what was a farm, a house, a kitchen, without a family and a community?

Jeb shook his head. "No, it's no better. Menno hates me. And I understand why."

"He's wrong," Leah replied earnestly. "I know this is a complicated situation, but he has no right to be passing around these rumors and trying to sway the community's opinion of you for the sake of some land. Your uncle made the will clear. Menno didn't want to farm. And if he'd cared about his father more in life—"

"He's not all wrong," Jeb replied, cutting her off. "Will I give up the farm for him? Even if I wrote over half the land, he'd sell it. Giving up half is like giving up all. I can't run half a farm, and at least I want to farm."

"Are you feeling guilty?" she asked softly.

"A little. He asked me to give him the money in the bank account. He knew about it. He didn't know how much was there. He thought it was thirty thousand. Still, he said he wanted to grow his business—get his own carpentry shop away from his brother-in-law. And that money would help him do it. He asked if he could just have that, for now. I have a feeling if I had, he might have left me alone with the rest. . . ."

Leah's stomach dropped. "But you used it for Simon."

"Yah."

She saw how it was now. The little bit that would have smoothed things over between the cousins had already been syphoned off. Because of her. Because of Simon.

"There will always be someone who sees you as the bad one," Jeb said. "Like you and Simon. Have you done something wrong? Of course not, but your brother still resents you. You have to know where you stand, have a clear conscience, and let the rest fall where they may."

"It helps to have the community's support," she said. "Their reassurance that you've done all you could."

"If you can get it." He met her gaze, then shrugged. "When you meet your Maker, you won't have the community by your side. It will be just you facing God."

"Like you now?" she asked.

He laughed softly at that. "I might be alone, but I'm not facing judgment yet."

"True . . ." She smiled at that. "Is that where you get your strength—knowing you did right, even if no one else seems to know it?"

"Part of it," he agreed. "I have a clear conscience, but I also have God. I'm not quite so alone as I look."

Maybe God made up the difference for him, filled in the spaces for all he'd lost. And looking at him sitting there with his Bible on his knee, he didn't look alone. He looked like any other Amish man—strong, satisfied, thoughtful.

"I'm not sure I'm strong enough to do what you do, Jeb," she admitted quietly. "I can't face life alone."

"I don't think anyone really chooses this . . ." he said.

"Isn't it a choice now?" she asked.

"Not anymore." His voice was low, and she wondered what he meant by that.

"Maybe Menno does think badly of you," Leah said after a moment. "But I don't. I think you're kind. And I'm so deeply grateful for what you've done for Simon. I know he's not seeming worth all this trouble . . . not to you at least. And I understand that. But he's worth it to me. And when I see you, I see—" She swallowed. "A good man."

Jeb closed his Bible and put it on the table next to the lamp. "Yah?"

Leah nodded. "Yah. So, if one opinion could hurt you, maybe another one can make up for it. A little bit at least."

Jeb reached over and touched her cheek with the back of one finger. He met her gaze with a slightly flirtatious smile. "It helps. Are you ready for bed yet?"

The question would be an ordinary one between any other married couple, but it gave Leah pause. Was he suggesting something more tonight? Her heart sped up, and he didn't break eye contact. He raised an eyebrow, waiting for her response.

"I was going to bring in some wood," she said. "I'll need it for breakfast in the morning."

She was evading—purposefully.

"I'll do that." He rose to his feet. "That's a man's job."

Jeb cast her one more smile that she couldn't quite decipher, then rubbed his hand down the side of his leg. He limped toward the kitchen, and she heard his uneven footsteps head for the side door.

If she could convince the rest of the community of what she saw in Jeb, maybe she could bring them all back together again. He deserved a community, an extended family, and the hope that came with a group of people who cared. He shouldn't have to keep going on alone like this.

Maybe he just needed help coming back again.

Jeb loaded up the last pile of wood in his arms, the rough edges scraping against his arms. The sun had set and the stars pricked through the semidarkness. The sky was still velvet gray by the horizon, and he paused to look in that direction.

He'd come out to get the wood for two reasons, the first of which was that his wife wasn't going to have to carry wood as long as he was in the house with her. The second was that those dark brown eyes fixed on him with such honesty shining in their depths were making him feel things he wasn't comfortable feeling.

Leah was his wife, and she was on his side. That was a good thing—the way things should be. But it also made a strange well of tenderness rise up inside him. It was like all the gentle, warm, protective feelings that had lain dormant the last fifteen years were suddenly drawn to Leah.

And that wasn't safe either. This was loneliness making him feel these things—nothing more. So, he'd come outside to get his head on straight. The only other option had been to pull her into his arms and kiss her. And right now, he wasn't sure it would stop at that.

You're lonely, he reminded himself. *That's all this is. Don't mess up a good thing.*

He headed around the side of the house to the door and let himself back in. The wood pile for the kitchen was just outside the mudroom for easy filling, and he let the wood roll down into the box, then brushed off his hands.

Leah stood by the kitchen table, the sugar bowl in her hands. She looked at him silently.

"Done," he said, breaking the silence. He looked down at the scrape on his arm. It was a bit worse than he'd thought. Small beads of blood broke through the scraped skin.

"Thank you, Jeb."

Those eyes . . . What was it about her clear gaze that drew him in like that?

"Did—" Jeb cleared his throat. "Did you mean that? What you said about me being a good man?"

"Yah. I wouldn't say it if I didn't."

He smiled at that. There weren't many people out there like her—utterly honest. Or perhaps there were, but they didn't tend to be on his side.

"Did you hurt yourself?" she asked, and she stepped closer to inspect his forearm. Her light touch moved down his arm, making his skin tingle. He should pull away . . .

because she was innocently enough inspecting a scrape, and she had no idea what this was doing to him.

"It's not bad," he said, but he didn't pull his arm back. "Hold on—"

Leah pulled away first and headed across the kitchen. He exhaled a slow breath. The kitchen smelled like her. This house had changed since her arrival—the very scent of the air had grown sweeter somehow. But he also knew what it was like to want something so badly and have a wife who didn't. It didn't matter how she made him feel if it wasn't mutual.

She pulled out a cloth napkin from a drawer, soaked it under the tap, and wrung it out. Then she came back to where he stood and pressed the cold cloth against his skin. She cradled his arm, one hand underneath it and the other on top. Her touch was cool and gentle. She lifted the cloth, peeked underneath, then pressed it down again.

She'd feel his goose bumps, he realized belatedly. She stood so close to him that he could feel the warmth of her body emanating against him, and he could smell the soft scent of her shampoo. He stretched out his hand, the backs of his fingers brushing against her apron. She froze, but she didn't move away. He stretched his fingers out again and let them linger there against her soft stomach.

"You don't need to do this . . ." he breathed.

"Maybe I want to," she murmured back. Still, she didn't move away from his touch, and he felt all his focus moving down to the spot where he touched her. He wanted more than that—to run his hands around her waist, to pull her against him. . . . Lately, at night, he'd been dreaming of her skin against his. If she weren't his wife, he might feel guilty for those dreams—those fragments of hope in his mind.

"Leah . . ." he whispered.

And this time she looked up, her lips slightly parted, her gaze meeting his. But there was no question in her eyes.

He pulled the cloth from his arm and tossed it onto the table, then brushed a tendril of hair that had escaped her *kapp* from her forehead. Her skin was so soft against his fingertips, and he looked down to her lips. He slid his hand over her cheek, tugging her closer. She settled against him, and he could feel the patter of her heartbeat against his chest. It was like her entire body trembled with the force of it.

He'd regret this—he always did—but he couldn't quite keep himself from dipping his head down and catching her lips with his. She crumpled his shirt into her fingers as he kissed her. His mouth moved over hers as he nudged her closer and closer to parting those lips again so he could deepen the kiss. She didn't seem to quite understand what he was pushing for, and that made him feel just a little more tender toward her.

She'd pulled away by this point last time, but she wasn't pulling back this time. Jeb slid his hand down her side, feeling the gentle give of her figure under his touch. Then his hand finally settled on the small of her back.

He broke off the kiss, his breath ragged. Leah's eyes fluttered open and she looked up at him blearily. He hadn't ever left a woman looking quite this mussed before. Her lips were plumped from his kiss, and somehow in the course of kissing her, he'd loosened more of her hair around her face. He'd been married before, but a moment just like this . . . it was a first for him, too. He let his fingers trail down her cheeks, down her neck, and stop at the barrier of her dress along her collarbone.

"Is this okay?" he murmured.

"Yah . . ." A smile tugged at the corners of her lips.

"Can I . . . kiss you again?" His gaze dropped down to her mouth once more, and his heart hammered in his head. All he wanted was to taste those lips. She didn't answer, but she reached up and caught his shirt in a handful at his chest and tugged on it.

He'd take that as a yes. He wrapped his arms around her, and this time he lifted her up toward his lips, covering them as a wave of desire crashed over him. She fit into his arms perfectly, and with his emotions coursing through his veins like this, the tug of his sore arm and leg were like a dull rhythm in the background of his mind. He could deal with that—all he wanted was to hold her closer.

He pulled back, tugged her *kapp* free—it was only hanging by one pin now anyway—and tossed it toward the table, not even seeing where it fell. He loosened the last of her hair, letting it cascade down around her shoulders, and he pushed his fingers into the warm, fragrant depths of it.

Leah lifted her lips toward his, and he let out a moan as he kissed her again. She didn't know how she was firing him up—he could almost guarantee that. But then he felt her push up against him, and the last of his logical thoughts crashed down around him. He wanted her—all of her. He longed to get closer to her . . . to feel her soft skin against his fingers . . .

It would make things so much easier if they could just do what other married couples did and move upstairs to the smooth expanse of a bed.

"Leah—" He pulled back, his voice husky and low. "We are married, you know."

She nodded. "Yah."

"We could—" He swallowed, licked his lips. "We could just go on upstairs—it might make this easier."

This—he wasn't willing to say it out loud. He knew what he was asking for, and she did, too. Was this fool-hardy? He wouldn't blame her if she said no, but there was something glittering in her eyes. She nodded.

"Okay . . ." she breathed.

Was that a yes? He looked down at her, and color infused her cheeks. He wanted this—more than anything else, he wanted to carry her up those stairs and make love to her for hours in the quiet privacy of his bedroom. He wanted to hold her the way he'd dreamed of holding her . . .

But it would change things for him. It would open parts of his heart that he'd been trying to hold shut. It would make him want things he hadn't been asking for yet—intimacy, growing closer, opening up . . . a shared bedroom.

He wanted to just scoop her up in his arms and carry her up those stairs without giving it another thought, but he knew himself too well.

"I have to ask just one thing first," he said softly.

She looked up at him, mute.

"Are you happy like this?" he asked quietly. "With me. Alone on this farm. Just us—" He swallowed. "Are you happy like this?"

Leah pulled away from him ever so slightly, and he loosened his hold on her.

"I—" She frowned slightly. "I'm still hoping that you'll join our community again, and I can help you to—" She stopped speaking when she saw his face.

"So you aren't," he clarified.

"Jeb, I can't just live alone without people in my life," she said pleadingly. "I know it's hard for you, but I need more than this. That doesn't mean I'm not pleased with you, but—"

And those were the words he needed to hear to get his logical mind back in control of himself again. He dropped his hands, and a nearly crushing wave of disappointment flowed over him.

"No, I get it. I just had to ask."

"There is more to life than a husband, Jeb," she said. "And more than a wife. I'm not enough for you either. I know it. You'll find out."

And maybe she was right about that. And maybe she

was wrong. He'd been on his own for so long with only his uncle as company that he was used to the dull loneliness that sometimes came over him. But she wasn't.

"Maybe we shouldn't go upstairs," he said quietly. "It's a big step, you know—" He tried to hide the rising sadness in his voice. "I think it's best if we wait."

Leah nodded, red flaming across her cheeks. He'd embarrassed her—led her on and then pulled back. And that hadn't been his intention.

"Leah, my last wife slept with me from time to time—but she wasn't happy," he tried to explain. "Women might think that the act is enough, but it isn't. It gutted me—that combination of physical expression and deep resentment. Yah, I've got desires and needs, but there is no rush for this step between us. We can take our time."

"You don't want to," she whispered.

Is that what she really thought—that he didn't want this? He wanted it so badly that it nearly choked him. That was the problem.

"Oh, Leah," he said, his voice lowering to a growl. "I want you, every inch of you, and I want things that would very likely scandalize a good woman like you . . . but I only want it when you're sure that you're happy with me. That I'm enough. Just as I am. Let's wait . . ."

Leah stepped back, and her hands went up to her loosened hair. She ran her fingers through it, pulling it away from her face again.

"I should go up," she said, her voice shaking.

"Leah—"

"No, it's okay," she said quickly. "I understand."

She turned for the stairs, and it was like his heart tugged out of his chest to follow her. If that was how he felt now, what about after making love to her? What about then?

Leah's footsteps padded softly up the stairs, and he heaved a sigh, shutting his eyes. Had that been the smart choice or the stupid one? He wasn't even sure. If he'd just kept his mouth shut, he could have her in his bed right now.

Jeb bent down and picked up her white *kapp*; it had fallen on the floor next to the table. The fabric was neatly starched, and he ran it through his fingers. Yah, he wanted her—so much that he was aching for her right now. But he also knew what heartbreak felt like . . . and it started with this kind of longing.

Chapter Seventeen

Leah lay in her bed a long time that night, her mind spinning. What had just happened down there? And would she really have gone upstairs with him? Would she have thrown all her caution out with the potato peels and gone to bed with her husband?

The truth was, in the moment when her body longed for more, with his lips on hers and his muscular arms holding her so gently, she would have. She wanted it. She wanted it now! And lying in her bed, alone on those cool white sheets, hot tears began to flow.

Maybe she was lonely, too. Jeb was very much alone in his secluded life, but so was she . . . and to be held in her husband's arms, to be kissed like that, to be desired like that—yah, she'd have gone to his bed . . . if he hadn't changed his mind.

She lay there in the darkness, her tears soaking into her pillow, until she finally fell into a heavy sleep.

Breakfast the next morning was hurried and somewhat awkward. Jeb looked like he wanted to talk, but Leah wasn't interested. Whatever he had to say would only explain why he'd pulled away—and she knew why. Nothing had changed, and there was nothing else to say about the matter.

"Leah, I'm sorry," he said before he left for chores that morning. "I am. Deeply."

"There's nothing to be sorry for," she said quietly. "We should have known better."

She should have known better.

"I'll see you later on, then—" He paused, looking like he wanted to say something else, then pressed his lips together and headed out the door.

Expecting Jeb to be an ordinary Amish husband had been a mistake on her part, and as she turned back to her work in the kitchen, the letter from the school board crinkled in her apron pocket.

There was a place where she was wanted, where she could contribute with her head held high. Rimstone was asking her to come back, and it was looking more and more appealing.

An hour later, when Leah had just finished mopping the kitchen floor, Jeb's boots came clunking up the steps, and the side door opened. Leah wrung out the mop and wiped her hands on a cloth. Jeb came inside, but he stopped at the edge of the clean floor.

"Have you seen your brother?" Jeb asked. "He didn't show up to help me today."

Leah blinked at him. "He didn't?"

Jeb shrugged. "I've got to get back to work, but . . . he's not here."

"I'll see if I can find him," she replied.

Jeb was silent for a moment.

"Are we okay, Leah?" he asked.

"Yah, of course," she said, and forced a smile.

"Do we need to talk?" he asked. "Have I messed this up too badly?"

No—the last thing they needed was to rehash all of that again.

"It's fine, Jeb," she said. "You go back to work, and I'll try to sort out my brother."

Jeb retreated again and the door shut after him, leaving Leah alone in the kitchen. If Simon wasn't at work, he was either sulking because of yesterday's drama or it was something much worse.

So Leah left her mop leaning in the corner and headed for the door. Simon needed some sense to be drilled into him, and right now, she was the only one who cared enough to do it.

The day was overcast, so much cooler than it had been the last week. A stiff breeze promised rain, and Leah watched the tops of the trees thrash about in the wind as she walked briskly toward the cottage.

Simon was the one who needed her right now, but her mind wouldn't stay on her younger brother. She was still thinking the same thoughts that had been overrunning her head all morning—what it had felt like to be in Jeb's strong arms.

Strange how in this short time of marriage she'd started to see the older, scarred man so differently. He'd gone from intimidating to . . . how did she feel about him? She found herself remembering his touch when he wasn't around, thinking about just how it felt to be pulled against him. She'd started to wonder when he might do it again. . . . He wasn't frightening anymore. She understood him better— the community that meant so much to her was the one that had crushed him. And she could accept that dichotomy because she truly believed he could come back again. It just might take time.

It wasn't the logic that filled her mind anymore, but the memory of his touch, the longing to feel his lips on hers again. The curiosity about what it might be like to share her husband's bed . . . This was the very thing they'd meant to avoid, because he'd been right—she wanted more than a man in her bed. She wanted him to join her in the community. The closer they got physically, the more she wanted in other parts of their relationship.

Suddenly, the Amish advice to young people to sort out every other aspect of their relationship before marriage and deal with the physical parts after the vows made a lot more sense. Passion didn't fix the other problems, it only magnified them.

When Leah reached the cottage, a spattering of warm rain had started to fall, the scent of moist, rich earth rising up around her. She put her hand over her *kapp* to keep it from blowing in the wind, and she hurried toward the front door. There was a buggy parked under the stable awning, the horse still hitched up and waiting. A crack of lightning lit up the sky, and she ducked her head and rapped twice on the door, then let herself in.

The clouds opened up as she stepped inside and rain pummeled down. She swung the door shut behind her and looked up to see her brother standing in the kitchen, but as she suspected, he wasn't alone. Standing next to him, his arms crossed over his chest and an irritated look on his face was Matthew Schrock. Leah blinked, then smiled hesitantly.

"Sorry to just let myself in like that, but the rain . . ." she said.

"It's fine," Simon muttered.

"Hello, Matthew," she said, and she glanced between the two men. She'd definitely interrupted something, and she'd gladly retrace her steps right back out the door if it weren't for the current deluge.

"It's just as well your sister is here," Matthew said, turning to Simon. "I'm sure she'll agree with me on this anyway."

"Let it go," Simon snapped.

"No, I'm not going to do that!" Matthew retorted. "Leah, I came to talk to him man-to-man about his gambling. It's not like he's listening to me anyway."

Leah smiled weakly. "I came to discuss the same thing."

"The both of you can leave me alone," Simon snapped. "Am I gambling right now?"

"You were yesterday," Matthew said, then glanced over at Leah. "Someone saw Jeb haul him out of the pool hall, and word flew around town."

Leah sighed and rubbed her hands over her face. "The thing is, Simon, we *can't* bail you out again. We don't have that kind of money."

"What do you know? You're barely married!" Simon shot back.

"I'm well and truly married," Leah said.

"Are you?" Simon shot her an irritated look. "Because there have been some rumors around town about that, too."

Leah's heart skipped a beat, and she felt the blood rush from her face. What exactly did he mean by that? And he'd heard this *around town*?

Leah glanced over at Matthew, and his face colored. He dropped his gaze. "Leah's marital problems aren't our business, Simon."

"Marital problems?" she breathed.

"Leah, don't you come here and start telling me how to live," Simon said. "We're both grown, and I'm not telling you how to live your life."

"Seriously? I don't have any marital problems!" she burst out.

Simon looked away, and suddenly, he wasn't the grown man anymore, he was the boy—embarrassed, upset, out of her reach.

"Of course," Matthew said quickly. "And while this really is not my place to talk to you about, I could suggest that you speak with the bishop's wife, perhaps, or an elder's wife. A new marriage isn't always easy, especially when the husband and wife don't know each other well—"

Anger bubbled up inside her. To be lectured about marital issues by her ex-fiancé was almost unbearable.

"Please, stop talking," Leah said, her voice strangled.

Matthew fell silent, and Leah swallowed. How much did people know? How far had these rumors gone? The worst part was that they were entirely truth. This wasn't some painful exaggeration—she and her husband were sleeping in separate bedrooms, and so far, they had not consummated their relationship. If they stuck to their original plan, they never would.

"The bishop's wife has spoken with other young women," Matthew said. "And after I say this, I won't ever bring it up again. But she talked to Rebecca, too. Rebecca didn't want a baby right away because we didn't know each other terribly well, and—"

"That obviously worked well," Leah said bitterly. Their issues were very different.

"I'm just saying," Matthew said. "It might help. She's been married a long time, and she's counseled many newly married women."

Apparently, Matthew had some interest in counseling newly married women as well, but Leah clenched her teeth.

"I thought we were here to discuss my brother's problem?" she said.

Matthew nodded. "The thing is, I have an idea of something that might help—something the bishop agreed would be a good solution."

"Fine. What is it?" Simon asked.

"The Englishers have a group that meets to help people trying to get over gambling addictions. Several Amish men in our community have gone, the bishop says, but he won't name names, obviously. The point is, it's effective. It worked for them, and it can work for you."

"An Englisher group," Simon said bitterly.

But it wasn't a terrible idea. Leah didn't know what else they could do for her brother, short of asking the community to donate to bail him out of his future debts, and that was a ridiculous request. Simon needed more than punishment if a severe beating wasn't enough to keep him away from those vile card games. He needed help—more than his sister could provide. And for the first time in the last year, she was grateful for Matthew's interference.

"Simon, this is serious," Leah said quietly. "I'm afraid for you."

"I'm fine. I'm actually good at cards," Simon said.

"Not really," Matthew replied. "Besides, it's a game of chance, isn't it? It doesn't rely on your skill so much as the hand you're dealt. You've gone too deep, Simon. I'm taking the risk of losing my friendship with you because I'm scared for you. Those men are violent. Next time they might break a bone, or you might find yourself stabbed. They're Englishers, Simon!"

Leah exchanged a look with Matthew, and she realized that he did look older with the married beard. He sounded older now, too. A year had changed a great deal.

Simon sank into a kitchen chair and slowly shook his head. "You said it worked for other Amish?"

Did the mental image of his potential injuries mean more coming from Matthew? Was it that Matthew was a man and Leah wasn't? Or was it just that Simon simply tuned her out? Was her effectiveness here at home over now?

"The bishop says it worked. So, you'll go, then?" Matthew pressed. "Because I'll drive you there myself. And I'll pick you up. The meeting itself is private, I understand, but—"

"Yah," Simon said. "Okay, then."

Leah looked out the window. The spontaneous shower had let up, and the trees were dripping, but the rain was back down to a drizzle. A few rays of sunlight punched through the clouds, illuminating a stretch of rainbow through the haze.

Their community was going to be a help to Simon, and even Matthew, for all his faults, was turning out to be a solid friend to her brother. Maybe these meetings would help him—give him some perspective, perhaps, or give him the answers he needed to keep him away from those card games.

But for her? For the first time, Leah realized, this community that had cradled her since babyhood was no longer her answer. They knew too much—they knew the worst. Her marriage would no longer bring her the respect she longed for, because they'd see a woman with a problematic union. They'd all know that she went home to her own bedroom, and they'd be whispering behind her back. Apparently, they already were if Matthew knew about it and the bishop's wife was being suggested.

Was that why Matthew had been in such a rush to come tell her about her brother? Was Jeb right that he'd come to check on her?

As Leah looked out the window at the misty rainbow that formed across the gray sky, she slipped her hand into her apron pocket and touched the letter she'd received from the school board. Rimstone was the one place that didn't know the worst—the town that respected her for what she contributed, the *kinner* she taught.

"Simon," Leah said, "Jeb has given you this job to work on his farm, and I'd appreciate it if you didn't take advantage of his kindness. Either go back to work with him this morning and make up the lost hours or I will ask him to hire someone else."

Simon looked over at her, and she could see the blatant shock on his face.

"Is this coming from Jeb?" her brother asked.

"This is coming from me," she replied. "If he doesn't

tell me about your surprising new dedication to your job by dinnertime, you won't need to bother coming in to work tomorrow."

Simon compressed his lips, the old, defiant look in his eye back again. Would he do as she said? Or would she be forced to follow through? Regardless, it was time Simon got serious about something, and a job wasn't a bad place to start. The Amish worked hard—it was what kept them close to home and close to the land. Simon needed more labor in his life, not less.

"I'm going home," she said, turning toward the door. "Nice to see you, Matthew."

And as she pulled the door open, she realized she didn't have the desire to look over her shoulder again. Whatever she'd been feeling for Matthew was gone.

And whatever Simon had ahead of him, he'd better start facing it like a man, because Leah had done him no favors these last years. He was now in the arms of the Amish community.

Jeb stood at the back door of the horse barn, a stick in his hand as he whittled away at it, a braid slowly forming in the wood. It was a simple technique Menno had taught him years ago when they'd shared a bedroom. Funny, the things that comforted. Whittling helped him to focus his thoughts.

He still wasn't sure if he'd done the right thing last night with Leah. This morning was awkward enough between them. It didn't feel like any of his options were the right choice. If he took his wife to bed, they'd start expecting things from each other that hadn't been part of their original arrangement, and he knew what disappointing a woman felt like. And having chosen not to take that step yet, he'd embarrassed her. That was plain as day, and he felt like a fool for having done so.

A small curl of wood followed his knife as he traced around the shape of the braid. Little by little—that was the secret to whittling. A man couldn't rush. The piece was done when it was done. And yet taking his time with Leah felt . . . not exactly wrong, but not right either. He was messing this up with Leah—he could feel that much.

If Peter were here, they'd talk it out. Peter had insight into people, into what made them tick. He'd come home with gossip about the community, and it was never the mean-spirited kind. Peter didn't just repeat tales. He always sympathized.

A man is never as strong as he wants to be. Peter had said that over and over again. And he was right. Jeb wasn't as strong as he wanted to be either.

What would Peter say about Leah? What would he say about Jeb's fear of stumbling again into the resentment and anger of his first marriage?

Peter would have had a word of wisdom . . . but he was gone, and his wisdom was gone with him.

How do I fix this, God? Or was this marriage unblessed from the start?

The front door to the stable opened, and Jeb turned to see Simon coming in.

"I thought you were sick or something," Jeb said.

"I'm—um—feeling better," Simon said. "I'll work longer hours today to make up for this morning. I'm sorry about that. If you'll let me know what you want me to do, I'll get to it."

Jeb raised an eyebrow. He hadn't expected that, and when Simon came closer, he squinted at the younger man.

"What's going on?" Jeb asked.

"Nothing," Simon said. "I just want to work, is all."

Something had changed. Jeb nodded. "Fine. You can

start by watering the cattle in the west pasture. I was going to head out there next."

Simon didn't move, though. He met Jeb's gaze uneasily. "My sister is going to suggest you fire me."

"You think?" Jeb asked.

"She might. Man-to-man, I want you to know that I'm willing to work. I won't mess this up again. I'm going to attend some meetings—these Englisher meetings for men who gamble. It's supposed to help."

"That sounds like a start," Jeb said.

"I didn't think it was possible to get to the end of my sister's patience, but I have. She's got a big heart, she's got integrity without bounds, but she has her limits." Simon gave him a meaningful nod. "For what that's worth."

"All right." What else was he supposed to say to that? But he saw something in Simon's face that softened him just a little. It was the frustrated look of a young man who'd just seen how hard life could be.

"She'll forgive you, Simon," Jeb said.

"It's not always about forgiveness," Simon replied. "I've got to change my ways, Jeb. I've got to be better."

Funny—standing here in the stable with a newly humbled young man in front of him, Peter seemed closer than he'd felt ever since his death. This was what Peter had been to him—an older man who had seen more life than he had. And yet Peter hadn't demanded that he change. He'd just worked alongside him, and listened when he talked, given advice when he could.

"You know what," Jeb said. "I'll go with you to water the cattle. It won't take as long with two of us."

Simon paused, then nodded. "All right, then."

Jeb would help his wife with Simon. The young man needed guidance, and distraction. Maybe the answer wasn't in sending Simon off to do the work on his own, but in going with him to do the work shoulder to shoulder.

For Jeb, any healing he'd experienced hadn't come through the broader Amish community, but through the steady companionship of one good man.

Funny, how after all these years of diligently keeping to himself, he was considering this amendment to his ways. But Leah couldn't shoulder this burden by herself much longer. It was a husband's job to carry the firewood, to do the heavy labor that was too much for a woman . . . It was Jeb's job to make her life a little easier.

He had a feeling that Uncle Peter would approve.

Chapter Eighteen

Leah watched out the kitchen window as Jeb and Simon drove the farm wagon down the muddy gravel road, the horses plodding along in that unflappable way that workhorses had. The wheels bumped into a water-filled pothole and the wagon clattered with the jolt.

So, Simon had decided to work.

She watched the wagon as it continued on, Simon sitting next to Jeb on the seat, Jeb taller and broader. Simon's hat was a little bit crooked, but they looked like regular Amish men in their white shirts and suspenders. *Her family*.

This was what she'd prayed for, wasn't it? And she had it—a husband of her own, a man who belonged to her.

And yet it wasn't real, was it? Because while Jeb was her husband, they weren't truly husband and wife—not in the way she'd prayed for at least. On the outside, God had answered her prayer. In her heart, she ached with loneliness.

Leah went down the hallway and opened the door at the end—the laundry room. A wringer washer stood along one wall, and there was a bank of cupboards topped with a length of counter. The room was bright—no curtains on this window—and outside, it looked like it might rain again. Leah would do the washing, but she'd hang their clothes indoors to dry. She could transfer them outside later if it cleared up.

She pulled some clothes from the hamper—two of her own dresses and some of Jeb's shirts. His clothes were so much larger than Simon's, and as she shook out Jeb's shirt that still smelled like him—hard work and hay— there was a faint knock. Leah paused, listening. There was another knock—louder this time. Someone was at the front door, it sounded like. Friends and family always used the side door, so her curiosity was piqued. She hung the clothes on the side of the wringer washer and headed toward the front door.

When she opened it, she was faced with a gray-bearded elder—she knew him well enough—and his wife. They were Methuselah and Trinity Beiler, and they smiled cordially. Trinity, who was about ten years younger than her husband, had some considerable gray in her hair, too. She held a basket in front of her.

"We've come to say hello," Trinity said. "And I've brought some baking."

"That is so kind," Leah said, stepping back to let them in. "Thank you so much."

"Well, I know how busy it is as a new wife, and I wanted to take some of the burden off you for today."

Trinity and Methuselah came inside, and Leah gestured toward the sitting room.

"Please, sit down. I'll get some tea started. My husband is doing chores, but if he sees your buggy, I'm sure he'll come inside."

Actually she wasn't sure of that at all, but it was the wifely thing to say, and she couldn't imagine that they'd come to see her exclusively. Likely, they were here to be kind to her husband and start a process of drawing him back into the community.

Methuselah went into the sitting room as he was bid,

and he sat down in the one high-backed chair, looking around himself slowly. A Bible sat on the table next to him, and he nodded at it approvingly.

"Actually, dear," Trinity said. "If we could just talk first . . . while you're alone."

"Oh . . ."

Trinity put the basket of baked goods aside on one end of the couch and then sat down, patting the seat next to her.

This was no ordinary visit, then . . . and there were a few things they might have heard from the community grapevine. Her brother, most likely.

"What's happening?" Leah asked, but her heart was already hammering in her chest. "This is about Simon, isn't it? I know he's been in trouble, but he really does seem to be making a good step forward. Matthew Schrock—"

"It's not about Simon," Methuselah said, his voice a quiet, reassuring rumble. "Although we have heard of his struggles. We're more concerned about how you are today."

"Me?" Leah glanced over at Trinity, looking for some clue about what this was about, but the older woman appeared calm and collected.

"You are newly married," Trinity said quietly.

Was this about their sleeping arrangements, then? She felt the color bleed from her face and the room spun for a moment.

"Dear—" Trinity reached out and took her hand.

"Normally a young woman will spend at least the first few months of marriage in her parents' house," Methuselah said. "There is wisdom in that—it sets an expectation of how the young wife will be treated under her parents' supervision. But your parents are gone, and we as your community have a responsibility toward you."

"Oh . . ." Leah looked between them. They were right—things would be very different if her *mamm* and *daet* were still alive. She wouldn't be quite so alone in any of it, and the kindly older faces made grateful tears rise in her eyes.

"I have been missing my *mamm* and *daet*," she said.

"As you would," Trinity said with a kindly smile. "Now, please feel free to be as open and honest with us as you would be with your own *mamm* and *daet*. No one wanted to stand between you and a chance at marriage, but we do want to make sure that you're—" Trinity glanced toward her husband. "—safe."

"Safe?" Leah frowned. "Yah. I'm fine."

"Your husband was married before," Methuselah said. "And his first wife found a home with him to be quite unbearable. Now, people change. They grow. And fifteen years is a long time, but we wanted to make sure that you aren't in a similar situation. We wouldn't forgive ourselves if that happened a second time."

A little late now that she'd married him, she thought bitterly. Was she considered so far past hope at thirty that a marriage to a monster wasn't half bad? But that wasn't her only concern here.

"My husband is a kind man," Leah said. "We're adjusting to married life. That takes time. But he is considerate, a hard worker, grateful for what I contribute to our home."

"Has there been any suggestion of violence?" Methuselah asked quietly.

"Violence?" Leah started to smile, then stopped. "Why would you ask that?"

"We have to check."

"Do you check on this with every newly married couple?" she asked. "Who has suggested that Jeb is violent?"

Methuselah pressed his hands together. "I don't mean to suggest anything, Leah. But I feel I owe your father some caution on your behalf. When you were a teenager, your husband was married to a vibrant young woman. She tragically died in a fire. I'm sure you remember. And while there was no reason to suspect that the fire was anything but an accident, now that he is married again, we need to make sure we are vigilant on your behalf. Katie didn't flourish in her marriage with Jeb. It was very likely a terrible mistake from the very beginning, but—"

"She didn't flourish?" Leah shook her head. "So, everyone thinks that Jeb is the reason for the unhappiness there? Katie was in love with an Englisher—you know that, don't you?"

"Marriage changes these things," Trinity said, shaking her head in dismissal. "Many a young woman has been in love with another, and a sensible marriage has set her straight."

"It didn't," Leah retorted. "Apparently, she really loved him."

"Even you had a special friendship with another man before your marriage," Trinity said delicately.

"We were engaged actually," Leah said tightly. "And you're right—time moves on. We're both married to other people. But it wasn't like that with Katie."

"You were rather young at the time—" Methuselah began. "And sometimes the version of the story can change over a few years."

"This isn't about the version of the story told about a dead woman," Leah said, leaning forward. "You seem to think my husband is abusive and cruel—yet you didn't bring this up before our wedding! Do you really think that of him? He's been nothing but considerate to me. He's kind. He works hard. He's been very, very kind to my brother, too. He's not the monster you seem to think."

"Monster is a strong word," the older man said slowly. "And all I want is to make sure that you're okay. That's all."

"I'm fine!" Leah capped her rising voice. This was an older man, an elder. She owed him her respect and she should be grateful that he was trying to do what her own *daet* couldn't, but she couldn't let them go on believing these things about her husband either. "Jeb has been pushed out of this community. I know that everyone thinks he just hid himself away—even I thought that. But it isn't true. It's rumors like these that keep him away."

"At your age, you can choose for yourself who you marry," Trinity said, her voice firming ever so slightly. "But you can't blame the community for Jeb King's oddities. Is this how you want to live?"

"Do I want a normal life, you mean?" Leah asked. "Of course I do! I want to be able to go to social events with my husband. I want to have guests come visit! I want something normal!"

And it was the community that stood in the way of that happening. Jeb had said that there were times that a person couldn't change another's view of him. And this was what he meant—rumors that dogged a person for over a decade.

"And you don't have that . . ." Trinity said quietly. "Is he refusing to allow you—"

"No!" Leah shook her head. "You are so certain that he's a particular way that you aren't listening to me!"

She saw the warning look that crossed Methuselah's face, and if she wasn't so infuriated right now, she would heed that silent warning. Instead, she plunged on. "Katie was in love with an Englisher, and that never changed. Her relationship with that Englisher didn't stop either. She wasn't being faithful to Jeb, and she was leaving him. She was going English. He didn't find out about that until after her death."

"How did he find out?" Methuselah asked, frowning.

"There was a letter she left. She was in that barn that night to meet up with her Englisher boyfriend. I don't know what became of him, but in that letter, she was telling Jeb she was leaving him."

"A convenient story," Methuselah murmured.

"I found the letter!" she insisted.

"Can I see it?" the older man asked.

"Jeb has it now," Leah said. "And even if he didn't, he'd be angry if—" She stopped. She was making him sound like that monster again, being afraid of his anger. But it wasn't fear. It was respect for his privacy. But she could see the older man's eyebrows furrow.

"Jeb only found that letter after he got home from his stay at the hospital," Leah said. "And he was glad he didn't know. He went into that fire to save his wife, and he didn't hesitate. My husband is a good man, but his own community has been treating him like a secret criminal. He was the one who was wronged in that marriage, not Katie!"

"I see . . ." Methuselah said quietly.

"You came here because you wanted to help me. Well, Jeb isn't the problem. If you want to help me have a proper Amish life, then you'll help to make a place for my husband in our community again," Leah said, her voice choking with emotion. "He's been pushed out. How do you expect him to come back? How?"

"You've given us much to think about," Methuselah said. "I'll bring this to the bishop."

Leah's stomach clenched. Already Jeb's secrets were moving outside of this home. She'd said more than he'd have liked—she knew that very well—but someone had to defend him. Katie's memory had locked her into some sort of angelic state for the community. And she was dead— no one wanted to speak ill of her. It was easier to chastise the living.

Methuselah rose to his feet and his wife followed his

lead. He walked to the door with the slow gate of a man with authority.

"Leah . . ." Trinity caught Leah's sleeve and leaned in close, her voice low. "I have heard about your own bedroom, and I know there will be pressure to change that. But you don't have to. You're being cautious, and I can understand it. I want you to remember that while ideally a husband and wife should never refuse each other, it isn't a sin for a wife to say no if she has a good reason. You are allowed to say no. Do you understand that?"

Trinity looked earnestly into Leah's face, and she felt her cheeks flood with shame.

They knew. Everyone knew.

"Yah . . ." she said weakly.

"Good. I hope we'll see you at service on Sunday." Trinity went to the door, where her husband waited.

"Goodbye," Methuselah said with a nod. "Tell your husband we gave our regards."

Their regards—loaded with their judgment. Leah forced a smile and nodded.

"Good day to you," she said.

As the door shut behind them, Leah put her hand over her mouth and squeezed her eyes shut. She'd said far too much. And maybe shouldn't have . . . But if she didn't, nothing would change, and the community's judgment would continue. Someone had to stand up for Jeb. Someone had to make them see what they'd been doing to him.

Maybe this would only make things worse . . . but there was also the chance that it might make things better, and they'd finally stop whispering behind Jeb's back, making him out to be some sort of monster that he wasn't. Because she had been serious in her request—and she did hope they would come to her aid. If they really wanted to help her, they needed to make it possible for her husband to come back.

Jeb pushed back his chair. Simon was still mopping gravy from his plate with a dinner roll—the fresh-baked bread being the gift of an elder and his wife who had stopped by, apparently. Leah hadn't eaten much, and she stood up to start clearing the table.

"You okay?" Jeb asked.

"Yah. Not hungry," she replied with a wan smile.

Simon's gaze popped up and he stopped chewing for a moment, then continued. So, Simon saw it, too. Something was up, and as her husband, he'd have to figure it out.

"Tomorrow morning we're going to head out to the east pasture to check for calves," Jeb said. "So we'll want to get moving early."

"I'll meet you at the cow barn fifteen minutes early, if that works," Simon said.

"Perfect."

Simon's attitude had improved drastically. Working with him instead of sending him off on jobs seemed to be relaxing the young man, and they'd chatted a bit while they worked today. Simon had his eye on a young lady, it would seem. But he had a lot of work to do to clear up his reputation before she'd ever let him drive her home from singing.

Simon rose from the table. "I'll see you then."

Jeb gave him a nod, and Leah turned and smiled at her brother before he headed out the side door. Then Leah rose to her feet and began to clear the table, but her hand shook as she lifted a dish.

"You should eat," Jeb said quietly.

Leah paused with a serving dish in her hands, her dark gaze landing on him somberly.

"I'm going to have to tell you something, and you're not going to like it," she said, putting the dish back down on the table. Then she folded her hand in front of her in a tight grip. "But I have to explain myself first."

"Okay . . ." Jeb eyed her uncertainly. "Explain what?"

"The elder—Methuselah. He and his wife, Trinity, weren't just here to congratulate us on our wedding."

"Why were they here?" he asked, and he heard the wariness in his voice.

"They were worried about me," she said. "I told them that you're a kind husband, and that I have no complaints, but apparently news has gotten out about our sleeping arrangements, and—"

"What?" Jeb's expression darkened. "*That* got out?"

"I don't know who would have said anything, besides your sister," she said. "Because I haven't breathed a word, and I know you wouldn't have. But Matthew knew about it—I saw him at my brother's place . . . It isn't a secret anymore."

"So, people are discussing our sleeping arrangements?" he asked hollowly. "The elders are discussing it?"

"Yah." She felt the pain of that fact, too. "It would seem."

"I'll be speaking to Lynita, trust me," he muttered. Because he couldn't see who else might have leaked that information either. But Lynita? She, of all people, knew how private that was. To use it as idle gossip . . .

"That's not the worst of it, Jeb. . . ."

"There's more?" His stomach sank. It was hard to think of anything worse than their privacy being a topic of common gossip.

Leah folded her hands in front of her in a white-knuckled grip. "Methuselah was concerned that I didn't know about Katie, and that perhaps there was some mean tendency in you that they'd missed in your first marriage." Her voice trembled. "And I know how insulting that is, even repeating it. And I was angry on your behalf. I didn't want them speaking about you like that. And I told them they were wrong, that you weren't some monster who'd terrorized his young wife. She was the one—" She sucked in a breath, and her words faltered. "—who was leaving you."

Jeb stared at her, his heart hammering in his ears. She'd told them his personal business? She'd told them the secret he'd been keeping all these years and entrusted to her as the only person living he could trust with it . . . She'd told them?

"They won't believe you," he said woodenly.

"They didn't," she agreed. "So, I . . . Jeb, you have to know that I only wanted to protect you! It wasn't fair! Fifteen years of rumors and assumptions, and no one knowing what was really going on!"

"What did you do?" he asked hesitantly. It was better to know it all.

"I told them about the letter," she said weakly.

His heart thudded to a stop and he stared at her. She'd revealed his letter? It was no longer in the drawer; it was now upstairs in his bedroom. So, she wouldn't have shown it to them, would she?

"That won't fix things," he said. "They won't believe I found it too late. It will only fuel their suspicions."

"Then why dive into that fire after her?" Leah demanded. "Jeb, *I* believe you! And if I do, others will, too!"

Jeb shook his head bitterly. "You have great faith in these people. I know them a little better."

"They're taking the information I gave them to the bishop."

"Yah, that's no surprise," he muttered. "Is that all? Or is there more?"

"That's all."

Silence stretched between them, welling up like rising water, sucking the air from the room. So, people knew . . . everything. He felt like the very walls were closing in on him, and he shook his head, trying to clear his thoughts. He'd told her how important his privacy was, and he'd trusted her more than he'd trusted anyone else . . .

"Why would you do that?" he asked at last. "You knew how I felt about keeping my life private—"

"Because I can see what they did to you!" Leah sank back into her chair and looked up into his face pleadingly. "They were in the wrong, not you! And Katie wasn't the innocent dove they all assumed she was. They messed up, and afterward they let everyone blame you!"

"Yah. I'm clear on what they did," he breathed. But they'd never own up to it, and there was nothing more dangerous than people protecting a popular lie.

"They pushed you out," she said. "They made it impossible for you to come back. And what is life without your community? You did what your community told you was right in marrying her, and then they abandoned you! I told them because—" she dashed a tear from her cheek—"you can't come back and be part of the community until *they* fix it. It's not on you."

And then it all fell together in his mind, tumbling into place. He could see it now, clear as day—why she'd talked to them, why she'd spilled his secrets.

"And that's your goal," he said quietly. "That's what you're trying to make happen—to get me back into the community."

Leah paused, then nodded. "Of course! I understand exactly why you're angry. I know why you don't trust them. But if they could see what they've done . . ."

She went on, but he'd stopped listening. It was her goal to get him back into the bosom of their Amish community.

But he wasn't coming back. What part of this didn't she understand? He wasn't some lost lamb waiting for rescue. He'd been through hell and back again, and he'd never be a well-meaning Amish fellow who believed the best of his brethren again. Those days were gone, and he was now a hardened, wiser version of himself.

"I'm not some broken man waiting to be fixed," he said, cutting her off. "I know who I am! Why can't you respect that?"

Leah put her hands on her hips, meeting his gaze with glittering intensity of her own. "I do respect it, and I see that they're the ones who are wrong. This is bigger than one man's experience, Jeb. This effects everyone!"

"And do you see that I will *never* open myself up to them again?" he barked. "Do you see *that*?"

Leah blinked up at him, and he felt a wave of remorse. She'd just been told what a monster he was by the people she respected, and here he was bellowing at her.

"I'm sorry if I scared you—" he started, lowering his voice.

"You don't scare me!" she retorted, her own voice rising. "Maybe you did before, but not now. Did it ever occur to you that God might have brought us together for a reason?"

Did God do this? Did he bring people together, just to hold them apart? Did he use money to chase people into marriages of convenience?

"God didn't do this, Leah," he said quietly.

"God works in mysterious ways," she said, but he saw the tears mist her eyes. He'd hurt her with those words, and he hadn't meant it like that . . . But he highly doubted that God had put her in his arms to erase the last fifteen years. God had taken him through mountains and valleys, journeyed with him for years . . . just to flick him back to the beginning? What was the purpose of it all, if it just got erased?

"I didn't mean that the way it sounded," he said hesitantly.

"And how did you mean it?" she asked, her chin trembling.

"I meant . . . this is more complicated than that."

"You *need* our community."

"I don't need people I can't trust!"

"You need people, period! Before Peter died, you had him, didn't you?"

"And now I have you!" Jeb said, and as the words came out, he felt a flood of those confusing, overwhelming emotions he was starting to associate with her. "I thought I'd be alone. I didn't even think I'd have this farm at the end of the day. . . . I was okay with being by myself—because at least I knew who I could count on . . . but then you came along and we came up with this crazy plan to get me some land and your brother his money, and—" Jeb sucked in a breath. He wasn't even sure he should say everything he felt. "Leah, I have *you*."

Didn't she understand the depth of that? Did she feel what he felt? He didn't need a community full of do-gooders if he had a wife he could count on. She was the one he needed.

"I'm not enough," she breathed.

"You *are*." He caught her hand and tugged her closer. "You have no idea what you've brought to my life, Leah. I thought a marriage could be distant, but the vows change things between a man and a woman. And I find myself thinking about you when I'm not here. I find myself wondering what you think about things. I look forward to coming home to you, and not just because of your cooking. It's you. It's sharing a home with you, a life with you . . . I was lonelier than I knew before you, and having you here is like opening up shutters that have long been closed, and having sunlight come flooding in."

"I'm like sunlight?" she whispered.

"Exactly like sunlight . . ." Jeb touched her cheek and ran his thumb over her bottom lip. She didn't pull away, and when her gaze met his, he bent down and kissed her tenderly. When he pulled back, her eyes stayed closed for a beat longer, then they fluttered open.

"God knows how I tried to stick to our agreement, Leah," he murmured, meeting her gaze in agony. "And I can keep trying, if that's what you want, but . . . I love you."

Chapter Nineteen

Leah's breath caught in her throat, and she stared at Jeb in silence. She was still stuck on her worry about how angry he'd be . . . but he loved her? She opened her mouth to answer, then closed it again.

Her feelings for him had been growing, too. It was why she'd defended him so passionately. It was why she wanted him to rejoin the community so badly. . . .

"I think . . . I love you, too," she whispered. There really was no other way to explain how she felt for her husband. Her longing for his touch, her longing to help him . . . And somehow these tender feelings had been building.

"Yah?" He reached out and took her hand, tugging her off her chair as he rose to meet her. "Is that even possible?"

"It's why I tried to defend you, Jeb. . . . We weren't supposed to love each other, were we?"

Jeb bent down and lowered his lips over hers. His kiss was slow, tender, and she could feel his frustrated longing. She wanted to stay there . . . melt there . . . But then he pulled back again and rested his forehead against hers.

"I need to be enough," he breathed.

Leah pulled back, forcing him to meet her gaze. She knew what he wanted from her—to join him in this lonely life cut off from everyone else.

"A community and a husband are two different things," she whispered, begging him to understand.

"The thing is, I'm not going to change," Jeb said. "This is me. I'm stubborn and tough, I work hard, and I love deeply. But I can't go back to being the man I was before Katie. I can't. It doesn't work that way."

"I'm lonely," she whispered. "Jeb, I can't just live like you have. I need people. I need worship services, game nights, strawberry parties, and visitors! I need to attend weddings, and celebrate other women's babies, even if it hurts. I want to make quilts around a circle, help neighbors in need, play with *kinner*, and—" She cast about, looking for the words. "Happiness for me is shared."

"They know too much," Jeb said woodenly. "They'll only dig deeper, trying to figure out what's happening over here. That's the thing with a tight community. All is fine if you appear exactly like everyone else. They can accept that. But if you're different in any way, you won't be a part of things. No matter how much you want it. And there won't be any pregnancies to put their minds at ease. They'll talk about us behind our backs. They already are, and the elders have started coming. Do you think that will stop? Leah, I know what you want out of this community, but you won't get it."

"And I can't be happy without it." Her chin trembled, and she looked away. "Jeb, I'm not as tough as you. I'm Amish—and what are we without our community?"

"It won't happen here!" he said, his voice hardening. "I'm sorry! I wish I could tell you otherwise, that if you just attend enough weddings and quilting circles, they'll stop worrying about me. But that isn't going to happen!"

He stepped away from her and tossed his hat onto the table. Then he rubbed his hands over his face.

"Then you come to the weddings and the parties!" she pleaded. "This isn't impossible! If they can see you, get to know you again . . ."

"I'm doing my best with Simon," he said, his voice low. "I'm going against my instincts to keep to myself, and I'm taking him with me to work. I'm trying to be something to him. I'm trying, Leah. I thought that would mean something to you."

"It does!" she said. "But Jeb, is sitting on this farm alone good for him? He needs community now more than ever, too. It's the community that's going to help him get over this gambling problem. Not me. I'm not enough! And I'm not too proud to admit that. We all need people. We need leadership and friendship . . . we need this community, Jeb, even when we don't want to admit it!"

"Even when I don't want to admit it, you mean," he said.

Leah sighed. "I can't live alone, Jeb."

He dropped his gaze, and they stood there in silence, the only sound that of their breathing. How had this happened? They were supposed to avoid this. She'd known his ways when she agreed to this marriage, and he'd known what she needed, too. So how had they gotten to this point?

"We shouldn't have given in to those feelings," Jeb said quietly, and she realized he must have been thinking the same thing she was. "We knew this all along, and it wouldn't have been a problem if we'd just kept things—" He shrugged his broad shoulders, not finishing.

"Practical?" she supplied.

He met her gaze sadly. "I thought if I didn't take you to bed, I wouldn't fall in love with you."

"I'm sorry," she whispered. But it was the same for her. "We need to get our balance back."

"Yah." He nodded.

Leah reached into her apron pocket, and her fingers brushed against the letter from Rimstone. They couldn't make each other happy here, and they'd known that all along. Jeb had been right. They'd want more, they'd *long* for more . . . and they wouldn't be able to give it.

"I got a letter from the school board in Rimstone," she said, her voice choked. "They want me to come back . . . as early as possible."

"But you're married," he said.

"They don't know that," she said with a weak shrug. "And if they find out, all you need to do is give your permission for me to teach."

"You want to go?" he asked. "You want to leave?"

"I want to see those *kinner* again," she said, tears rising in her eyes. "And I want to be a respected part of a community. If I stay here, I'll be the wife who does it all wrong—I'll be a morality tale for the younger women, and I'll be talked about constantly. But if I go teach—"

She left the thought hanging. It was a lot to ask. There wouldn't be anyone to do the women's work around the house anymore. There would be no meal waiting for him on the table, and that thought nearly broke her heart.

"It wouldn't have to be for forever," he said, his voice tight. "We could do it for a year. Get our balance back."

Leah nodded. "And I'd send the extra money home to you. You could buy some preserves, maybe even hire out the laundry and some of the other work."

"I could get Simon to move in here," he replied. "We'd work together, and I'm sure we could do our own cooking and cleaning between the two of us. Might let me keep a better eye on him."

"Would you do that?" she whispered.

"For you, yah."

A tear slipped down her cheek and she brushed it away.

"I thought my own bedroom would guard against this, Jeb."

"Yah. I thought so, too." He nodded, then swallowed hard. "When do they want you to start?"

"As soon as I can," she said. "There are *kinner* who need extra help with their studies, and they've said they'll pay me for tutoring before the school year starts if I come now."

"Okay." He nodded. "When do you want to leave?"

"Tomorrow," she whispered.

"As soon as that?" He stared at her, his dark gaze pleading. "Are you sure?"

"If I don't go tomorrow, I won't go!" she said, her voice shaking.

Jeb licked his lips and turned away, staring out a window. She couldn't see his face, and she wondered if he'd refuse. Maybe she wanted him to. If her husband said no, she wouldn't have to say goodbye, and she could stay here, and they'd . . . They'd make each other miserable, because their needs weren't going to change, but their feelings might. And after a love like this, feelings got mangled and bloody. They turned to resentment and anger, oh so easily . . .

"Tomorrow, then," Jeb said, his voice thick with emotion. "I'll take you to the bus station."

"Maybe it's better if my brother does," she said. Saying goodbye in public would only make it harder.

He nodded. "Okay. Yah. I could see that."

They were being practical now, just as they should have been from the start. They shouldn't have been playing with something so volatile as attraction. Wasn't that what they warned the young, single people against? *Don't toy with it! It's fire.*

It was fire inside a marriage, too . . . to warm or to devour.

She couldn't say she hadn't been warned. At least Rosmanda had tried to warn her . . . Marriage was never quite so simple, was it? There was something about saying those vows before God and community that changed things.

"A friendship lasts longer than passion anyway," she said, and the words sounded feeble and hollow in the agony of the moment. "It's what they say . . ."

And sometimes all a woman had was the wisdom the community had told and retold the young people . . . That a marriage should be entered into with practicality in mind, that a friendship needed to be developed, because it was the part of the relationship that lasted the longest.

So, she and Jeb would have to focus on a friendship—something they could both manage that would be longer lasting than whatever this passion was that kept trying to boil up between them.

Maybe then they'd stop longing for more. It was the longing that hurt the most.

That night Jeb listened to the sound of his wife's sobs from behind her bedroom door. She was trying to muffle them, he could tell, but the unmistakeable shuddering breaths gave her away.

He lay on his bed, his throat thick with unshed tears and his chest aching. He'd done it again . . . made another woman miserable in her marriage to him. What was wrong with him that he kept hoping for someone to love the broken man he was? He didn't have what an Amish woman wanted—he never had.

Jeb rolled over, putting his back to the door. The springs squeaked under the weight of his body, and he wished he could cry. It would let all these jagged feelings out of him, but it wouldn't solve anything. It wouldn't make her tears any less real.

He loved her . . . and if he'd just been able to keep those feelings under control . . . He might still have fallen in love with her, but maybe he could have hidden it. It was his hope for more that always seemed to burn him. Look at him! He was a man with scars so terrible that they made *kinner* cry. Who was he to hope for the kind of love that Jacob and Rachel had, or Isaac and Rebecca?

Eventually he fell asleep, still in his work clothes, sleep stealing over him like a broken promise that it was just a moment to rest his eyes. He awoke the next morning before dawn, startling himself awake in the silence. His throat ached, and he felt like his chest was filled with water. But it was morning and there were chores to do.

Simon arrived fifteen minutes early as requested, and while Jeb mucked out the first of the calf stalls, he explained the situation as best he could.

"Your sister is going to take that teaching position again," Jeb said.

"Yah?" Simon sounded surprised. "But you're married now."

"Well, they need her help, and she wants to do it," Jeb said.

Simon pushed back his hat and scrubbed a hand over his forehead. "When is she going?"

"Today. She'll need a ride to the station. I was hoping you could take her."

Simon leaned on his shovel and squinted at Jeb in the light of the kerosene lamp. "Today? And you're not driving her yourself? What happened? Tell me the truth."

"She wants to teach," Jeb said. "I don't know what else to tell you."

The rest wasn't Simon's business. It wasn't anyone's business, and if he'd learned anything, it was that breathing a single word to someone else was as bad as announcing his secrets in the middle of town.

"So, when am I supposed to drive her?"

"After breakfast," Jeb replied.

"And that's it?" Simon demanded. "I drop her off and we both pretend this is normal?"

Jeb shook his head. "It isn't normal. Nothing about our marriage is normal. You know that well enough. But she wants to go, and I'm a private man. So I'm asking you to drive her for me."

Simon stared at him, then shrugged. "Fine."

And Jeb turned back to his work. He didn't trust himself to say anything more. Likely Simon already suspected the truth—that he and his sister had had a falling out and she was running as far away as she could. And that's what the community would believe, too.

When they headed back to the house for breakfast, Jeb's heart was in his throat. He wanted to ask her to stay, but for what? He couldn't give her what she needed—a place in her community. So asking her to stay would be selfish, meant to ease his own pain, not hers.

Leah had fixed a proper breakfast of eggs, fried potatoes, oatmeal, and bacon. The cooking dishes were already washed when Jeb and Simon came tramping in. Leah's suitcase was packed and sitting beside the door, and Jeb looked over the laden table toward his wife. Her face was pale, her eyes red-rimmed. She'd been crying recently. He wanted to hold her, but something in her stance told him the physical gesture wouldn't be welcome.

The food was a peace offering of sorts—he recognized that. It was more food than they needed for the meal, especially considering that his stomach was like a rock and he wasn't going to be able to eat much.

"Eat up," Leah said, forcing a smile. "Before it gets cold."

Simon glanced between them. "So you're really going?"

"It's a good-paying job," Leah said. "And there will be no *kinner* coming in our marriage, so I might as well help earn."

"That's what this is about?" Simon squinted at his sister. "Your ability to have children? Jeb knew about that before he married you!"

"This isn't about that," Jeb growled. "Look, we just think it's best to have a bit of space for a while."

Now he was the one saying too much. But it wasn't like Simon was going to be placated with their official story either.

"And we want people to just think that I'm going to earn some money," Leah said quietly.

"Oh." Simon swallowed. "Are you okay, Leah?"

"I'll be fine," she said. "We'll talk on the drive, okay?"

They sat down at the table, and Leah turned those red-rimmed eyes toward him, waiting for him to say the blessing. He swallowed hard and bowed his head.

"Lord, thank you for this food we are about to eat, and for the hands that have prepared it."

Thank you for her . . .

They didn't eat much of the food, and Leah started to gather up the plates when Jeb reached out and put a hand on her wrist.

"I'll do that," he said quietly. "You've done enough already."

Leah met his gaze and tears misted her eyes. "I don't want to leave a messy kitchen. I do have my pride."

"I'll go get the buggy hitched," Simon said, standing up. He glanced between them again, then headed for the door.

He seemed to sense that they could use some privacy. When the door had shut, Leah's shoulders relaxed a little more.

"Do you want to stay?" he asked softly.

"I don't know what I want," she said, her voice trembling. "And I think I'll only figure that out when I can get back to where I have some balance again."

"Yah." He nodded. "But a year's a long time."

"It's not so bad," she said, but he saw the lie in her eyes. "Many engaged couples wait as long as that. I'll be back before you know it, and you'll be annoyed when I touch your things again."

"This is your home, Leah," he said, his voice rough with emotion. "Remember that."

Leah didn't answer him, and she rose to her feet.

Life had changed him, and while the innocent often thought that God's healing brought a person back again, the truth was that God's healing brought a person through. And maybe Jeb wasn't through yet. He could admit to that. But he also knew that his journey wasn't going to drop him back where he'd started. That just wasn't how life worked. Even if a beautiful woman desperately longed for it to be so.

"I don't know what to say," Jeb said quietly. "I wish I had words to express . . . and I know I'm sending you off without anything proper from me, and . . ."

"This is the address where I'll be," she said, pulling a slip of paper from her apron. "You can write me."

"Yah." He nodded and looked down at the slip of paper. Rimstone . . . where it all had started.

"Jeb, I'm sorry," she said. "I won't be the woman you long for either. And sometimes that's how marriage works. You don't get the person who fulfills all your deepest needs and desires. I haven't done that for you. And that's okay—"

"You do fill my desires, Leah," he breathed.

"But your needs, Jeb. Those are more important, don't you think?"

Outside, the rattle of buggy wheels drew her eyes, and he saw her steel herself, her spine straightening.

"They can't know," she said, turning to Jeb again. "Okay? We have to make them all believe that we are perfectly happy with this and all is well. That's the only way we can ride this out."

"I agree," he said.

Leah crossed the kitchen and stooped to pick up her bag.

"Leah—" Her name caught in his throat, and she turned back. "Can I carry that for you?"

A tear escaped her lashes and she shook her head. "I'm okay."

Then she opened the door and disappeared outside. He followed her and watched as Simon tossed her suitcase into the back of the buggy, then handed his sister up into the seat. She leaned over and looked back, her dark gaze meeting his once, and then Simon hopped up, flicked the reins, and they jolted forward.

It took everything inside him to stay in that doorway and watch his wife drive away.

But this was better for her, and he couldn't be the man who would chain her to a life with him just to fill his own heart. He loved her too much for that. It wasn't the kind of man he was.

He stood there until the buggy turned onto the main road and was out of sight, and then he leaned his head against the doorframe, and all those tears he'd been holding back for years came flooding out in racking sobs. His shoulders shook with the force of them. He'd found out what it was like to be loved, but it hadn't changed the outcome one bit.

He was going back to being alone. The solitude. The

lonesome nights . . . He'd said he wanted it—and maybe he would again, but right now it felt like the cruelest irony. He'd said he wanted solitude and he would have just that. Be careful what you pray for, people said, because you just might get it.

Chapter Twenty

Leah thanked the Rimstone cab driver and handed over her fare. It felt good to be out in fresh air again. Her stomach was queasy from the drive in the musty back seat of that car. How the Englishers spend so much time in those vehicles, she had no idea. They couldn't be good for a person—the smell, the motion, the way her body physically recoiled from the experience. It was worse than the bus.

She sucked in a few breaths of fresh, summer air, and she felt her nerves start to relax. Her suitcase was in the trunk, and the driver pulled it out for her and handed it over with a nod. She accepted her bag and returned his nod, then looked away. The Englishers could be overly friendly if allowed, and she had no interest in making small talk.

The driver got back into his car, and Leah looked around at the neat property. The apples were growing well on the low, gnarled trees, and she could see the small, green pears forming on some trees close by the white-washed fence. She'd only been gone a few weeks, but it felt like longer. So much had happened . . . changed. She wasn't the same schoolteacher who had left Rimstone for the summer.

It was strange. She remembered her mother telling her that a man couldn't fill all the corners of her heart, but she'd never guessed just how true that was. The Bible said that man didn't live on bread alone, and perhaps they could add that women couldn't live by marriage alone either. The human heart needed more. And maybe God could make up that difference for her, too, because she didn't know where else to turn.

All the same, she missed Jeb. Her heart ached with the loss of him, and she'd seen him that very morning. So, while a woman couldn't live by marriage alone, it certainly did tug at parts of her heart she'd never known existed. That made it harder still. They said that a husband gave a woman position, children, and a home to live in by the sweat of his brow. They said a good husband was like a well-built barn—he stood up to storms and sheltered his wife. All those images of husbands and wives were practical, and she could appreciate that, especially after Matthew's desertion. But she hadn't been prepared for the depth of feeling she could develop for a man in such a short space of time.

It's like being partners in a battle—having a warrior defending your back. That was how Rosmanda had described it. And in the most heartbreaking way she had likely never anticipated, she'd been right. Because Leah would have Jeb's back until death parted them. She'd protect him yet, even if they needed to tamp down their emotions to do it. But she wouldn't have a lover for life, as Rosmanda had predicted. That part couldn't be for them.

How had this happened? If she loved him half as much, she could have lived her own life and appreciated the home he provided her. But love him like this? It was misery.

"You're here!" Cherish Wittmer called, coming out the side door of her little house with a broad smile on her face. "We weren't sure if we'd see you again, my dear. You must have gotten the letter from the school board, then?"

"Yah—and how could I not come?" Leah said, forcing a smile. "I'm glad to be back."

The taxi reversed, and Leah hoisted her suitcase in one hand.

Cherish paused, eyed her for a moment. "Are you? You've been crying."

"Allergies." Leah's smile slipped.

"It isn't Christianly to lie," Cherish whispered. "But then, it isn't Christianly to pry either, is it?"

Cherish had always had a strange, balanced wisdom about her, and Leah's eyes welled with tears despite her best effort to keep herself stoic.

"Come on inside," Cherish said, linking her arm through Leah's. "I have fresh cinnamon buns on the counter and I'm making a chicken tonight with the gravy you like so much."

"Thank you, Cherish," Leah said, and they went up the steps together and into the house.

Leah glanced around. The mudroom and kitchen hadn't changed a bit. The same containers lined the counters, the little step stool Cherish used to reach her upper cupboards was still in an awkward location—right where Cherish had left it the last time she used it.

"Is it Matthew?" Cherish asked.

"No . . ." Leah realized she hadn't been thinking about Matthew lately. It had been a while now since she'd shed a tear over him. "His wife is pregnant, so he'll be a *daet* soon. They seem very happy."

"I'm sorry, dear," Cherish said softly.

"Don't be," Leah replied. "It isn't Matthew."

"That's a good thing," Cherish replied. "Then who has broken your heart? Oh . . . the pregnancy . . ." Cherish's cheeks pinked. "I know how hard that must be, to see another woman—"

"It's another man!" The words burst out of her before

she could think better of them. But she couldn't go through this—the guesswork, touching on every painful spot she had.

"Do you want to talk about it?" Cherish asked.

"No," Leah said. "I'm glad to be back where I can be respected. That's all."

"He didn't respect you?" Cherish frowned.

Leah sighed. Cherish was like a mother—loving, tender, sweet, and as persistent as a woodpecker when it came to personal issues.

"Shall we pretend there is no problem?" Cherish asked, putting a weathered hand on Leah's arm. "I can do that. I think so at least. I would try very hard."

"Cherish, I did something crazy . . ." Leah sucked in a breath. "And you'll have to keep my secret, because I want to teach this year. I *have* to teach this year. It's the only way I'm going to keep myself level."

"What did you do?" Cherish whispered.

"I got married."

A smile spread over Cherish's face, then it faltered. "Why are you here, then?"

Why indeed? Leah rubbed her hands over her face. "Because it wasn't for love, it was for money. And I know that's terrible. I do! But my brother was in trouble and I didn't have the money to help him, and this man needed to have a wife to inherit a farm, and—" Leah couldn't look Cherish in the eye as she confessed all this. "It's a marriage of convenience. That's all."

Cherish was silent, and she nodded slowly. "All the same . . . why are you here?"

"Because we need different things," Leah said. "He keeps to himself. He wants nothing to do with our community—"

"He's not Amish?" Cherish choked out.

"He is, he is . . ." Leah laughed softly. "He's just . . . a hermit. He was badly burned in a fire and he's been through a lot, and . . . I'm not saying it was all a mistake because we both got what we needed from this marriage already, but I need to work this year so I can get my emotional balance again. He's my husband, but we both want very different things."

"A little late to be considering that," Cherish murmured.

"I know."

"And he's fine with this?" Cherish asked. "You working here and not taking care of him?"

"Yah. He's fine. Please don't tell anyone, Cherish. I just need to teach, have some space. Marriage is long, they say. I have time to sort it out."

"So, you're running away from him . . ." Cherish said.

"No."

Cherish raised her eyebrows.

"I'm not," Leah insisted. "It isn't like that. Marriage is long, and sometimes two people need time to find their balance. That's all this is. But I'd rather do that without the judgment of all of Rimstone wondering why I'm not with my husband."

And again, here she was saying too much—unburdening herself when she should be stoically holding it all inside. She didn't suffer well, it would seem.

"Please, Cherish," Leah said, reaching out to take the older woman's hand. "Please don't tell them . . ."

"I won't say anything to anyone," Cherish said. "Let God be my witness to that."

Leah nodded. "Thank you."

Could she trust that? Only time would tell. She'd begged Lynita not to tell anyone what she knew, too, and look how that had gone. But she couldn't go through life isolated—at some point a woman had to trust someone. . . .

"Eat." Cherish dished up a cinnamon bun onto a plate

and pushed it toward her with an encouraging smile. "Our teacher needs some meat on her bones."

Leah smiled through her tears. "I've missed you, Cherish."

"Me too." The older woman stood up and went to the gas-powered fridge for some milk. "And while they tell you that marriage is long, dear, this is one thing they don't tell you because they expect you to figure it out the natural way. But I sense that you aren't going to do that any time soon . . ."

"What's that?" Leah asked tiredly.

"There is more than one way to communicate with your husband," Cherish said. "And while a relationship takes time, it also takes proximity. You'll learn things about him while in his arms that you'd never discover anywhere else. Marriage can also be incredibly sweet if you spend your marriage in each other's arms instead of miles apart."

Leah's gaze moved toward the window. So far, in her experience, marriage was heartbreaking, lonely, and confusing. Pillow talk couldn't be the answer to everything that went wrong between two people, could it?

She roused herself and sucked in a deep breath.

"Do you know a woman named Ruth King, Cherish?"

Cherish's eyebrows raised. "Why?"

"She's a relative," Leah said, boldly meeting Cherish's gaze. "I only recently found out about her. I was hoping to visit her."

"Yah, she's in town. She works at an Amish inn—she works the front desk." Cherish didn't say anything else, and neither did Leah.

Leah's husband's secrets were safe with her. She'd be the warrior at his back . . . even from here. All the same, she did intend to meet her mother-in-law.

***

That night, Jeb didn't sleep well. He went into her bedroom and looked around. It was as neat and nearly as empty as the day he'd given it to her, but it was different now. He could smell the soft scent of her around this place—her lotion, her soap. There was a bar of softly scented soap in the bathroom, and he wouldn't touch it, because it reminded him of her. . . .

"I'm an idiot," he muttered.

The truth was, he missed her desperately, for all the good that did him. He knew this would be the fallout of letting himself feel too much, but it hadn't felt like a choice. Leah tugged these complicated emotions out of him, like a thread pulled through fabric at the end of a needle. He was drawn along . . .

But he didn't need to draw her along with him. He could have kept his hands to himself. He didn't need to complicate things for her. In fact, if he hadn't, she might still be here. The exquisite agony of sharing a house with her could have been his alone to bear, and it would have been far preferable to having run her off.

Because he wasn't fooled—she'd left because of him.

A day's worth of work hadn't improved matters, and neither had trying to make small talk with Simon once he'd gotten back from the bus depot.

"You've made a mistake," Simon had said. "Both of you."

And that's all he'd say on the matter.

Maybe the kid was right. But it was a little late now. Leah was in Rimstone and the community there would be thrilled to have her back to teach their *kinner*. It was what Leah wanted.

The night, Simon declined coming in for dinner. He had promised to go to that Gamblers Anonymous meeting, he said, and Matthew was picking him up to drive him. Apparently Matthew wasn't going to give Simon a chance to back out—not a bad thing, Jeb had to admit. Simon, at least, could benefit from this community.

After a hasty dinner, half of which Jeb didn't eat, he sat at the kitchen table, his heart still feeling heavy and sodden inside him. Outside he heard the rattle of a buggy, and Jeb pushed himself to his feet and looked out the window. It was Bishop Yoder with another elder—Methuselah? Yah, that looked like him. The very elder to have visited his wife the other day apparently. They were worried about her . . . and they'd likely come to check up on her. And he'd have some explaining to do.

Jeb sighed. They'd find out eventually that she'd gone to teach in Rimstone again, and it was like his heart was drawn to that town doubly now—the town he'd grown up in, where his *mamm* still lived, and now the town where his wife worked to keep her distance from him. Today wasn't a good day for a visit from the bishop. His emotions were too raw. But they were here all the same, and Jeb resignedly headed through the mudroom and pulled open the side door. The men had reined in the pair of horses and they jumped down from the buggy.

"Good evening, Jeb," Bishop Yoder called.

Jeb gave him a curt nod but didn't answer.

"We're glad we caught you at home. How is married life treating you?" The bishop smiled.

"Fine." It was the acceptable answer, wasn't it? No one told the truth if their heart was in shreds anyway.

"We hoped to speak with you," the bishop said. "May we come inside?"

Methuselah still hadn't spoken, and Jeb looked over at him quizzically. The older man looked down uncomfortably, and his discomfort was welcome at least. The last time Methuselah had been here, it was to undermine his marriage. He should feel badly about that.

"Come in, then," Jeb said, standing back.

The men came up the steps, wiped off their boots on the mat, and came inside. They glanced around, then pulled up chairs at the kitchen table. Jeb was expected to offer them something, so he picked up the basket of baked goods Methuselah's wife had brought and plunked it onto the center of the table. He looked at Methuselah meaningfully.

"Have some of your wife's baking," he said, and then sat down, too.

"Jeb, I want to apologize for that," Methuselah said, breaking his silence for the first time.

"Yah?" Jeb raised an eyebrow. "Coming to a man's home, spreading tales about him, trying to convince a man's wife she's in danger."

"Where is your wife?" the bishop asked quietly.

"She left," Jeb said, his throat thickening with emotion. "Ask your elder about that."

"Where did she go?" Methuselah asked, frowning.

"She's gone back to teach in Rimstone," Jeb replied. "And you can confirm that with her brother, if you don't believe me. He's the one who dropped her off at the bus station."

There was silence around the table, and Methuselah cleared his throat awkwardly. "I didn't mean to do that."

"It wasn't all you," Jeb said. "So, are you done, then? She's safely away from me."

"We didn't actually come for that," Bishop Yoder said.

Jeb eyed them uncertainly. If this wasn't about his wife, why were they here? "Menno?" he asked.

"Yah." The bishop nodded.

There it was. If they couldn't ruin his personal life anymore, it looked like they'd meddle further into his relationship with his cousin. He clenched his teeth and closed his eyes for a moment, looking for some way to lower this rising anger inside him. He should have left the Amish years ago . . . He still could! What kept him linked to this community when they kept ruining every part of his life?

Except he was Amish. Angry, resentful, heartbroken, ugly . . . whatever he became, he was also Amish. It was the last tie he would not cut himself. But maybe that was being taken from him now, too.

"We came here because Menno has been saying some rather incriminating things about you, Jeb," the bishop went on. "He's claiming you manipulated his father into changing his will in your favor. He wants this land. I'll tell you that straight."

"And you're here to demand I sign it over, I take it?" Jeb said bitterly. "And if I refuse, I can face the wrath of the community?"

"No." The bishop shook his head. "I'm here to reassure you that we're on your side in this. I knew Peter well, and I was aware of that will. It's all perfectly legal, and your uncle wanted you on this land. He also wanted you married— so it looks like Peter managed to get things sorted out."

"Wait—" The word caught in Jeb's throat, and he cleared it. "You're saying . . . you're on my side?"

"We've looked into it," Methuselah interjected. "You're in the right here, Jeb. And we stand for what is right. Menno is angry—maybe even understandably so. He lost his father, and he truly believed he'd inherit this farm. It was a blow to him. But it wasn't right of him to slander your name behind your back." Color tinted the older man's cheeks. "Neither was it right of me to do the same, Jeb."

Jeb stared at them, the words still sinking in. He hadn't expected this show of support. If anything, he'd expected to have to throw them off his property . . . He sucked in a breath, then released it, words still not coming to him.

"We want you to know that we've visited with Menno, too," Bishop Yoder said. "And we've told him that he needs to stop the rumors he's been spreading, or we'll have to address this with more of the elders. We are an honest and truthful community, and we must treat each other fairly."

"I don't know what to say," Jeb said.

"It's been a long time since you've been to service," the bishop said.

There it was . . . the demand. "So, there's a price for your support, is there?" Jeb asked.

"A price?" The bishop shook his head. "No, I was just going to say that we'd like to see you, Jeb. It would be nice if you'd come out with the rest of us. And I do understand if you're not up to going to other gatherings, but when we worship God together it's healing. I don't know how to explain why, or how. But it seems to be."

"And if I don't go?" Jeb asked gruffly.

"You'll be missed." The bishop smiled. "And from time to time I'll invite you. Our community should have done better by you, Jeb. We've missed opportunities to be the neighbor you need. We want to do better. That's all."

Jeb was ready for a fight, but not for this. He swallowed a lump that rose in his throat. He dropped his gaze and looked away, not wanting to expose the emotions that flowed through him.

The bishop tapped the table, and both men rose to their feet.

"We should be off, then," the bishop said.

"I see you still have my wife's baking," Methuselah said quietly. "Please enjoy it, Jeb. And with your wife away, I'll have her bake extra and we'll drop it by for you."

"I don't need charity," Jeb said brusquely.

"Then call it friendship," Methuselah said.

Jeb looked up at the older man uncertainly. Friendship. He looked in to the basket—the braided loaves of bread, some blueberry muffins. They were getting stale.

"I have a broken wheel on my buggy," Methuselah added.

"I know it might be a lot to ask, but I could use a hand in fixing it. If you had the time."

Jeb nodded. "Yah. I suppose, I could. Sure."

Methuselah smiled. "Much appreciated."

The bishop headed for the door, and Methuselah put out his hand. Jeb reached out and shook it.

"Sometimes when you're having a rough time," Methuselah said quietly, "you just have to ask for the help you need. So I thank you. You're a good neighbor, Jeb."

Yah . . . a lesson for the *kinner* almost, in what it meant to be Amish, but a reminder he needed, too. He didn't mind helping Methuselah out with a wheel. It could be fixed easily enough between the two of them.

The men saw themselves out and headed back to the buggy, but Jeb stood in his kitchen for a long time, his mind whirling.

Was it really so simple, to just ask for what he needed? Because right now, he didn't need baking or company. He didn't need neighbors even . . . he needed his wife. He missed her, and even having her across the hall was preferable to this emptiness in his home.

But Jeb wanted more than having her across the hall. He wanted her in his arms. He wanted her in his bed. He wanted to pull her close and fall asleep to the soft scent of her hair on the pillow. He wanted a marriage—a true, soul-deep kind of marriage—and he'd been afraid to ask for any of it because he'd never gotten much of what he wanted in that respect before.

He'd asked for more . . . she'd said she couldn't live his solitary life. But she'd asked for what she needed, too, and maybe it was time to take a chance on community again. For her.

Abundance might have done him wrong, but they'd also come and apologized, admitted it, and backed him in his dispute with Menno. Before they'd even spoken to Jeb.

Before they even knew if he could forgive them . . . they'd given him their support because it was just and right.

They'd done the right thing. The difficult thing. Maybe it was time for Jeb to do the same.

So he'd help fix that wheel, and if he had his wife next to him, he could go to service as well. He couldn't promise to go to strawberry parties, but he could give a little more to the woman he loved. He could help a neighbor with a broken wheel. He could pitch in during harvest and barn raisings. He could find his place here again . . . a different place than before, but a place all the same.

Jeb sucked in a breath, his heart hammering in his throat. His wife was in Rimstone, and before anything else, it was time to see if she'd come home.

Chapter Twenty-One

Finding Ruth King had proven easier than Leah had anticipated. First, she'd gone into town and checked at the Rimstone Inn, where she worked, but the manager there said that Ruth had the day off. So Leah had gone to her home—a little apartment in the back of an Amish house. It was small but neat, with wide windows and a tiny garden out back that was flourishing.

"You're my son's wife?"

Ruth King's face was lined and browned from the sun. She slid a mug of tea across the table toward Leah and eyed her uncertainly.

"I'm Leah King," Leah said with a nod. "Did Jeb write to you?"

"Yah, he did." Ruth frowned, pressing her lips together. "Where is he?"

Leah felt the accusation in those words, but she wouldn't look down. "He's in Abundance still. I'm teaching school here."

"And you're here alone? Even though you're married?"

"Yah." Leah smiled sadly. "I am."

They were silent for a moment, and Leah could see the

older woman weighing the situation, and then she leaned forward, her gaze locked on Leah's face.

"How is he? How is he really? Because he writes to me, and I just sense—" Ruth sighed. "He doesn't tell me everything, and as a grown man, that is no surprise. But I worry."

"He's very, very alone," Leah said softly.

"Ah." Tears misted Ruth's eyes. "I was afraid of that . . ."

"What does he tell you?" Leah asked.

"Oh, that he married you. That the farm is his. That Menno is giving him grief. Facts, not feelings."

Leah nodded. "He hates if I talk about his business."

Ruth dropped her gaze to her hands. "I know. He's always been like that—very reserved. Some people deal with pain by lashing out. It was like Jebadiah lashed inward. But he used to talk to me at least. But that was a very long time ago . . ."

"How long?" Leah asked.

"Before I sent him to live with his uncle. He was barely thirteen then. It was never the same after I sent him away. He begged to stay with me. Did he tell you that?"

Leah shook her head.

"Well, he did. He wanted to be with me. He didn't care if he never got a fresh chance at a decent life. But I couldn't let my son try to protect me! He had to live his own life. And sending the *kinner* to be with their uncle was good for them. For Lynita, at least. She found a good man and married him. You know them, don't you—Lynita and Isaiah?"

"Yah," Leah said with a quick nod. "They're good people."

"But it didn't go so well with my son," Ruth said, and she leaned back in her chair. "If I knew then what I do now, I'd have kept him with me."

"You did your best," Leah said softly.

Ruth nodded slowly. "All the same, I never should have sent him away, Leah. I wanted to give him a community—a chance to really start his life—and I don't think that was what he needed after all. He needed me." Ruth wiped a tear from her cheek.

Was Leah so very different? She'd left him, too. And ever since she'd arrived in Rimstone, all she could think of was her husband. She loved him—and while he didn't fit into the proper Amish life she'd always imagined for herself, did she want that life without him in it?

And he'd asked her to stay . . .

A lump rose in her throat.

"Ruth, can I ask you something?" Leah asked.

"Yah. Sure."

"Did your community forgive you? I hope this isn't offensive, but . . . did they ever decide they'd punished you enough and let you back into the community again?"

"Yah, of course." Ruth laughed softly. "I'm not the same young woman who made those mistakes anymore. We all grow. It took time for them to forgive me, as these things do. But I also had to realize that *I'd* changed through it all. I was different, and my place in my community would be different, too. You see, you'll always have a place in the Amish community. It's just a matter of where you fit. Life changes you—that's inevitable. People make mistakes, or they get married, or they don't get married when everyone expects. Maybe it's the birth of a child, or a grandchild, or they get sick, or they get old. Your place in the community is constantly changing, but there is always a space for you. It just isn't always in the same place as before. That's all. I suppose that's the wisdom that comes with age. I didn't understand that when I was younger, so take it for what it's worth."

Leah was silent as she rolled Ruth's words over in her

mind. Was it really as simple as that? Maybe it was time for Leah to change a few of her own expectations, too. If she loved Jeb this much, then maybe she'd need to let her place in the community change. If he couldn't join her in the busyness and community, then she'd join him on the periphery.

But loving Jeb had changed her—there was no turning back there. Maybe it wasn't a question of having her community or not. Maybe her place with the Amish could change, too . . .

It would mean adjusting her vision of her future—the active Amish life she'd longed for wouldn't be hers, but she'd have her husband's love. There wouldn't be *kinner*, but they would still be a family. It wouldn't be what she'd expected . . . but did she really want to push the man she loved away?

Outside, there was a rumble of an Englisher engine, and Ruth rose to her feet and looked out the window.

"Oh . . ." she said, her fingers coming up to her lips.

Leah's heart leaped to her throat and she hurried to the window, looking over Ruth's shoulder. There was a taxi idling in the driveway, and Jeb stood there next to the driver's side window, peeling bills off a roll to pay the driver. Ruth opened the door and went outside.

There was a murmur of voices, and Leah watched from the steps as Jeb embraced his *mamm*. Ruth stood on the tips of her toes to wrap her arms around him, and for a long moment they stayed like that. Then Jeb looked up, his gaze landing on Leah.

He released his *mamm* and she stepped aside. Jeb stood there in a pool of afternoon sunlight, his hat pushed back on his head, and his gaze locked on her.

"Leah . . ."

Before she could answer, Jeb strode across the gravel and gathered her up in his arms. He looked down at her for a moment, then dipped his head and caught her lips with his. His kiss felt warm and safe, like coming home. She leaned into his embrace, his beard tickling her face as he tightened his arms around her, holding her close against the deep, strong beat of his heart.

Why had she ever gotten on that bus to begin with? She belonged here—right here—in her husband's arms.

It was such a relief to have her in his arms again, but when Jeb looked up, he saw his *mamm* standing there with her arms crossed and a funny little smile playing across her face.

"What are you doing here?" Leah asked, looking up into his face.

"I could ask you the same thing," he said with a short laugh. "But I came to find you. I went to the address you gave me first, and she said you'd come to see my *mamm*, so . . ."

"Oh." Leah smiled at that. "I wanted to meet her. I hope you don't mind."

He should have expected as much. That was her way, wasn't it? She was better with people than he was.

"Leah, I need to talk to you." Alone . . . the words were jumbled up inside him, and he wasn't sure how he'd express it all, but he had to try. Jeb caught Leah's hand and led her toward the neat little garden, rows of leafy lettuce and twisting vines of green peas.

"I love you," he blurted out.

"I love you, too." She looked up at him, her brown gaze melting as it met his.

"Still?" he whispered.

"Still." Tears misted her eyes, and he felt a flood of relief. "I missed you."

"Methuselah and the bishop came by . . ." He swallowed. "Methuselah asked me for help with his buggy, and . . . they're siding with me when it comes to Menno."

Leah blinked at him. "What?"

"I'm not telling this very well, but they said I'm in the right." Jeb dropped his gaze. "They've told Menno to stop spreading tales about me, and they're in support of me inheriting the land. The bishop knew about the will apparently. It was no surprise to him."

"I'm glad," Leah said.

"They've invited me to come to service Sundays, and I said I would," he went on. "I'll help out Methuselah with his buggy wheel. . . . Leah, I know you need your community, and I'll try to find a place again."

"Really?" she breathed.

He was giving her hope, but he had to be clear. She had to understand him—all of him.

"The thing is, I'm not perfect," he went on. "I'll still be me. . . . I'm not going to be good in groups, and I'll probably make people uncomfortable still, but—"

Leah didn't say anything at first. She just looked down at her hand in his, and he saw what drew her gaze—the puckered, scarred skin.

"I really missed you," she whispered at last. "I've been holding on to my own idea of what a proper Amish life looks like, and it's okay that the one I have looks different than I thought. My place in the community is going to change, too. I just want to come home. I don't want a year without you. I'd be miserable. Community or not."

Jeb reached up and put his hand against her cheek. She leaned into his touch, and he leaned forward, kissing her forehead.

"I'm going to take a chance here," he said quietly. "I'm not asking you to come back halfway. I'm not asking for our old arrangement, where we have separate rooms and we try not to feel all this. I'm asking for all of it—a real marriage, for you to come home with me as my wife in every way."

Pink touched her cheeks. "All of it?"

"Yah," he said. "You know how I feel about you, you know what I'm wanting. And I promise to respect you, to protect you, and I'll always be kind. You can count on that. But I want a wife in every sense, Leah. I want you to move into my bedroom."

She was silent for a moment, and for a split second he thought she'd say no. But then he saw the tears shining in her eyes, and she nodded before she said, "I want that, too."

"Are you sure?" he asked hesitantly. "Because I don't think my heart could take any miscommunication on this."

"I want to come home to you," Leah said. "And I want to share a bed with you, and to wake up with you . . . I want you to be my husband in every way."

Jeb slid his arms around her and crushed her against him as he kissed her thoroughly one more time. She twined her arms around his neck, and when he looked up, he saw his *mamm* standing in the doorway again.

"Mamm, maybe I should introduce you to my wife," he called with a grin.

"We've met, son," Ruth called back. "I've decided I like her."

Leah shook with suppressed laughter, and she tugged herself out of his arms. He hated to let go of her, but what could they do? It wasn't like they were at home, with privacy.

"Come inside," Jeb said. "I want you to meet my *mamm*. Properly."

As they headed up the steps, hand in hand, he realized

he hadn't gone back to the way things were long ago. Instead he'd come through the pain and heartbreak and come out the other side. It was amazing how beautiful it was out here with his wife's hand in his and his heart yearning toward her.

It felt like sunshine.

Epilogue

Leah awoke the next morning to the feeling of Jeb's arms tugging her against him. He held her close, one hand moving in a slow circle over her back. She blinked her eyes open, Jeb's broad chest coming into view. She tentatively ran her hand over the swirls of chest hair. *Her husband . . .* It still felt amazing to think that this man next to her was hers. She would never tire of the sensation of being held and loved. It was intoxicating, and right and pure in every way.

They'd taken a late bus back last night, and her suitcase still sat fully packed in one corner of Jeb's bedroom . . . *their* bedroom.

Jeb ran his hand down her arm and onto her hip, his touch firm and confident. She looked up at him. His eyes were still closed, but there was a little smile tickling the corners of his lips.

"It's morning," she said softly.

"I know . . ." He opened one eye and looked down at her. "I don't want to move yet."

"You might want breakfast," she said with a low laugh. Downstairs, she had a fire to kindle, cooking to start. It took a little while for a stove to heat up sufficiently.

"Nope." He rolled over onto his side, the whole bed creaking and groaning with the sudden movement, and he pulled her close against him. "I want this."

He kissed her temple, his beard tickling her eye, so she shut it, enjoying his embrace as his lips traced the side of her face.

"We have a farm," she reminded him, but only half-heartedly.

"Yah, we do." He smoothed her hair away from her face. She hadn't braided her hair last night. He'd tugged her into bed before she had the chance, and told her he liked it better like this—loose, wild. A woman's hair was her husband's glory, he'd said, so let him glory in it. . . . This morning her thick hair was tangled.

Leah pushed herself up onto her elbow, and Jeb let out a groan, then smiled up at her.

"I like this," he murmured. "Having you here, in our bed, together."

"Me too," she agreed.

"I'll make a deal with you," he said. "If we get up now, then we go to bed early tonight."

Leah laughed softly at that, then leaned down to kiss his lips. "Okay."

"Very early."

"Okay," she repeated.

"Yah?" He caught her gaze. "I'll hold you to that."

"I hope you do." She grinned back.

Jeb sat up and swung his legs over the side of the bed. She watched him, enjoying the sight of his muscles, his skin, even the play of the scars over his left side.

This was marriage. This was what it was like to be loved by a husband, to be enjoyed by a husband. . . . It was more than she'd ever imagined.

"Jeb?" she said quietly.

"Yah?" He looked back over at her, doing up his pants and then reaching for a fresh shirt. He stood there, his shirt in his hands and that warm, dark gaze meeting hers tenderly.

"I do love you," she said.

A smile touched his lips. "I love you, too. With everything I've got."

Leah believed him when he said that. She'd felt it in his kiss, in his touch, in the way his gaze moved over her face like that. . . . They had a lifetime to prove it to each other, a lifetime to explore this new domain of marriage and where they'd fit into the larger community. This was just the very beginning, and her heart was already full to bursting.

She couldn't imagine how much better it would get as the years rolled by.

With one last smile cast in her direction, Jeb headed out of the bedroom, his footsteps creaking down the stairs. Leah stretched out beneath the sheet, a smile toying at her lips. Her friend's words came back to her:

Like a warrior at her back, a lover for the rest of her life . . . a man who cherished her.

Suddenly all that advice the women had been trying to give her made a whole lot more sense. Perhaps the community would have to wait a little bit before they saw much more of Leah and Jeb. She had a feeling the women at least would understand.

The honeymoon was only beginning.

Connect with Us

Visit us online at
KensingtonBooks.com
to read more from your favorite authors, see books
by series, view reading group guides, and more.

for sneak peeks, chances to win books and prize packs,
and to share your thoughts with other readers.

facebook.com/kensingtonpublishing
twitter.com/kensingtonbooks

Tell us what you think!

To share your thoughts, submit a review,
or sign up for our eNewsletters, please visit:
KensingtonBooks.com/TellUs.

More by Bestselling Author
Hannah Howell

__Highland Angel	978-1-4201-0864-4	$6.99US/$8.99CAN
__If He's Sinful	978-1-4201-0461-5	$6.99US/$8.99CAN
__Wild Conquest	978-1-4201-0464-6	$6.99US/$8.99CAN
__If He's Wicked	978-1-4201-0460-8	$6.99US/$8.49CAN
__My Lady Captor	978-0-8217-7430-4	$6.99US/$8.49CAN
__Highland Sinner	978-0-8217-8001-5	$6.99US/$8.49CAN
__Highland Captive	978-0-8217-8003-9	$6.99US/$8.49CAN
__Nature of the Beast	978-1-4201-0435-6	$6.99US/$8.49CAN
__Highland Fire	978-0-8217-7429-8	$6.99US/$8.49CAN
__Silver Flame	978-1-4201-0107-2	$6.99US/$8.49CAN
__Highland Wolf	978-0-8217-8000-8	$6.99US/$9.99CAN
__Highland Wedding	978-0-8217-8002-2	$4.99US/$6.99CAN
__Highland Destiny	978-1-4201-0259-8	$4.99US/$6.99CAN
__Only for You	978-0-8217-8151-7	$6.99US/$8.99CAN
__Highland Promise	978-1-4201-0261-1	$4.99US/$6.99CAN
__Highland Vow	978-1-4201-0260-4	$4.99US/$6.99CAN
__Highland Savage	978-0-8217-7999-6	$6.99US/$9.99CAN
__Beauty and the Beast	978-0-8217-8004-6	$4.99US/$6.99CAN
__Unconquered	978-0-8217-8088-6	$4.99US/$6.99CAN
__Highland Barbarian	978-0-8217-7998-9	$6.99US/$9.99CAN
__Highland Conqueror	978-0-8217-8148-7	$6.99US/$9.99CAN
__Conqueror's Kiss	978-0-8217-8005-3	$4.99US/$6.99CAN
__A Stockingful of Joy	978-1-4201-0018-1	$4.99US/$6.99CAN
__Highland Bride	978-0-8217-7995-8	$4.99US/$6.99CAN
__Highland Lover	978-0-8217-7759-6	$6.99US/$9.99CAN

Available Wherever Books Are Sold!

Check out our website at
http://www.kensingtonbooks.com